D1825933

Neither Piety Nor Wit

Dennis Alsop

Dedicated to a wonderful family

The Moving Finger writes; and, having writ,
Moves on: nor all thy Piety nor Wit
Shall lure it back to cancel half a Line,
Nor all thy Tears erase a Word of it.

Rubaiyat of Omar Khayyam

Acknowledgement

With thanks to F.

CHAPTER 1

Sheffield, England

Of the three complete strangers, the teenage girl was the happiest that morning. Sophia had showered earlier, and had sung spiritedly as the water splattered onto her shower cap, and down her body.

At her bedroom window, she gently pulled the chord and peeped through the partly-opened vertical blinds. The glorious sunlight streamed through the slats and into the room. It was to be another beautiful summer day, an early summer weekday, and it would definitely provide the chance to wear her new, thin summer school uniform which was so much better than the dreary thicker uniform that had been necessary for weeks.

The sunlight which blazed brightly through the vertical slats and cheerfully illuminated her bedroom, formed straight strips of light on the plain wine-coloured bedroom carpet. She grinned as she regarded the configuration and made an association. Mr. Penbourne the physics master, in yesterday's lesson on quantum physics had been describing interference patterns. A mischievous thought came into her mind. Sophia speculated what her teacher would think if he could see her now, one of his female students, naked, remembering him and his lesson. She remembered how unfathomable the reaction of those electrons had seemed, and how illogical that they behaved like waves. Luckily it did not matter. She was dropping the subject next term.

The thought was fleeting, forgotten as she selected clean clothing for school and thought ahead. It was Wednesday and tonight was skating night. Tonight she could dress as she liked. With her parents abroad on holiday and her brother working up North, she had the run of the house. As she put on her school uniform she sang softly to herself and pictured in her mind's eye how she would look as she and her friends glided out onto the rink.

Across town, the second of the three strangers, the woman, was also in good spirits, but additionally, Philippa was nervous. She had already dressed and she intended to be "on station" in good time. Detective Sergeant Philippa Tate had no intention of walking late into the room when it would be already full of men, her new male colleagues. She had been promoted and transferred to Sheffield. She was about to begin her new duty. She was anxious to get off to a good start and had been informed that she would be the only female in that office. Sheffield was not the centre of excellence when it came to apprehending wrongdoers, but South Yorkshire had a sizable detective force, and one of the very best of them was her new boss Detective Chief Inspector Mallard. She had yet to meet him.
Philippa checked her appearance in the full-length mirror. Taking a deep breath she opened the door of her flat and stepped out to begin the new phase of her life.

Pensive, did not quite describe the mood of Joel Bush, the third one of the trio. He was already at work. The owner of a Sheffield butchery shop, the man was uneasy, troubled, as he carried on the routine business in own little empire in that neighbourhood High Street. His two assistants said

nothing to him. They watched him furtively as was their policy. Of course they knew their boss as well as anybody; knew his various moods, and endured his sarcasm and vitriol at times. They put up a show of laughing at his occasional joke, and did their best to avoid the sack.
This mood was new. Today Joel Bush was silent. He was on autopilot. In body the big man was there, but he was definitely not there in spirit. Something was up. There was a problem. Were they involved? They thought not. Had somebody somewhere, or had something somewhere, upset him? Probably.
They were correct.

*****

All his life, butcher Joel Bush had been too scared to do anything but play by the rules, obey the law, and lead a blameless life - until he had set eyes on that schoolgirl. She had been just another new customer stepping into the shop. When he had seen her that first time he was bewitched. Some phenomenon overcame him. Never in his entire life had he been so affected like that. He was stupefied. It was to be some time before he would even know that her name was Sophia, but an overwhelming desire for her had engulfed him. Not in his whole life had he known anything like that powerful longing. It welled up in him and tormented him.

For two weeks after she had first come in, he had watched his shop entrance all the time for her to return. Two more times over those two weeks he was rewarded, but that randy little sod, his junior assistant, Darryl, got to serve her first both times. On the third, Joel Bush was lucky. He hastened to serve her. Smiling, prognosticating, making helpful suggestions and being generally ingratiating, he prolonged the serving experience as much as possible. Smirking, his two assistants witnessed the schoolgirl's discomfort and saw her reaction. Young or not, she knew about men. Sophia realised what he was about. It was unwelcome.

When Bush handed Sophia her change his hand had deliberately brushed against her slender fingers, but she had not noted that. She was looking at Darryl who had just winked at her.

Bush had seen the girl turn and step out of his shop. How long would it be before her next visit? Would he actually ever see her again? Why was schoolgirl shopping straight after school anyway? Was her mother ill? She would surely get better and maybe this girl would not need to come anymore. This might be the last time.

Guts churning, Bush took a decision. As soon as she had left, Joel Bush went swiftly into the back of the shop and took off his apron. Donning his jacket he left by the rear exit and followed the girl. Darryl noticed him go and went to the window to watch what the boss was up to, but the road curved and Bush disappeared from sight after just a glimpse.

She had stopped at a bus stop. Running to his van, Bush had ample time to calm himself, wait and then follow her bus. Doubt and fear ran through his mind for the length of the ten minute journey. This was completely out of

character. Never before had he been caught up in a commotion like this. This was stupid. She was a schoolgirl and he was at least twice her age. This was wrong. His brain sent all the right messages throughout the agitation of the crazy drive. He must turn back!
Bush did not turn back. It was not his brain that was in charge.

When she alighted he parked his van and followed the girl at a distance, on foot. It was a quiet suburb of Sheffield. Obviously an expensive area, all of the houses were detached, set well back from the road, and had generous curving drives. Little of each house could be seen from the road. Bush had no trouble in following and identifying her house when she walked up its drive.
Now he knew her address. He could see her again now.

For several evenings that week and most of Sunday Bush kept watch on her house. Initially he just wanted to catch sight of the girl. She came and went frequently but there was no sign of anyone else. She must live alone.

On the next Wednesday evening it was after dark when she arrived home. This time she was with a friend. Earlier he had walked up the curving drive and stood in the garden at the back of the house. It was not dark when he had arrived and it had been necessary to be careful, but the garden was not overlooked. Hiding in some bushes he could see the back of the house quite clearly. When darkness had come he felt it was safe to stand and ease his aching limbs. It was shortly after dark when he heard someone approaching.

Bush watched as two girls came round to the back of the house, both carrying skating boots. They were in high spirits and their girly giggles and laughter entranced him. Her friend was an attractive girl too. The girls made no attempt to keep their voices down, and as they chatted away, he learned the girl he followed was called Sophia, and her friend Karen. They had obviously been to the Skating Arena in town.

Incredibly, though, he learned where the spare key was kept. All the house doors were fitted with Yale locks. Sophia had left her house keys in her other bag, the every-day handbag that was just not chic enough for a night out downtown. Always leaving things to the last-minute, Sophia frequently forgot to take her house key after she switched handbags, but it was not a problem because they always left a spare in the garden. Speaking unmindfully loudly, Sophia explained to Karen about the backup as she retrieved it from beneath a white rock. Three rocks had been painted white so they could be better seen in the dark. The key was always under the centre rock. That rock was six feet from where Bush was concealed.

If Sophia had not forgotten her keys the girls would have entered by the front of the house. Upon such small matters can destiny turn.

In the subsequent few days the obsessed Bush went every evening to be near Sophia. Sometimes he would catch glimpses of her through the window. She was definitely alone in the house. Unusual that, for a young schoolgirl, he thought. During many hours of usually fruitless vigil to fill, his mind began to speculate how he might contrive to do more than just catch sight of her from a distance. Within three days Bush had convinced himself he should do something. On the fourth, he decided he could do it, knew what he would do – he just had to. With that key, there was no reason to hold back. The die was cast.

*****

At exactly midnight in San Diego, California, Francis Ulanski reached for another beer and made up his mind. Switching the phone to hands-free he pressed a cool beer glass against his brow. His father lying prone in his bed just two miles away slept little at night, so Francis knew that the phone would be answered.
It was. Seriously, Francis conveyed the welcome news. His father breathed an emotional few words of gratitude and, with a sob, ended the call.

Francis Ulanski began to plan his undertaking. Using the internet for the hour he had allowed himself, he learned all he could of the best way to trace those people. Highly competent with computers he soon had what he wanted. Tomorrow he would make travel arrangements and rearrange his business appointments.

*****

At midnight in Sanorias City, Mexico, Catalina Cruz left her small apartment to walk to work. The nineteen year old cleaner would meet her colleagues there, and for five hours they would spruce up the offices of a car-hire company. At 6.00 a.m. she would begin her main job at the local supermarket; then at 4.00 o'clock in the afternoon, her check-out duties finished, she would hurry home, snack, and sleep for a few hours before the routine began again. Catalina was happy. She had a plan.

CHAPTER 2

Detective Chief Inspector Mallard was deep in thought as the train effortlessly ate up the miles back to Sheffield. The carriage was very hot and some others inside were trying not to doze off, and miss their intended stations: not Mallard. He was wide awake.

His disappointment that the suspect held by the West Yorkshire police had yielded no fresh information to help his own case was for the time being forgotten. A different murder case of the other police force would have been of little interest to him as in his years of participation as a detective he had seen most things. The surprise had come when the West Yorkshire police had revealed to Mallard a brand new technique that they had used to confirm their supposition of their own suspect's guilt. It was a major breakthrough. Using Mass Spectrometry they had been able to identify which of two suspects had held the knife that had been used in the murder.

There had been two suspects who both admitted breaking into the empty house intent on burglary. Both blamed each other for the stabbing when the householder had returned home unexpectedly early and disturbed them. The householder had died on the way to hospital, but had given enough information before he died to establish that only one of the two burglars had actually harmed him. One had fled immediately they had heard him return; the other had waited for him and stabbed him three times. The police recovered the discarded knife but had no usable fingerprint on it. There were only smear traces of the hand which had held the knife. A major breakthrough by Sheffield Hallam University had been used for the first time. Analysis at the university by Mass Spectrometry revealed that the blurred traces found on the knife, had been left by someone who used cocaine. None in the victim's household used drugs. The police soon established beyond dispute that only one of the two burglars used drugs: ergo he was the murderer.

A graduate in Chemistry from Manchester University, Mallard was fascinated that this technique was now possible, and he determined to discover much more about it.
He was also really miffed. Once the Leeds detectives had realised Mallard did not know that Mass Spectrometry had advanced to the level of being able to carry out analysis like that, they had ribbed him all afternoon. The clincher was that the frontrunners in the UK for the breakthrough, was Sheffield Hallam University. The university laboratories were situated less than two miles from Mallard's station – and Mallard was in the dark.

The middle-aged lady who was dozing across the aisle from Mallard shot into the air when Mallard slammed his fist down with a bang onto the table at which he was sitting.

CHAPTER 3

The cold knife at the young girl's throat precluded the otherwise inevitable screaming. Although Bush wore a mask over his upper face, there was enough of it exposed to reveal the bloated lips, and the chalky pockmarked skin. At her age Sophia took scant notice of men of his age. Had she been more interested in people she would have recognised the butcher, partially masked or not.
He stared down at the girl, watching her futile attempts to free herself. It was the girl's eyes which had first mesmerised him when she had entered his shop. Pale blue eyes with a mere hint of grey, her eyes were clear and sparkling. What is more they were honest eyes. They looked at you and did not search, examine, or assess. They saw and did not find flaw. Bush knew there was much about his looks to dislike. The eyes of the girl were beautiful eyes. He had seen no hint of disapproval when she first saw him.
Now, as he was able peer into her young eyes, so close that his rank breath swept over her face, their look of terror stirred and thrilled him.

"God, she is even more incredible like this!"

Aged sixteen and full of hopes and dreams of happiness, Sophia was revolted, as well as utterly terrified, by those peering eyes staring down so intently into her own.
There were no observers, so when his exposed podgy cheek pressed against the smooth softness of the girl's, and when his wet lips forced against her dry mouth and held it in an enforced clasp; no-one knew.

13

The pair, Sophia petrified, Bush engrossed and caught in a desire-filled turmoil, were in a private shared world. The world of nightmare for the girl, was a new awakening for him.

This was his tragic first step along a path that was to lead to destruction for several travellers.

*****

In San Diego, Francis Ulanski sat at a desk in his apartment. Skillfully his fingers darted over the keys of his top-of-the-range computer. Having earlier booked the flights, he was searching the internet for a suitable hotel in London. He had never been to England. In the limited time available he was eager now to see something of the UK, as well as trace those people for his father. Even if it proved to be a waste of time, he was determined to enjoy the tourist part.

*****

Catalina Cruz replaced the telephone on its hook, ignored the landlord who she knew was watching her, and walked happily up the stairs which led to her own room. Her sister was keen for Catalina to visit her and her husband in the USA. It was not going to be automatically possible to be granted a visa to enter America. Catalina had almost scrimped together enough money for the bus journeys. She just hoped that when she applied for the visa she would be successful.

For months the young woman had been dreaming of leaving Mexico just for two weeks, and seeing America. To be with her sister again, a visit to America, and to be in San Diego would be marvelous.

CHAPTER 4

"You have let the side down."

A shocked constable was jerked out of his reverie when he realised that the remark by his Chief Inspector was addressed to him. Trevor Higgs-Whitethorn replaced the coffee cup onto its saucer and looked nervously at his boss.

"In what way, sir?"

"You are supposed to have your fingers on the pulse of new scientific techniques so that we can use them here in the steel city and not be upstaged by those dozy sods in Leeds."

Police Constable Higgs-Whitethorn had no inkling of what Mallard was talking about and he looked at his two colleagues hopefully. The blank faces of both Detective Sergeant Philippa Tate, and Detective Constable Frank Cropper, assisted him not at all.

"Sorry gov. I don't understand."

"Do you think, Detective Constable, that you could keep abreast with the universities of, shall we say, Sheffield? To be au fait with their discoveries might that be within your capacity?"

"That sounds like a rhetorical question, Chief Inspector." Mallard stood.

"If you can make the time, perhaps you would be kind enough to stick a wet finger in the air and see which way the wind is blowing in Sheffield, in the vicinity of the two hallowed establishments that are pleased to call themselves universities."

When he had gone Mallard left behind him three subordinates with a shared sense of bewilderment, but each with different attitudes to the situation. Higgs-Whitethorn was downcast and silent. Tate was sympathetic. Cropper was practical and became the shedder of light. It was some years since Cropper had been a detective in West Yorkshire, but there still remained some former colleagues at Leeds.

Cropper had correctly deduced that the likely reason for the atypical display of displeasure would be something connected with Mallard's visit to Leeds the previous day; in fact Mallard's remarks about the dozy sods there made it almost certain. A five minute phone call was all it took to give him the answer.

When he told Trevor, the young man brightened substantially. It should not be difficult to discover the basics of Mass Spectrometry that could be of assistance in crime detection. For a graduate it should be well within his capability to understand sufficient detail and be able to advise his superior on its practical application to themselves. With any luck he hoped to be able to organise an immediate visit to the laboratories and find out sufficient to be in a position to quickly return to his boss with the facts. He put down what he had been doing, explained where he would be, and left his two colleagues.

*****

"It works by vaporising the sample, and then firing it through an electric and magnetic field. Particles of different mass behave differently under these conditions and this means our team can specifically identify molecules found within a fingerprint, or smudged traces. The kind of information we can find is not only precise, it is also very diverse."

"For example, by looking at the proteins found in the mark, we can find out if the suspect is a male or female. We can understand whether or not a person has dealt drugs or actually taken drugs. We can detect ingested substances, so we may be able to reconstruct what that person has been eating just before committing the crime. All kinds of exogenous substances can link to the lifestyle of the person or their activities."

When Trevor Higgs-Whitethorn left Sheffield Hallam University after his meeting with Dr Fraser, he felt he had enough information to report back to his chief inspector. The breakthrough technique had impressed him and he could see it having a part to play in aiding the identification of suspects. Significant amounts of time could also be saved by eliminating the innocent. The detective constable felt pleased with himself. Just seven hours had passed and he had more detailed facts to add to what Mallard had learned the previous day.

Where was she, Sophia wondered? Attacked yesterday at home in the early evening, groped, stripped, and raped, he had bundled her into a van and brought her to this evil place. He was keeping her naked. It was July so the cold was not a big problem, but it had grown colder during the long night. She knew she was below ground level for there was a slight dampness in the room. He had explained the procedures and house rules. She had food and water on the floor beneath the bed but there was a substantial restriction. One ankle was shackled by a metal chain to the leg of the iron bed.

She had been awake most of the night but had just fallen into a troubled sleep when he had entered the room that morning. After he had done to her what he had done and had left, she had begun screaming again. Sophia screamed as loud as she was able, but she realised it was probably useless: she had been screaming for most of the day out of desperation.
Morning or night, what time is it? How long have I been here? It seems an age. They must be looking for me. He can appear at any time. This room is awful. Somewhere below ground and with no windows there is hardy anything in here. Is this the basement of a house? Are there other houses nearby? I scream but no one comes.

How did he know about that key? He was already in the house when I got home from school. I saw the spare key on the dressing table when I went into the bedroom, but he was onto me before I realised. He is not one of my friends so how did he know about the key. Surely he cannot be a friend of Tomas.

When I try to talk to him he just laughs. My clothes are in the corner over there but he keeps me naked. He is disgusting.

CHAPTER 5

A grey 6.2L engined Hummer eased smoothly into a lonely lay-by on the outskirts of Sanorias City, Mexico, and parked there with no lights. The powerful engine was kept running whilst the two grim-faced Mexican government agents awaited the arrival of "the pigeon". Each of the agents had a Heckler & Koch MP5 gun in his hands, resting across his knees. They knew he would come.

Although where they were was pitch black it was still evening. There was a strong breeze blowing in from the west which could have been a welcome relief on that humid night if the agents had stood outside. They did not. Familiarity with this routine had not brought careless relaxation and the dangers that could be associated with this business were appreciated by both of them. That welcoming breeze they could have had would also have made the driving rain most unpleasant. On other nights, clear moonless nights, whilst they waited patiently in the silence, both men occupied with their own thoughts, they would have seen a sky full of stars. One of them would enjoy the sight, and wonder some of the thoughts that had absorbed the minds of men since time immemorial: but only one of them. His partner would continue to steadily shovel small portions of Cacahuates Japoneses into his cavernous mouth. True he would stare up at the cosmos, but his mind such as it was, would have no interrogation as to creation, destiny, or infinity. It was there; that was enough. Any interrogations he would have an interest in, in his little world, would have a completely different character.

Diego Tamayo was the senior, the one with the eye for opportunities, the one who had devised the "business". The other, Rufino Rivera, was the muscle. A big man with a small intellect, he removed objections and obstacles that may hinder their smooth progress. After a few minutes with Rivera, people became "helpful". Working as a team of federal agents now for six years they complemented each other. Their team worked well in official paid legitimacy. Their pursuit that night was unofficial – it was also illegal.

For three years their "business" with one Alfred Walberg, had prospered. The man, Alfred Walberg dealt lawfully in tractor spare parts. His was a legitimate business. Walberg sold spares to several garages in San Diego. He had worked hard in the business for five and a half days a week, and had taken only public holidays for four years. On Saturday afternoon every week, Walberg would close his depot and drive over the border and collect the tractor spares, in northern Mexico late Saturday evening. He would sleep in his cab and on Sunday morning travel north driving his lorry loaded with those spare parts until he reached Sanorias. There he would park his vehicle in a Truck Stop, and in a nearby establishment catering predominantly for solo males, take a few hours relaxation on the Sunday evening. The Mexican ladies of *El Retiro* know the type of relaxation that many American men like him appreciate. After a huge steak meal, an ample quantity of cheap local firewater, and a willing wench, Walberg would sleep like a baby in his cab, to make an early start back to San Diego Monday morning.

Until one morning when his start was delayed by six unnerving hours. The two government federal agents Tamayo and Rivera were themselves frequent partakers of the amenities of *El Retiro*, free gratis. In fact a recruiting arrangement with Alegria, the proprietor, a woman not yet forty years of age, had been formed. The two agents had been observing Walberg in *El Retiro* for some weeks. In the early Monday morning, they would follow him and watch him cross the border without difficulty. At that time of day the border was quiet. The border guards on both sides knew Walberg as a regular who was always "clean". On that particular Monday morning, Tamayo and Rivera pounced before Walberg reached the border, and they took him and his lorry to the police station. In a search of the vehicle, they "found" a quantity of cocaine. It was sufficient to keep him locked away for the majority of his normal, natural life. In Mexican jails, the length of life expectancy varies in inverse proportion to one's decency. Walberg knew, and the agents knew, he would not survive long. There was however a possible way out.

Each time he crossed into the USA he would take a parcel with him. That parcel would be collected from his depot in the USA on the next evening. He would hand it over and be given payment for himself, and be given another parcel which he would deliver to the agents in Sanorias City on his next trip. Then the cycle would begin again, and continue weekly. Not only would he be freed without charge, he would also be paid handsomely for his efforts. The promised weekly payment was extremely significant. They would not tell Walberg what the parcels would contain, but they would not contain drugs. Sniffer dogs at the border would detect nothing. Walberg reluctantly but rapidly had to agree.

The agents made sure no checks were carried out at the Mexican border, but they had no sway in the USA. Walberg was checked for drugs on every journey, and nothing was found. Whatever was in those parcels, it was not drugs. With the money from the smuggling, Walberg soon expanded his business and reaped the rewards that its success brought him.

After two years of this association Walberg felt he deserved more leisure time. He also wanted to be free of the nerve-wracking border crossings. Together with the two Mexicans he agreed a plan. Walberg would take on an employee whose duties would include the Mexico collection. The agents would arrange sound references and papers, for a certain known Mexican resident to have a solid chance of being able to emigrate to the USA. Walberg would have a job waiting for the man in San Diego. The two agents knew one petty criminal who would be perfect for the job. He had no police record. Tamayo and Rivera had seen to it that he had never been charged or even listed as a suspect. The man, Vasquez, had enjoyed the protection of the two agents for a share in his "earnings".

All had gone well and "the pigeon", Luis Vasquez, had been used for the past seven months, as the courier. He would be arriving shortly. The agents were relaxed.

CHAPTER 6

Every Wednesday evening the four of them would have a night out to skate at the Skating Arena in Sheffield. Of course they took their crucial gear. Skylarking and chatting as they whooshed along the ice in their outfits: own white boots purchased from pocket money and presents; their Bows and Beads sleeveless dresses with tiny skirts; and naturally, because *simply everybody wears it mom*, a concoction of make-up, as carefully applied as brush strokes on a Caravaggio canvas: always noticing and giggling at the stares they attracted from males of all ages. In the first few weeks before they were in-the-know, they borrowed boots and dressed in normal jumpers and jeans. Hardly a glance had come their way. The gear transformed that. It had been worth every penny.

As always, that Wednesday night, they had confirmed the arrangement by telephone before setting off to catch their respective buses. Karen Clayton could not understand why her best friend Sophia had failed to arrive. At the Arena they had all tried to phone her, but just heard the recorded answering message. Harumi had been nervous and wanted to phone the police, but Courtney just wanted to get straight onto the ice.

Neither did Sophia attend school on Thursday. Sophia was never sick, and she was not so gifted that she could freewheel whenever she fancied. Something was obviously wrong. After school, Thursday afternoon, having made several more fruitless attempts to contact her friend by phone, Karen Clayton reported her concern in person, at the local Police Station. She was treated politely – then promptly ignored after her departure.

In the evening she decided to ring Sophia's older brother, Tomas Pearson. Karen had, as long as she could remember, fancied the tall athletic Tomas with those dreamy blue eyes like his sister. She would go round to see Karen whenever she could, in the hope that she might be able to be near the brother for a while. Sometimes she was lucky. Although he was always friendly, he had never shown any interest in her, in that way. She had earlier recognised that she was too young for him, but now she was sixteen and had developed – well, things might change. Other males had been eying her for some years, but not Tomas – not yet.

It was not to be. As Karen dialled, a hundred miles away on business in a hotel room, Tomas was sighing happily. They would meet whenever Tomas' sales visits brought him to that part of England. It was by lucky chance that during one visit he had met this lover, and now he celebrated the freedom that his job afforded.
Regrettably his sales manager would ring him every evening to check up on him and require a progress report. The call could come at any hour for the bastard seemed to delight in inconveniencing his Reps as much as he could. When his mobile rang Tomas cursed and reached for the phone. Beside him, Steven too cursed - forcefully.
As a result of what Karen Clayton had told him, Tomas kept ringing Sophia. Disheartened, at midnight he decided that in the morning he would ask a neighbour to go round to the house. Tomas Pearson had become concerned. This was most unlike his sister.

*****

The mirror had been telling him all his life that he was luckless in the looks department. Girls did not want to know. The only two he had properly been with, two years apart, as a teenager, had been boozed up and almost legless at the local nightclub. It was likely that neither would remember much the next morning, who it was that had taken them home or what had happened. This little beauty, though, would definitely remember. That though, was going to be a problem.

Nothing in life is perfect though, at least not for long. This Sophia had that unexpected damage. Shame that. Soon Bush slept.

Sophia cried and did not.

*****

An unexpected morning phone call was a rarity in her house, and it was a puzzled lady, early that Friday morning, who answered the call from her neighbours' son, Tomas. The couple were on holiday. After replacing the telephone Margery Wilson, spinster, went next door to her brother Colin. Always a nervous, timid woman, that phone call from Tomas had worried her. Margery wanted support in case she was really heading for some unpleasantness at the family house where Sophia remained alone. The two of them knocked and rang, and peered in windows, but of young Sophia there was not a sign: nor of anyone else. The postman had already been and, looking through the letterbox, they could see two letters on the floor beneath the letter box. Although all the curtains were pulled back downstairs, in Sophia's bedroom they were drawn. Had she slept in? Was she ill? It was by now nearly 9.00 a.m.

They went to Margery's home and phoned Tomas. What to do?

Tomas told them about the spare key under a rock in the back garden. Would they please get it and go inside? Of course they would. Curiosity mounting, back the pair went. No key. He said the white rock didn't he, the one you could pick out in the dark? Check them all, you know what youngsters can be like.

No key.

Back home, they phoned Tomas who now became really alarmed. The system of that key, under that rock, had been operating since they could walk. How could it not be there?

Sophia could have told him.

*****

It was a different police officer who took the call from Tomas.

"When did you last see her, sir?

Wednesday, just two days ago sir? Not unusual this, sir. Summertime and young girls go off all the time. Probably gone to stay with a friend.

What bird? Canary? What about the canary? Oh. She probably left it enough food for three days, sir.

Shits itself daft, what do you mean, sir? Ah, right – eyes too big for its belly?

What about the phone, sir? Have you left a message?
OK calm down, sir. If you can't get a response from the
phone what about Skype, email, a computer message?
Can't get a floor-mounted computer in her bag. Right, sir. I
understand, sir. Try to calm down.
Tablet then? No tablet, just the phone.

Well, sir I will note it down and someone will go round
there and investigate. Don't worry, sir I am sure it is
nothing."

With a sigh, PC Wallace made the appropriate entry and
set the wheels in motion for "somebody to go round there
and investigate".

*****

There was always plenty to arrange in the shop. Joel Bush
whistled happily and was in obvious good spirits. The
butchers shop was well located. His side of the road caught
most of the area's business. In the centre, his decently
sized premises were next door to the post office on one
side; whilst on the other was a popular small greengrocer.
The car park was thirty yards away. His father had made a
brilliant choice and had successfully developed and
expanded the business.

Last week he had been bristly and hard. His two assistant
butchers were grateful for the improvement. Whatever had

caused this welcome change in the boss had done them a favour. They cared not what it was.
Sophia could have told them.

After closing the shop, he used a supermarket where he was unknown to buy the extra provisions he now needed. As he loaded the provisions into the van he remembered he had not sanitized it since the Wednesday night. There will be traces of the girl. It was days now and he had only just realised he had overlooked it. Alarm welled up inside him.

Now he was on the verge of panic as he stared at the interior of his van in which he had transported the girl. Terrified of the thought of discovery, he scrambled into the driving seat and raced home.

Two hours later, with the van thoroughly cleaned he was calm again. Then he had another thought. Yes, he should certainly do that. Rummaging in the linen basket, full now, for his leisure time had been taken up with more agreeable activities than laundry; he extracted every item of clothing he had worn on the Wednesday night. He took them down to the garden. After lighting the Bar-B-Q and waiting for it to burn fiercely enough, he placed each item onto it. It was an hour before he was confidant they would all be destroyed by the time the fuel was burnt. Hungry by then, he went in to prepare meals for himself and Sophia.

As he ate he cast his mind back over his recent actions. "If I ever do this sort of thing again, I will be more careful." As he gulped down the last of his fillet steak, it dawned on him what had just passed through his mind.

Bush went outside and checked that the clothes had been destroyed on the Bar-B-Q.

When he went inside for an evening of entertainment with his young beauty, his tread was unusually slow. He was re-thinking that surprising thought about being more careful *next time*.

CHAPTER 7

Sergeant Benjamin should have been off duty two and a half hours ago. A meeting at his station to arrange for the policing of a march by a pressure group had forced the delay. Sergeant Benjamin was a patient man who had seen a lot in his time. The pressure group this time was WASPS.

Urging harsher measures for sex offenders, the march through Sheffield city centre was to take place the next day, Saturday lunchtime. This timing was designed to create maximum disruption to traffic on the main Market Day. Why target markets was not clear as there was no apparent correlation between sex offenders and market customers. Still, solutions MUST be found, they advocated.

As the wife of the Assistant Chief Constable was known to be an active supporter, this must be a priority policing operation.

On his way home at 4.30 p.m. it came to Sergeant Benjamin that he had not even looked at the log of non-urgent matters requiring attention. Sod it; he would do it in the morning. Hopefully there would be time before he deployed his detail for the Women Against Sex Predators Society demonstration.

*****

Sergeant Benjamin did not look at the log the next morning, or any other morning. During the night he suffered a stroke and never returned to work.

On that Saturday morning, the earlier than expected arrival at the Station of the wife of the ACC caused a little panic. Brave, community-loving, conscientious male officers of the law, hastened to straighten out the office and conceal any hint of sexist printed matter, and better appear to be over-stressed and over-worked heroes of the people.

The fact that sixteen year old Sophia Pearson had been reported missing was on no-one's agenda.

*****

The agents watched the lights of a lorry with US plates pull into the lay-by. As always the agents were alert looking for any other vehicles in the vicinity. If they had seen anything which looked as though their man was being followed, they would simply have sped away. He would have to take care of himself.

"The pigeon", Luis Vasquez, switched off the motor and quickly approached the waiting Hummer. Watching him carefully, the government agents kept their hands ready on the MP5s. In Vasquez's hand was the parcel given to him on Saturday morning by Alfred Walberg. Hatless, the rain ran down the back of his neck as he handed it over. He in return was given a parcel for Alfred Walberg. "The pigeon" would be given his payment in the USA by Walberg.

Vasquez was content with his life. Now that he was living in the USA, his standard of living had risen beyond what he had dreamed. With just his decently paid job, earned honestly working at the tractor depot, he had more money than he had ever had thieving. With his extra bonus for the Mexico run on top, he was creaming it. Vasquez and his wife had started in a two-roomed apartment in downtown San Diego. After the first two months, convinced they had hit the jackpot, they moved into a rented 4 bed-roomed house in Encinitas. Already they had made friends with some of the neighbours.

Luis Vasquez recognised, though, that his biggest blessing was his wife. He adored her. She had been always there for him through their difficulties. With the Mexican police as partners, keeping out of jail had not been his major fear in Mexico. It had been the other crooks, like him, who were the danger. Competition for prey was fierce and frequently it was their own kind that were targeted.

On the prompting of his wife, he had agreed to chance a request to agent Tamayo, to help her sister. Now he gave details of Catalina Cruz to Tamayo. The agent slipped the items into his pocket with barely a glance. The two agents monitored him all the way, smiling, seeing him trying to shield the parcel as he scampered to his lorry.

Back in his lorry Vasquez concealed the parcel and drove to *El Retiro*. There he too would enjoy their full hospitality. Mexico is far enough from San Diego for a man to be able to enjoy a degree of liberty. The girls at *El Retiro* are not only wise to the preferences of American men. The ways and susceptibilities of men of every nationality, and they see plenty, are largely consistent. As a curvy Mexican female nibbled his ear, his adored wife Rosa Cruz slept alone in their bed in San Diego.

In Sanorias City her sister, Catalina Cruz, was singing quietly to herself whilst she polished a desk at the car-hire company. She was wondering what she would buy to take to her sister if she managed to obtain the visa to the USA.

CHAPTER 8

"Sophia."
Silence.
From the hallway, louder now. "Sophia." Silence.
Into the lounge. Empty, no sign of life – literally.
Stiffening on the cage floor, the canary was motionless, never to sing again.
"Jesus! Please don't let her be dead upstairs."

Heart pounding and mouth dry, Tomas ran up the stairs two at a time. Bedroom – no sign, bathroom, nothing, toilet with its door wide open, obviously was empty.
He checked all the rooms. He went outside and into the garden. Warily he checked the shed, managed to find the key for the garage – nothing. Sophia's bike was propped up at the end of the garage. The car that would customarily have been there would still be parked at Robin Hood airport. Their parents had flown to the Costa del something or other for their two weeks holiday from that airport.

Not dead or unconscious at home, anyway. "Thank God, thank you, Lord."
Tomas stood and slowly regained his composure.

Back in the empty house, Tomas made a cup of coffee. It had been a particularly difficult week. His sales manager was fearful for his own job, and was therefore piling more and more pressure and insults on his staff. Steven was becoming more demanding and wanted Thomas to move north to be closer to him. And now his little sister. He had promised his parents, in fact guaranteed, that he would keep a watchful eye out for the girl. There was no doubt he loved her dearly, but what more could he have done when he had to be away for his job?

Miserably, Tomas sat to consider the possibilities one more time. He thought he had already been through them all, over the past two days. There were sound reasons to rule out her staying with friends, a traffic accident, illness, or a last-minute flight to join their parents. The one he had, in dread, pushed firmly away, was that she had been killed or kidnapped. Now, he had to admit, it was at least possible.

And where was that missing key?

*****

The pain was still there. The man had come to Sophia early that morning. It had taken him several minutes but he had hurt her so much that she had sobbed her surrender. It had been so easy for him to hurt her, and he had grinned the whole time he had pinched the soft flesh under her armpit which had hurt her so much.

At junior school Bush's best friend was Stuart whose father was an amateur wrestler. When he caught them misbehaving he would take hold of the boys and hurt them. Once the man had described at length, a few of the tricks of the trade. Later, at senior school, after Bush had blurted out that his parents were from Poland, some of the boys had decided to victimise him and label him a foreigner. The tricks Stuart's father had taught them came in very handy. Using one of them one day soon stopped the ringleader and hence the rest.

Twisting and pulling the girl's flesh whilst gripping it tightly, had been so effortless for him; but for Sophia the pain had been wicked. The thought of complying with his new demand had kept Sophia awake all night. She wished during those sleepless hours that he had not given her advance notice of it. She had cried bitterly and wanted to die.

That morning had been the worst yet. She guessed he would be back for her later that day.
"Please, please, please someone come and rescue me."

Sophia still had no idea where the monster had brought her. Her mind went over and over that initial ordeal. After the rape in her own bed, she had been wrapped, and tied in some sort of bag. She had been unable to see anything during the journey.
Here, underground, there were few outside noises, except for a few birds, a few cars, and occasionally a dog barking in the distance. The sounds were so remote. Probably a detached house, Sophia reasoned
"Tomas where are you? He is here again. Help me!"

*****

By Saturday evening there was a more relaxed air at the station. The ACC had been seen actually smiling as he departed for his weekend of wedded bliss. The demonstration had proceeded satisfactorily. The WASPS had returned to their respective nests. There was initial annoyance when Tomas Pearson arrived at 18.30 enquiring of the progress of the investigation. Investigation?

Fobbed off with platitudes and promises by the police, Tomas went round again to the family home. The quiet empty house in that early evening had a portentous air. For a few minutes Tomas wandered around hoping for inspiration. In Sophia's bedroom the curtains were still closed and he decided to leave them that way. He picked up her mobile by the bed. There was still adequate battery life and a strong signal. Replacing it on the table his misery grew.
He buried the canary.

The blank looks at the police station had indicated that very little, if anything had actually been done. Despite the late hour he went in person to the two local hospitals and checked with them. From the evening staff he heard they had no knowledge of Sophia.

At a loss what else to do, Tomas went home.

CHAPTER 9

Today would have been his father's birthday. Joel Bush was sitting at the kitchen table, with his recollections. The father had done well. Coming, from Poland to England with his pregnant wife, he had correctly reasoned he would be better accepted with an English name. Ryszard Bushmanov had changed his name to Richard Bush. He had soon learned enough of the customs and language to be taken on as an assistant butcher at one of the Sheffield City centre butchery shops, which was owned by a national chain. By the time he was thirty years old, he was manager of that shop and for two more years it thrived. Fortune is fickle. It smiled on Richard Bush. One particular regular customer was an aging man who was obviously lonely and liked to linger and talk. Of the three men in the shop, only Bush made time for him and, with the passage of time, the man would loiter until Bush was free to serve him.

One day, some three years after their first gossip, the old man whispered to him that he would like to discuss something outside work in private. It would be, he had emphasised, to the advantage of Bush. It was a reluctant young butchery manager who, after church the following Sunday, set off in the opposite direction to his wife and son, heading to the house of the aging Mr Howard. When he arrived home some two and a half hours later, he informed his agitated wife what had occurred. Mr. Howard had no living relatives and was a wealthy man. The village, on the outskirts of Sheffield, in which Mr Howard had lived all his life, was small and the sole Butchers shop which had closed five years earlier was now a Chinese take-away. With walking becoming increasingly difficult, Mr. Howard's future journeys into Sheffield would soon have to cease. He proposed to buy the premises of the village Post Office which was also about to close, and convert it to a Butchers.

Mr. Howard wanted Bush to run it and in return, Bush would receive a salary of fifty percent more than he was currently being paid. Further, in his will, Mr Howard would leave the shop to Richard Bush. There was one more item. Mr Howard owned another bungalow. The Bush family would move into his village and would live rent free in a bungalow a few doors away from the house of Mr. Howard. Upon his death, the bungalow also would be bequeathed to Richard Bush. If the Bush family would look in on Mr Howard from time to time, that would be most welcome.

The remarkable Mr. Howard, ex cutler and gentleman, died peacefully in his sleep eight years later. He had seen his Butchers shop thrive. He had witnessed the young son, Joel maturing into a sturdy lad. As hoped, he had enjoyed frequent visits from the delightful Magdalina Bush and her friendly husband.

Subsequently, the Bush family sold the bungalow and business, and bought another established local business in a more convenient and busy area. Having the benefit of the Bush gregarious flair, the new business went from strength to strength. The three were regular attendees of the local church. It was there that the first sign appeared, of the illness that was subsequently to kill Richard Bush. The man liked to join in the Amateur Dramatics activities led by the wife of the vicar. On stage in a dress rehearsal one day he was taken ill. Seven months later he died.

Joel inherited the business when his father died, and also eighteen months later, after the death of his broken-hearted mother, their large detached family home in Dore.

It was there, finishing his breakfast, some three miles away from the Pearson home, on his late his father's birthday that Joel pondered his parents' life so far as he knew it. He had no knowledge of their life in Poland, no familiarity with the country of their birth or its language. To both his parents it had been a closed book. On his eleventh birthday, they had taken him as a birthday treat, just the three of them, to Wimpeys, his favourite burger bar. They had told him how they used to live in Poland, but gave few of the details of that life. From that day onwards, nothing else of Poland had ever been mentioned in his presence.

As he made his way again to the basement and Sophia, Joel was oblivious to the significance that that former life was about to have upon his own.

******

Just before Sunday lunch, PC Allen went with Tomas Pearson to the house. An agitated Tomas managed to keep his patience for a little time whilst the constable poked around and did all the things Tomas had already done. The bathroom revealed Sophia's toothbrush, toothpaste and the myriad of accessories essential for all teenage girls – and their mothers.

"She has apparently not planned to go away, sir" announced the constable, profoundly.

41

Tomas exploded. After a heated exchange, the PC departed to report back to the Station. Tomas Pearson would be kept informed.

PC "Noddy" Allen was a keen footballer. His name may well have had something to do with his propensity to use his skull on a member of the opposition if skill alone was proving inadequate. "Noddy" Allen was captain of his local side. It was some time after his normal finishing time, when PC Allen finished his report. He stood and stretched, picturing, in his mind's eye, the photographs in Sophia's bedroom. Apart from pictures of herself there were some of teenage boys and also men. Had she simply absconded with one of them?

A number of the pictures were of footballers. Back to the subject of his over-riding sport, he brooded over his team still being short of a decent centre forward. The plonker they still had, had cost them the trophy last season. Now that Tomas Pearson today looked the ideal type to make a centre forward. He was tall - big factor – and he looked very agile. Also he was probably strong enough to survive what the pansies at the BBC would describe as "a little bit robust" tackles which were the norm in their league – not that the BBC would be remotely interested in their standard of soccer. On the off-chance, he decided to ring him.

Replacing the phone some minutes later he concluded he had probably caught Mister Pearson on a bad day.

*****

For some in San Diego, night is a profitable time. Dealers trade, and working girls share their blessings. Money changes hands. Life is active for them at that time, and the good times roll – for a time. With luck, age, other criminals, and police as adversaries, times change.
The arrow of time would soon reach its journey's end for Lucek Ulanski, who that night lay awake reflecting.

Except for that one bewildering stupidity, he had led a reasonably good life.
That blemish had been completely out of character. Lifelong friends, it was he who had suggested to his younger cousin, Ryszard Bushmanov that he was convinced that they would find a better future in England. All over Europe people had become restless. The Cold War showed no sign of ever being resolved. In some countries people were building nuclear shelters, whilst in Poland people were striving to make enough money to feed themselves. There must be a better life elsewhere, and England which had withstood the Nazis and freed Europe, was rebuilding its economy and was the major country in Europe. It was also very cagy regarding Russia. England was the obvious choice if they were to leave.
So the two cousins and Magdalina had embarked on that journey of emigration. Magdalina had been just another pretty girl to Ulanski. Two weeks of close contact had changed that. Magdalina unintentionally captivated him. He fell in love with her. Married to his cousin Ryszard, the girl was obviously blindingly happy. Thumbing lifts as they made their way eastwards across Europe, they were cramped together, often overnight. Lying alone he was conscious of the pair, their amorous movements and

hushed noises. It nearly drove him crazy that Ryszard, and not he, was with Magdalina those nights.

A wave of pain swept through the body of Lucek Ulanski. He moaned loudly. Which was worse, this diseased paroxysm, or those nights of agony of wanting Magdalina?

In Calais they had found an abandoned house in which they had sheltered and rested before crossing the English Channel. The more intelligent and charismatic Ryszard was sent to try to find a free passage on any vessel that would take them. Magdalina was to do the shopping for food with the little money that remained, and Lucek would guard their belongings. Ryszard left first. Alone with Magdalina for the very first time, Ulanski declared his need for her. He tried to force himself on her but she had pulled free and fled. How could he face the couple now? In a despairing panic he had grabbed his meagre belongings and was almost at the door when he noticed the silver crucifix. It had belonged to Magdalina's mother, long dead. It was of very little worth to anyone but Magdalina. He wanted something of the girl for his own. Ulanski took it and fled.
His moist eyes could not see clearly, but he knew where it was. He looked towards Magdalina's crucifix which, down these subsequent years, had constantly hung on the wall opposite his bed. Before her death, Francis' American mother whom Lucek Ulanski had wed some years later, had tried several times over the years to replace it with something better. He would never part with it.
Ulanski crossed himself as he tried to focus on the crucifix.

At that moment the silver crucifix was in the suitcase of his son Francis, in England.

*****

Sunday had been a long and bitter day for Sophia. He did not have to work on Sunday. Before the church bells had started to ring he had come to her. Throughout the day he kept returning. Confidant now, his requirements were becoming more insistent. Finally, just before midnight the girl was able to sleep. It was not a peaceful sleep. She dreamt she was running down a never-ending tunnel chased by howling monsters. A young man appeared before her, faceless - Tomas. It must be Tomas. She ran towards him as fast as she could, but, however fast she ran, he never appeared any nearer. Was there no escape?

CHAPTER 10

England was enjoying an unusually hot dry summer's day. In the Sheffield police HQ at 8.30 a.m. on that Monday morning; all the fans in the building were humming. John Mallard was not. His tie had been loosened, and the top button of his shirt unfastened. Already he was feeling the heat. As she stood before his desk looking the picture of radiant health and composure, Philippa Tate showed no sign of discomfort.

"So the girl has been missing for 4 days."

"Five if you count Wednesday night, sir."

"Correct, I stand corrected. They teach you to count then, at Harvard?"

"No, sir. My father taught me when I was four, sir."

Detective Chief Inspector John Mallard looked up at his recently acquired detective sergeant. There was a blank expression on the face of DS Philippa Tate. This one was no shrinking violet, he decided. Would they be able to work harmoniously together?

The sergeant was average height and had a fairly pretty face. She looked fit; probably exercised at a gym regularly. Two aspects were not average. First, her intelligence was probably as high as anyone in the station, including Mallard: degrees gained at Harvard had to be earned. Second, her figure was not average. She wore a simple white, short-sleeved blouse and a dark blue skirt, it was apparent that Philippa Tate was an attractive woman.

"Quite right. A stupid remark. Let me say straight off, I am impressed with your academic achievements and I look forward to our association benefiting from your contribution. I hope your practical work is as significant."

"Sir."

A straight bat this one plays. Mallard inwardly sighed. His last DS was a useless bloke who eventually, after much acrimony, asked for a transfer. Good riddance, but would this girl – nay woman – cut the mustard? Only time would tell.
"May I ask why we are taking on a missing person after just 5 days absence?"

Whilst she waited for his reply, Philippa Tate was looking at Mallards hands. It was an unconscious habit. As a teen she had briefly dated a farmer's son. At a point of their relationship when he had judged it appropriate, his hands had wandered more than usual. Philippa liked him and was enjoying the attention of this lad. She knew where he was heading and only protested a little for the sake of propriety. His warm breath in her ear and his sigh of such longing for her were thrilling. She relaxed and allowed it. When the one striving hand won through, and eagerly cupped her bare breast, it felt like one of his Hessian sacks of animal feed was wrapping itself around her tender flesh. The rough work on the farm had had its effect on his rugged hands. His copping-a-feel had been staggeringly brief. Since then, hands became important. She had no intention of ever allowing Mallard or any other colleague to put their hands on her; but it was habit. Mallard had hands of a normal size. They were strong hands, a man's hands. Clean hands, with nails neatly but not professionally cut, they were still: they did not tremble, quiver, or drum the desk. The hands were average, appropriate – for a man.

"Normally we would not, but this one smells fishy. It may of course be a kidnapping. No sign of any ransom demand as yet. The plod asked around on Sunday and have come to the conclusion it is probably an abduction. Her parents are on holiday according to the brother, so she has been living alone in the house since they went, nearly two weeks ago. She is not the type to disappear AWOL. She is fit and healthy and fairly unlikely to have been taken ill. Also, says the plod, she is a beauty. Just the type, they say, to ignite unwholesome thoughts into the evil minds of ninety percent of the male heterosexual population. Most importantly, abductions have a nasty habit of turning into murders. Finally, my eager Detective Sergeant, we are in the doldrums. We are becalmed. The rogues are on holiday. They are slacking and I am p.....   cheesed off with twiddling my thumbs and dealing with undemanding matters. I want something to get my teeth into."
"What do the other ten percent do, sir?"
"Eh?"

"The ten percent of men who do not take unwholesome thoughts into their evil minds?"

The merest trace of a smile transformed the previous expressionless features of twenty-five year old DS Philippa Tate. Mallard stared, surprised. The young woman was taking the piss. Unexpectedly, the slight smile had changed her face. It now gave a hint of its own ability to ignite thoughts of a testosterone inflaming nature.

"Don't know. I am with the naughty nineties."
"Do we have a photograph?"
"Would uniform ever think of such a thing, sergeant? No!"

"How do we know she is a beauty, as you put it?"

Is the cheeky sod at it again? Give her the benefit of the doubt, this time.

"You understand of course, detective sergeant, that even the plod can produce reports?"

The sharpness was fairly mild by Mallard's biting standards. It still stung the young woman. She had been promoted just recently and assigned to the most successful Detective Chief Inspector in South Yorkshire. She was determined to impress him. She was new, obviously eager, and probably a vulnerable female – vulnerable that is, in that she would be sensitive to criticism. Mallard saw her expression.

"Sorry, sergeant. I hope you will quickly get used to my sarcasm. You will see it often. Don't read anything into it. It is just my way. Yes, it was in the report by the constable who went round Sunday lunchtime. There were photographs of her throughout the house. Any officer of normal competence would have snaffled one for us. Not PC "Noddy" Allen, oh no. I suggest you make time to read it.

Right now, I want a report on anything uniform discovers from their door-to-door enquiries. Go round there with Frank and have a sniff. See what that dozy sod of a constable missed. Is there a mobile phone? Were any messages left on an answering service or device? See if you can get any advance inkling from them while forensics are performing their miracles. Then I want you and Frank to do detailed checks of bank and financial records. I want all her friends interviewed. Find out what makes this girl tick. The school breaks up for summer holidays soon. By tonight I must decide how many teams to put in there. Where does she eat, drink, dance, socialise etc? I will have the plod search all outbuildings around there, and then I will interview Tomas Pearson and check up on all and any relatives they have. Maybe a prelim from Forensics will materialise today, or maybe pigs WILL fly. We meet here again to check progress at 5.30 p.m. Get on with it, sergeant."

*****

As was usual for a Monday morning, business was slow and he and time to think and brood. He could see it now in his mind's eye. The fool of a surgeon should be sacked. To commit such sacrilege on an otherwise classical beauty was unforgivable.
In his initial triumph and excitement, it had not dismayed him but now he was noticing it more and more. His eyes saw it; his fingers felt it, and the perfection he had beheld in that life-changing moment when she had first entered his shop had proved delusive. Although he was rejoicing in the sex, a rare treat in his so far lonely frustrated existence, there was this growing disappointment gnawing at his mind.

*****

It was a bright morning, but for Tomas who was due to be working even further from home than last week, it was anything but bright. He felt out of touch and impotent. His attempts to contact their parents had failed. Not for his father were the mobile phone companies' exorbitant roaming charges in Europe.

On route to Northumberland he had stopped off at a roadside mobile café just a few miles short of his destination. A Chief Inspector Mallard phoned him and demanded he return to Sheffield: demanded no less! After phoning his fuming sales manager he was about to begin his unhappy way back to Sheffield when a thought occurred to him. He had better talk to the secretary of his sales manager to make sure somebody cancelled his appointments for the rest of that day. The manager had said he would do it. Tomas knew the man well enough by now: better to be safe than sorry. At least the secretary was reliable.

Another pair not feeling bright on that morning was Margery and Colin Wilson. They had gone together to visit their mother who had fallen and hurt her back. All thoughts of Sophia had been replaced by concern for mother.

CHAPTER 11

Before Philippa Tate had arrived, the bedroom of Sophia Pearson had been examined and cleared by forensics. She was accompanied by DC Frank Cropper, fifty-one and as yet an unknown quantity to Philippa. She had been introduced to him the previous week and had been struck by his unimpressive appearance. True he had looked clean enough, even if his hair was marginally due for a trim. The tie he wore was neither central nor really tight enough; not thrown on in the schoolboys' deliberately loose fashion though. Leather shoes, which had been recently cleaned, were definitely his best feature. He had worn a sports jacket and slacks: nothing amiss there, but they were hardly impressive. Was he married or living alone? It was a ticklish question. She thought probably not married. He had got to the bottom of DCI Mallard's out of the ordinary show of vexation easily and quickly. He was a puzzle which would need solving sooner rather than later because they clearly would be working side by side for much of the time.

Today he looked smarter in a suit. He also stood more erect. The DC was a tall man, well built, and for fifty-one, a somewhat imposing figure. All in all DC Frank Cropper looked a different person. Why was he still only a DC at fifty-one, though? As she watched him rummage unenthusiastically around the roomful of the girl's belongings.

Sophia's bedroom was recognisably the bedroom of a teenage girl. If nothing else, the size and number of cuddly teddies and fluffy animals would have provided a hint.

Teddies and fluffies were not the sole preserve of teenage girls; they were frequently present in the bedrooms of women of all ages, who lived alone; and some who did not. Bottles and tubes promising guaranteed transformation into Aphrodite were carefully positioned on the dressing table. Pink carpet slippers in the shape of a baby lion were centrally located beneath the dressing table. They were what, size five? Decoratively arranged around the bedroom were photographs and posters in moderate number.

How would she describe the room? Cosy, welcoming, personal: my place!

DC Tate went to the large wardrobe with its expensive mahogany doors standing partially open. Forensics had probably left the wardrobe as they had found it. They would have photographed the contents first before interfering with its items. She opened the doors wide and stood quite still observing the items without touching anything. The articles were beautifully arranged inside the enclosed area. Sophia had organised everything so that it looked orderly, and the clothes would be very easy to identify and pick. Except for the singular neatness there was nothing remarkable, except perhaps the shoes. There were only three pairs of stylish shoes and three flat-heeled school shoes. Philippa Tate knelt and began to examine the three handbags which again were positioned precisely on a low shelf.

******

"OK." Mallard said looking around at his team assembled in the Incident Room. "First off there was no sign of a struggle. It is a possibility the girl has indeed gone off somewhere innocently. Perhaps she has developed some sort of mental aberration and is wandering around, lost and confused. Anybody want to say anything?"

He looked around making deliberate eye contact with each. Them waiting for him to do it all was not satisfactory: contribution was what he required.
First to speak was Sergeant Philippa Tate.

"I think she has been snatched, sir."
"Elaborate, sergeant."
"A female and her handbag are inseparable. Hers was in her wardrobe. There are three handbags but it is obvious which is the one currently in use. Inside the bag is her purse with forty-five pounds odd in cash. Additionally there is her card wallet containing two credit cards, and a debit card, all current. Her bank records show, in her bank account is two hundred and thirty-six pounds. There have been no recent transactions. Also, sixteen year old girls are wedded to their smart phones. Hers was by the bed. Sick or not, it is unlikely she would have left home without handbag, cash, bank cards and phone. I think she has been abducted from that house."

"Frank?"
"Probably just done a bunk with some feller who gave her the eye. Judging by the photo on the board she would get plenty of that."
"And the bag and phone?"
"Rushed off all eager, like."

"Are you bloody serious, Frank?"

It had been five weeks since Mallard had last used profanities. He had made a resolution, but lately Frank's attitude and lack of effort had been noticeably deteriorating.

"I am inclined to the sergeant's view. If she has been taken for money, and it is still a possibility, it is likely her cash and bank cards would have disappeared with her. For the moment, we will work on an abduction basis. Whether it is for sex or filthy lucre, I too say she has still been snatched. There is no information to the contrary. We must be doing our utmost from the start – even if the start was five days after the event.
Anybody else want to contribute?"

Feet shuffled. Eyes were averted.
Eventually, from DC Cropper "Did you turn up anything interviewing your people?"
"Frank's contribution is confined to asking me a question. Somebody must have something helpful."

The Uniform sergeant Harry Brownlow began. "My report on the door-to-door should be ready by 6.00 p.m. So far though nobody saw anything unusual. It is a well-to-do area and the houses are private, with big drives and fairly well apart. A few were not answering the door so we are still going round them. I have to say it looks very unpromising. Sorry, sir."
In the streets, on doorsteps, at bedsides, in fact wherever he was to be found doing his duty, this copper was liked. He was welcomed by ordinary law-abiding folk who found

his girth and smiling round face, with the bright rosy cheeks, reassuring and friendly. To wrong-uns he was the opposite. Whenever they could they would give him a wide birth. Many had not; and regretted it.

"Thank you sergeant – can't get blood from a stone. OK. I spoke to the brother, Tomas Pearson. Their parents are abroad on holiday. Sergeant Brownose here has people trying to locate them discretely, right sergeant – discretely?"

The smirks around the room were not shared by sergeant Brownlow. At 43 his name had been a source of irritation all his life. He had learned mostly to ignore remarks like that but he did not care for them. He liked Mallard; they all did even the erratic DC Frank Cropper, another one with a name he would rather not be blessed with.

"As quiet as a redundant train, Chief Inspector Mallard." Mallard liked Harry Brownlow, too and he smiled at his rejoinder. Philippa Tate had spent her childhood all over the globe. Her father was still in the British Army. She was the only one in the room left puzzled by what seemed to be a strange simile.

"Pearson is nineteen and lives alone in a rented flat in Nether Edge which is why his sixteen year old sister is fending for herself in that house in Bradway. I hope I am using the correct present tense. My initial fear that this could turn out very serious, heightens by the hour. Why the lad is prepared to fork out for a tiny flat there, when he could be rent-free in a beautiful house in Bradway, is something we may find has a bearing on the case. Bear it in mind when we find the parents."

The door opened and in strode a well-groomed, fit-looking male.

P.C. Higgs-Whitethorn was a twenty-three year old electronics expert with a good degree in Mathematics and Computer Science from Cambridge. Mallard smiled widely at Trevor. He knew the bloke was getting a hard time at the station because the others correctly perceived themselves to be intellectually inferior to him; so he had to be taken down a peg. Mallard had observed the pettiness, and went out of his way to be friendly. Except for the other morning which Mallard regretted, he had been supportive. He wanted him on his team which needed strengthening, and he had an inkling this lad had promise.

The ACC had decreed that Higgs-Whitethorn should be given the stimulating task of checking the computer, telephone and telephone records, of victims and suspects. The respectful Higgs-Whitethorn handed over the records from Pearson's phone and gave a concise summary.

"Nothing unusual about these, sir. Seem to be simply friends and such that are in frequent contact. I will further analyse the videos and music and check the internet links in absolute detail. If anything useful appears I will report immediately. So far the computer is just standard material, mainly schoolwork. It is only three weeks old and there is very little on it that is likely to be helpful. She did not spend much time on social websites, just the usual Skype and Facebook, and not even Twitter. There were emails of course – nothing in them of interest to us. There is no trace of a tablet. Do you know if she had one?"

"Frank?"

"Not as far as I know."

"The brother said no Tablet, just the computer and the phone."

"Thank you, Sergeant Tate. How do you know, you have not spoken to him, have you?"

"It was in the initial log last Friday, of the phone call that PC Wallace answered when Tomas first reported her missing."

Frank Cropper should also have seen that report but the tablet item had not registered with him. He spoke.

"The neighbours indicate she came and went a lot, an active girl, into sports, we are led to believe. Not a computer nerd, then."

P.C. Higgs-Whitethorn saw the twinkle in the eye of the Chief Inspector which told him it was not, yet another barb, to get under his skin. He left with more of a spring in his step than when he had arrived.

Mallard rang the ACC and informed him that the case needed to be upgraded to that of a major incident. He then rang for a HOLMES (Home Office Large Major Enquiry System) operative to come and see him.

*****

At this time of afternoon he was half awake and able to lie in relative ease. A nurse from the San Diego Scripps Mercy Hospital came twice-daily to ease the pain and clean Ulanski. His mind wandered over that blemished part of his life. Would his son succeed in time? He would not know for at least another week. The hospital had given him three months, but he was not a fool. Oblivion could come in three minutes or three months, perhaps a little longer. It did not matter as long as his son let him know he had succeeded.

CHAPTER 12

"So zero progress, Mallard."

Standing in the spacious office of the ACC, Mallard steamed inside and said nothing.

"Have you lost your bloody tongue, man? Have you no answer?"

"That was not a question, sir. If you ask me something of course I will reply. I do not reply to statements, sir."

Assistant Chief Constable Fisher would have noticed the deliberate emphasis on the "sir" – twice, but Mallard did not care. A decidedly able policeman was the ACC. He had been promoted on merit and his appointment had been applauded by the lesser mortals of the South Yorkshire force as they awaited his return to Sheffield from the Essex Police Force. Now, the unanimous view was that the problem was Mrs. Fisher.

Big Jim Fisher, handsome man, weight seventeen stones of mainly muscle, ex county rugby player, yard-of–ale supper's record (Sheffield Police) still unbeaten after twenty-three years, was dominated by his sub 9 stone wife. The male philosophers at the Sheffield station, there were many of course who put the world to rights and solved life's problems every day, knew the reason. Lucinda Fisher was fifty-two years of age, four years older than him, and must by now have been through, or was still going through, the big M. That would be it.

ACC Fisher deserved some sympathy, did he not? None did he get from Mallard. Menopause or not, the man should be the boss. That was the unspoken view of the bachelor Chief Inspector who now waited for an irksome Fisher to continue. Obviously his weekend had not been a serene triumph.

"What have you planned as the next step?"

"On the basis that it is an abduction, we will go public this evening. The parents were tracked down this morning and informed she is missing. They are trying to get back home this afternoon. It will be a rush but I want them to go on TV and beg Sophia to contact them. I do not expect that to accomplish much, but it will lead us into the appeal for information from the public. We are about to question her school-friends, teachers and teaching assistants, canteen staff, and the caretaker. It must all be completed this week before end of summer term. Tomorrow, when the news is out, pictures of the girl will be posted around the City, especially in the Bradway area. Routine enquiries will continue but quite frankly, sir it looks as if we will need some sort of break. It looks bad and there are no real leads."

Fisher nodded.

"We do not have Forensics' full report, they are still analysing some areas. The bed sheets were very crumpled but there were no obvious blood or semen marks. I am hoping Forensics will find something that is not obvious. They will have completed their work by morning."

"Nothing hit the newspapers yet, thank God."

"At this quiet time of year, after the TV appeal, it will make huge headline news tomorrow."

"Quite. I have already authorised extra resources as a major incident."

"I want to do a trawl of sex offenders in the area. We can search their houses and pull them in and check out their alibis once those additional officers assemble in the morning."

"On another subject, what do think of P.C. Higgs-Whitethorn?"

"Looks promising. Perhaps he should be additionally given some more demanding duties. His obvious talents and mental acumen should prove beneficial in investigations. We could do with more assistance."

"That is my intention. Didn't want to put Trevor too high at first. Not too high for him, I mean to avoid the rest of the blokes – and women – being given ammunition to fire at him. It will be hard enough as it is, being a Cambridge wiz. There was this WPC in Essex reduced to tears every night after the first week. An Oxford honours grad in classics; she stuck it three months, left and went nursing. Will it be helpful to you if I temporally second him to you? I still want him to keep his present responsibilities because his degree might unearth areas and possibilities which to us ordinary mortals are unfathomed. He is bound to have some spare capacity to help you. This is a good opportunity to broaden the scope of his work unobtrusively."

"Thank you, sir. Delighted to have him."

Mallard was impressed – crafty sod!

"Righto, John." Back to first names terms, to the relief of Mallard.

A wistful look appeared on the face of the ACC as he looked again at the photograph of Sophia Pearson.

"She reminds me of my Lucinda at that age. Get the bastard, John. Get him soon!"

In Mallard's mind's eye as he walked down the stairs to his own office, he pictured Lucinda, the wife of ACC Fisher, as she was currently. Still an extremely attractive woman, Fisher said at sixteen she was something similar to

Sophia. Big Jim would have been twelve when Lucinda was sixteen. She would truly have been much sought-after. A remarkable boy then to snare Lucinda, as well as a remarkably good copper. Shame his luck had deserted him on the home front, for the time being at least. Mallard welcomed the addition of PC Higgs-Whitethorn. Bachelor John Mallard was whistling by the time he reached his office.

*****

The TV appeal had finished. Neither Sophia Pearson nor Joel Bush had seen it. Together in body, in spirit their moods were poles apart. Sophia steeled herself to survive another horrible encounter with her captor. Though tears ran down her cheeks and her eyes were red, she was indeed lovely. That first time he had made her lie with him, she had refused violently. Now there was less protesting. Although there really was no need, for his current satisfaction Bush had fastened the girl's hands behind her back. The marks on her flesh were gone now, so the loutish encouragement which had achieved her obedience had left just a temporary discoloration. In this position he was free of it. He could not see the blemish. Briefly the girl was perfection again. The curve of her smooth white back and her haunches below thrilled him. For now he forgot the surgeon's damage and appreciated the sight and touch of her arousing form.

*****

For several days it had lain unseen in the top pocket of his jacket. He was alone in his office. There were matters that required his attention which he would get round to all in good time. First he needed a smoke. Searching for the book matches he had earlier confiscated during a search, he emptied his shirt pocket out onto his desk. As he lit the cigar from one of those matches and leaned back in relaxation, agent Diego Tamayo leisurely rifled through the other items and saw it. It took a few moments before he could recall how it got there. When "the pigeon", Luis Vasquez had made the request to help his sister-in-law, Tamayo had not the slightest intention of interceding. Now, looking at the photograph of the girl caused a sharp intake of breath, and a consequent unintended quantity of cigar smoke into his lungs. The teenage sister-in-law, who had smiled serenely into the camera lens, and whose image now lay exposed in the hand of the rascal coughing forcefully, was truly an attractive creature. It was simply an ordinary photograph of a girl standing outside a supermarket. The dress she wore was an inexpensive mass-produced item to be seen everywhere. It was not the dress that created the quickening of his pulse: what was causing it to curve like that, was evoking his reaction. Her smile as she looked straight at the camera was guileless, natural – lovely. Who was holding the camera he wondered? This girl was desirable.

With much justification in that particular area, the local forces of law were feared by the public. Men were often ill-treated and intimidated. Man-handling and violence of "suspects" were the norm and torture was commonly employed to extract information. Women were equally brutalised, and in addition usually ran the additional risk of sexual exploitation.

On the back of the photograph, "the pigeon" had scrawled her name and telephone number. After a few moments of trying, Tamayo could still not remember what "the pigeon" had said about her. This girl was worth a little effort. He reached for the telephone.

Catalina Cruz was in the shower in her room after finishing her shift at the supermarket. She was tired today and looking forward to sleeping after her quesadilla snack. Switching off the shower, she heard a loud banging on the door.

"Hello. Who is it?"

"You are wanted on the phone, senorita." The landlord was at the door. Catalina hastened to put on some clothes because the landlord wasted no opportunity to get close to her when his wife was not around to curb him. The wife seemed to work all hours. Out first thing in the morning, a quick dash home at lunchtime, and out again until late. What the woman did was a mystery. Her husband seemed to do nothing, except what he was no doubt planning as he waited for the teenager to appear. Catalina knew he would without doubt wait outside her door for her.

"OK, coming senor." The chaste, modest girl discarded the towel and dashed to the corner and her clothes. There was no proper wardrobe. What it consisted of, was a long sheet hanging on a piece of string in the corner. There was very little space, but then Catalina had very little to store there. One day, she hoped life would be better. With that hope the girl was banking her hopes on the visit to the USA;

who knows? She worked hard. She was a good, God-fearing girl. Surely she deserved more.

The landlord was indeed waiting outside her door for a sight of Catalina. Could he have seen the girl now, naked in the room that he owned, his dreams would have come true. He had imagined the scene often enough.
Dressed quickly, Catalina opened the door and squeezed past him as agilely as she could. She ran down the old creaking stairs to the gloomy, dirty hall.

"Hello, senorita Cruz here."

As the wheezing landlord arrived into the dreary hallway and hovered nearby, with her bare feet Catalina tried to cover the water droplets which had fallen from her hair.

"Good afternoon, senorita. My name is Tamayo, federal agent Tamayo, and I know Senor Luis Vasquez. He has asked me to help you."

Three minutes later the girl replaced the telephone and was totally absorbed with the good fortune of the offer of help. In a thoughtful daze, Catalina walked through the hall to the foot of the stairs. Very slowly the girl began to climb the two flights to her small cheap room, oblivious now to the forgotten landlord. His eyes remained fixed longingly on her, all the way, until she disappeared pensively into her room.

*****

66

As Bush ate he watched the end of Tuesday's national evening news. His priority, now, was to watch the local news broadcast which always followed the National. Since Sunday the lead story was that of the missing Sophia Pearson. He was relieved to see the police had obviously got nowhere. A new angle had been introduced. Two of Sophia's school-friends were separately interviewed on camera that afternoon. The second girl was known to Bush. She was the girl who was with Sophia that night she had misplaced her key and who had giggled with Sophia in the garden. Tuesday had been the hottest of the year and Karen Clayton was dressed for the heat. In her modest summer dress, to Bush, she looked fetching in the extreme. He froze the picture on the TV and stared at it for some minutes. The sun caught her blond hair and it shone a lustrous gold colour. The girl had an extremely attractive face, light blue clear sparkling eyes, and a lovely mouth. Her eyes were moist as she spoke earnestly of her friend. Bush wanted her. The lovely eyes should look up into his; as Sophia's did.

Sophia was gratefully astonished when he left her untouched that Tuesday night. When he had entered, all he had done was to talk to her about school and her school-friends. Why, she wondered, had he uncharacteristically wanted to talk? He had been particularly interested in Karen. Did she know that voice? Now she was hearing his normal voice and not his usual lust-filled menacing growl, it seemed she had heard it somewhere. As she had focussed on the voice, she had blurted out Karen's address without thinking. Her smirking captor had left.

Whilst Sophia was locked in the house, Bush drove to see the Clayton house. There were two cars in the drive and plenty of movement inside. This would not be easy.

CHAPTER 13

Using the internet before he left the USA, he had made good progress on tracing immigrants to England. Tuesday, at the British Library, had been frustrating and he had learned little. If he made no real progress soon, he was prepared to pay an agency in the hope of speedy results. His father's health gave him very little time to trace Magdalina Ryszard.

When he had arrived in London on Monday morning, Francis Ulanski had been intent on seeing some of its main tourist attractions. Speaking yesterday to his father, the voice coming down the phone line had been even weaker than just a few days earlier. His sightseeing would have to wait.

*****

In Mexico Catalina Cruz was cleaning an office and thinking of that brilliant phone call two hours earlier. Tomorrow she had a meeting with agent Tamayo at the Police station. He knew her brother-in-law Luis Vasquez, and could help her obtain entry to the USA. Catalina sang as she cleaned and planned what she would wear for the interview.

*****

The summer term finishes tomorrow. It needs to be done quickly. She might go on holiday. Tonight she would usually go skating with Sophia. Will she still go without Sophia? She very well might. Try it!

He went to his computer, composed a message, printed it, folded it carefully and went upstairs. Sophia was not expecting him this early. He had some news for her. For her good behaviour, he was going to offer her family the opportunity to pay a ransom to release her. He showed Sophia the folded paper and said it was the ransom note. So, was she going to be good?

Astounded by the thought of being set free soon, Sophia nodded. He crooked his forefinger and beckoned her to forward. When he told her of the new condition, Sophia yelled and pulled away. He made it plain it was non-negotiable.

Later, breathing hard, a gratified and exhilarated Bush put the folded note before the girl to sign. She wanted to read it, but he refused. It was her chance of release. How much would he ask for her? Her parents would want her back but could they procure the sum he would ask? After a short argument she signed it anyway. The signed note was placed carefully in his wallet and he left.

*****

There was more to DC Frank Cropper than met the eye. Having joined the Regular Army as a teenager, he had been ambitious and highly competent. Within 2 PARA, the Second Battalion Parachute Regiment, he became a sergeant and saw two spells of active service. He had started boxing in the army and had represented his regiment and done well. When he left after 7 years service, he joined the West Yorkshire police. Steady progress was made and he transferred to CID after four years. Again he did well, after seven more years he was made detective sergeant.

Cropper had married his childhood sweetheart whilst still in the army and the couple had only one regret, a massive one. They were childless. His wife was barren. Frank and his wife were devoted to each other and otherwise happy. However DC Frank Cropper was no saint. He liked women. Women recognised this and normally, at work, it was accepted and had never caused a problem. He was always correct and polite and never behaved inappropriately – unless given some encouragement. In that case, if it could take place discretely and temporarily, and pose no risk to his marriage or indeed any other relationship, Frank never looked a gift horse in its mouth, or anywhere else. DC Frank Cropper was one hundred percent a mans' man – who had a weakness for women.

His career was satisfying and all had been well until one day three years earlier, from Norfolk, and into the West Yorkshire police force had arrived a new detective inspector. The father was a Methodist minister; the inspector was teetotal, puritanical, and devoid of any sense of humour. Catastrophically for Cropper, the inspector was a woman. Worse, she was a good-looking woman of twenty-nine years of age. A graduate of St Hilda's College, Oxford, she was being fast-tracked for stardom. Within a year, Sergeant Frank Cropper was a detective constable in the South Yorkshire force.

D C Cropper had begun following fruitless leads brought on by the police and the family's appeals. There was nothing productive so far, plenty of response had been flooding in, but no firm leads at all.

Mallard replaced the phone and shouted. "Sergeant Tate, in here, please."
It was now a week since Sophia Pearson had last been seen and the mood was low.
"I have arranged for the lab tribe to send some fresh people to the Pearson house this afternoon to do another sweep of that girl's bedroom. Also two fresh uniform lads will again do the outside, this time with Mr. Pearson, the father. I want you and Higgs-Whitethorn to get back to that house and apply your respective superior brain power to check we have not missed anything. The curtains were closed in her bedroom. It is likely that she was attacked in that bedroom but there is nothing yet to show it. Sophia Pearson could be dead but we must proceed on the basis that we can find her alive. If and when she does show up, hopefully alive, I want to be sure our arses are not hanging out there in the breeze to be kicked by all and sundry, and especially our lords and masters upstairs. I want to end that girl's ordeal as soon as humanly possible."
"And we know for sure that Sophia did arrive home that night after school."

Mallard's face brightened.
"The phone call to Karen Clayton at approximately 5.45 p.m. Wednesday was made from the house. It must have been Sophia."
"Yes, that detective sergeant, is the most helpful information we have turned up. The girl came to grief somewhere and sometime, between **exactly** 5.37 p.m. in

72

that house, and the intended skating arena, last Wednesday night."

The phone rang. When Mallard answered he stiffened and stared sightless into his sergeant's eyes. Philippa saw his mouth tighten and tried to hear what was being conveyed to him but the woman's voice was too faint. "One man, you say? Can you be certain?"
Mallard nodded. "Greatly obliged to you, and it is being sent now?"

"We have another fact, Philippa," Mallard said quietly taking a deep breath.
That was the first time he had addressed his sergeant by her first name. She thought him very serious and uncompromising. Was he warming toward her, professionally?
Hopefully it was only professional. It was well known that Mallard was a bachelor. Still in his forties he was about six feet tall and of average build for his age. He was not bald or unduly grey, wore no glasses, and still played cricket for the local nick in inter-departmental competitions. Philippa could see no obvious disfigurements or character traits. Furthermore, she had observed already that when he looked at her, he obviously appreciated what he saw.
Her mind went back to when she was about eight years old. She had been crossing the hallway at home, when she heard her mother and some friends enjoying each others' company, drinking wine and laughing as they discussed men in general, and the local ones in particular. She had listened.
One had said, "I agree, you can always tell when a man likes women. I don't mean you in particular, but women in

general. They watch. Their eyes stay on you longer that necessary. When an attractive female walks across a room their eyes follow her."

He was looking at her now, professionally.

"Another fact, sir?"

"Forensics have found traces of sweat of a single male on Sophia's bed sheet. It is very recent, and quite possibly from Wednesday. We can't rule out the possibility she has had a boyfriend in there of course. Sixteen years old and very attractive, whilst her parents are away on holiday, in that house alone, it would be highly likely wouldn't it? What do you think, sergeant?"

"It would be a possibility, but from our enquiries there was no-one regular. The picture we have so far is that it would most likely have to be regular boyfriend because she was definitely not promiscuous. Why has it taken so long to find that trace of sweat?"

"Lord knows. Go over to that house again with the added knowledge that there has been a man on her bed, and look for signs, and anything that will assist us."

Philippa walked to the door. As she took hold of the handle she turned and looked back. Mallard already had his eyes focussed on a sheet of paper he was reading. She hardly knew whether to feel disappointed or relieved.

CHAPTER 14

The officer at the desk had been notified by federal agent Rivera that Sergeant Tamayo was expecting a visitor at 4.30. When the girl arrived at the Policía Federal, agent Rivera was to be notified. Catalina Cruz stood clutching her handbag in one hand, and a folder held together with a rubber band under her other arm. After finishing at the supermarket, she had run to catch a bus which had arrived with just minutes to spare. With no time to dash home to change, it had been necessary to go to work wearing the clothes she now wore for the interview. Catalina had few clothes that were not worn for work and normal daily activities. She knew she wanted some decent clothes for her visit to see her sister and had been saving up to buy some if she received a visa. The ones she now wore as she nervously waited to be seen by the agent were the best she had. The comments and questions from her colleagues about her appearance and make-up had been embarrassing and hard to deflect, making her ten hour shift seem an eternity. Minutes passed and there was no sign of anyone coming to see her. The officer at the desk had simply told her to wait, and someone would come. There was nowhere to sit. Catalina was hungry and thirsty, it was hours since she had eaten anything. Her stomach rumbled and she looked in embarrassment at the desk officer but he had not heard. He watched the girl covertly. He could see why the sergeant had agreed to meet her. Whether the desk officer knew what was likely to happen could not be read on his face. He knew all right.

Agent Rivera marched in and greeted Catalina. He simply told the girl to follow him to the sergeant.

Catalina could not have known that the actual office of Sergeant Tamayo was situated on the first floor. The desk officer knew, and as he had expected he saw them head in another direction. They descended two staircases into the lower basement level. Both levels below ground floor consisted mainly of prison cells, with the first level always being filled up first. Rarely was it necessary to use the bottom level. It was on the bottom level that the heels of the best shoes that Catalina possessed, clunked along the cobblestones. She hastened to keep up with agent Rivera; for a big man he moved along with a smooth haste. Surprised, but not alerted, Catalina stared into the empty cells as they walked along to the "office" at the far end. Rivera opened the door and the girl entered in front of him. The room was basic. Apart from an extremely huge desk, at which Sergeant Tamayo sat, there were just three chairs. Sergeant Tamayo did not look very smart for an officer on duty. He wore just slacks and a shirt open at the neck. He slowly looked the girl up and down, and very much liked what he saw. She wore a thin pink sweater and skirt. She had re-applied make-up on the bus and rearranged her shining black hair so that it now hung fully down her back. Catalina looked lovely.

He remained seated. Tamayo had learned during the phone call to Catalina that she hoped to visit her sister and brother-in-law.
"Sit down Senorita Cruz. As I explained on the telephone I may be willing to assist you obtain documents to visit the USA. First I must see your papers."
Catalina had half extended her hand expecting a handshake but quickly lowered it and sat. From the folder the required

documents were quickly extracted and handed over. In her agitation she dropped the folder.

"Many thanks, sir for any assistance you can give me to visit my sister. Is it permitted to ask how you know my brother-in-law senor Luis Vasquez?"

She retrieved the folder. The elastic band had skedaddled.

"No."

With barely a glance at her papers, Tamayo put them in the drawer of the desk where he sat. He then locked it.

"There is a price for my help, senorita Cruz."

"Oh, I have very little money senor. How much do you want?"

Tamayo stood.

"Not money, senorita, my services will cost not one peso." He was grinning.

"I am sorry, senor, I do not understand."

"Please stand up."

Quickly Catalina complied.

"Let me explain. You are nineteen years old and have a pretty face. Look at you. Your pink sweater is pushed out provocatively in two places. Your skirt fits tightly to your haunches in a way that gives men ideas. Also it ends at your knees and gives a view of shapely legs, and suggests of more above. Do you begin to understand me?"

Catalina stared at him open-mouthed. She was becoming alarmed. He knew her brother-in-law, didn't he? Surely Luis would not place her in a position of danger.

"So, senorita, you must reward me now for my help."

Catalina realised what he meant. She saw his face, the look in his eyes. She knew. Never!

"No I will not. Please give me back my papers and I will go. I no longer want your help."

"Your papers are in police custody. When I say you can have them, you will get them back: not before. First you must compensate two overworked agents for devoting their time on your case. Rufino assist the girl."

It was the way. Many times in their association together these two agents had used this room. Usually, as now, this whole floor was deserted. Several decades ago, some enterprising law enforcers had organised this facility for activities that they preferred to conduct in complete privacy. Today, this would be another. In many countries it was a crime. Here, in his world, to Tamayo, it was a perk of the job – and Rufino's naturally.

CHAPTER 15

The day had passed slowly at the shop and he was anxious to be there as early as he could to see Karen arrive at the Skating Rink - if she did arrive. The shop closed to customers, he took the bag he had prepared at home into the WC. From the bag he took the disguise items, and carefully applied them in front of the mirror. He had watched his father many times getting ready to go on stage and he had never thrown out the artefacts after his death. He did not know how clear the CCTV would be at the rink, but he did what he could to hide his appearance. He spent just five minutes on his face and was finished. Now he had a small scar on his right cheek, and a moderately-sized moustache. Quickly he put on thick glasses with clear glass, and a woolly hat.

From his fruit bowl at home he had brought a small bunch of cherries. As he ate one, he checked his appearance again in the mirror. Satisfied, he turned away and removed the cherry stone from his mouth. Taking the left shoe from his foot, he pressed some animal grease from the refrigerator into the inside at the heel. Then he pressed the cherry stone into the grease to keep the stone in place. When he replaced his shoe and took a practice walk. The cherry stone hurt his foot when he put his weight on it. Bush had a genuine limp.

Reflecting on what he was about to do made his mouth dry. Without enjoyment, he ate a sandwich and the remainder of the cherries. When he had finished Bush checked his appearance in the mirror, and rose to his feet. The essential item was in the back left rear pocket of his trousers. Bush knew very well that it was definitely there, but he felt for it and removed it. He scrutinised it carefully.

Satisfied he replaced it and, with a final glance around, walked to the door and locked the shop. He stood outside and took a deep breath. When he drove to the Skating Arena Bush was ultra careful to drive within the speeding limit.

Once inside Bush stood at the back and surveyed the whole ice rink area. He did not want to walk all the way around because his foot hurt. Also he wanted to avoid, as much as he could, being caught on their CCTV. As unobtrusively as he could Bush studied the whole area to locate the CCTV video cameras. He could see two cameras. He pondered where to sit. It needed to be near the exit, to have a view of everyone arriving, and to be as far from the cameras as possible. Decision made, he limped to his selected seat and positioned himself close to the entrance, and with a good view of it. He waited. His watch said it was 7.05 p.m.

Karen Clayton arrived with the two girls from her school. Both were younger than Karen. Bush sat rigid when he first saw them and quickly realised what he had done. He slumped back in his seat panicking that he had drawn attention to himself. The girls disappeared into the changing area. As casually as possible Bush looked around. No one was paying him any attention.

It was an age before they emerged. All three had changed into their full outfits. They looked charming. Karen was first onto the rink. Bush watched Karen skate around the ice, her short skirt wafting revealingly. The younger girls could not skate quite as well and stumbled frequently, but it was great fun and their laughter could clearly be heard around arena. They were dressed similarly to Karen. Giggling, they would try to stand quickly and elegantly. He saw them look around to see who was looking. He turned away quickly.

It occurred to Bush, and he should have remembered it earlier, that Darryl and his mates came here. Darryl was always talking about "the birds I've pulled there". If he came in and recognised Bush he would have no excuse or reason for the disguise. Bush kept looking back at the entrance, nervous now. This was far more dangerous than he had envisaged. His mouth was dry. What he needed, he concluded, was a drink; a real drink.

The rink was mostly empty. Bush was not the only one watching the girls.
A man about sixty years of age skated and watched the three school girls, paying particular attention to Karen as she whizzed across the ice, her golden hair floating pleasingly behind her. The man kept always on the opposite side of the rink to Karen. He was an average skater. Bush saw the man later sit down in the seating area and take out a camera from his pocket. The camera whirred away for a few minutes. It had video and a zoom lens.
A boy about Karen's age tried a couple of times to chat to Karen, but she and her friends laughed at him. When she stumbled and fell, the boy raced across and assisted her to her feet. She thanked him and sped away. He kept trying to be near her but gave up after a while. Karen was not interested.
Bush looked over at the man with the camera. It was obviously taking video and must have a decently sized

memory because he was still filming. It interested Bush. A later examination of the CCTV film of that night, by the police, would result in the subsequent arrest and profound grievance for that amateur Steven Spielberg.

Bush's opportunity came when Karen sat down to rest. Her friends had gone off somewhere and, as Karen sat alone he limped over so that he was approaching behind the girl. He retrieved the item from his left rear trouser pocket, and dropped the note in her lap. Bush swiftly limped away to the exit. He did not look back. Karen saw the paper and, smiling, looked around expecting to see her friends. Puzzled she unfolded the note.

> *Karen. It is me Sophia. Please, please don't say a word to anybody or show them this note.*
> *I need your help – only you can do this for me. Please meet me in the car park outside.*
> *Love Sophia.*

The shocked Karen, still in her skating outfit, went quickly to the exit towards the quiet car park.

*****

At 8.00 p.m. all 45 police officers involved with the disappearance of Sophia Pearson, assembled in the Major Incident Room pooled information and updated their notes with progress, events, and known facts. The forensic evidence was summarised with the key item being the DNA of an unknown man.

Excitement had mounted briefly that afternoon when a police dog had discovered a body in the garden of the Pearson home. A distraught Mr Pearson had fallen to his knees with relief when the canary was revealed. Further searches of the house had taken them no further forward. The identified sex offenders were being methodically questioned, and of the thirty-nine identified, seventeen with verified alibis had been allowed to go home, fourteen were being held whilst alibis were checked, two with no alibis were still being questioned, and six had not yet been found.

A bachelor male teacher at Sophia's school who had phoned in sick with a migraine that morning was not amused to have been visited at home by four police officers and two dogs with their handlers.
His graduate girlfriend, a Britney Spears look-alike, had revealed that she had been there to give him his medication.
With a smirk and a wink, she stood holding just a fluffy towel around her, enjoying the male officers' embarrassment, and that of her boyfriend. As the officers went on their way, the assessment was that the poor guy, drooping with infirmity, but being blessed with a nurse like that, would be up and about, in no time.

There was no shortage of enthusiasm or ideas from the officers who stood or sat desks,. Some sat on desks and some ambled around. Mallard knew from experience that on these occasions, out of the blue one of the team came up with an inspired suggestion which took the case forward. That night was not one of those. At 9.45 p.m. Mallard told them all they could go home.

He sat in his office chair and uttered a deep sigh. Aloud he said, "We need a development, a breakthrough – something."

There was no-one there to hear.

Neither, at that moment was there anyone there to hear Sophia, alone in that grotesque place. Had there been, there would have been nothing to hear. Sophia would never again make another sound.

$$*****$$

It was hot in back of the van and her head hurt. The July evening was sultry and humid, with dark rain clouds low overhead. Although the sun would not set until after 9.00 p.m. it had been almost dark outside well over an hour before that, when Karen Clayton had hurried into the car park of the skating arena. The car park was at the rear of the building away from street lights, and the car park lights were timed to switch on later. In the gloom, Karen had answered the beckoning of the smiling Bush. He had indicated that Sophia was in the van. She remembered him opening the doors. She had peered inside for Sophia, and then blacked out.

Now lying hooded and taped on the van floor she realised that he must have bludgeoned her. Her head hurt.

Who was this man? Why was he doing this, and how was Sophia involved? It had been her note for sure. Sophia was her friend. She cannot know this man was hurting her – can she? Karen tried to remember the last time with Sophia. Everything had been normal. But why had Sophia just gone away without telling anyone? Had she absconded with this man? Were they lovers? Never, the man must be forty – no never! Miserably Karen could only lay and wait.

Bush was in ferment. It was all happening so quickly. He wanted Karen out of his van as fast as possible, but the basement room must be made ready first. Nervous energy had carried him through and had been maintained until now. Suddenly a tide of weariness washed over him and he slumped for a few moments on the floor. There was an unexpected sadness too gnawing at his guts. Bush had not expected this chagrin. Resuming his scrubbing of the wooden floor he thought back to that morning. That brief time when Sophia was motivated to please him, even though he knew it was for her own purposes, it had been brilliant. He had given her a glass of pure orange juice afterwards and had felt really pleased to see the gratitude on her young face. Shame, though, about the flaw. It had to be done. She had felt nothing he was sure.

That time when he was fourteen and with his dad at that farm belonging to the friend of his dad in Derbyshire, he had seen the man put a sheep out of its misery. The three of them had been strolling through the field when they had heard the bleating. A sheep had tumbled into a gully and its rear legs had become trapped between two large boulders. In its efforts to free itself, the sheep had dislodged one of the boulders, and it had trapped and broken both rear legs. The legs were stuck immovably. It was dusk, they had no equipment or medications, and it would have been an impossible rescue without help. The sheep would be there all night in pain. In an act of kindness the man had straddled the back of the sheep and twisted its neck, breaking it cleanly with one wrench and killing it instantly.

In later years, in some films, war and spy films he recalled, he had seen men do the same to their enemies. They were not acts performed for the benefit of their enemies. They, like tonight, were to gain an advantage for the perpetrator.

Earlier that night, Bush had made the unsuspecting Sophia kneel on the floor with her back to him. It had been over in seconds.

A wave of shock suddenly made him shudder. It was not sympathy for the girl that he felt, but the suddenness with which death can arrive. One minute the girl was listening to him, watching, obeying him, kneeling still and compliant. But now she could do none of these things. She never would – ever again; because of him, because of that simple twisting.

Bush had gone terribly cold. It was so quick, and yet so final – so devastatingly effective. It could happen to him. It could be himself that dropped lifeless sometime, because of something quick, something utterly out of the blue. God Almighty, he was filled with terror. Bush the unimaginative had never considered his own mortality. Both parents had died after illnesses which had provided some warning. They had not gone quickly – not like this. He knelt transfixed.

In due course he regained some control.

Time was important now, he realised. That new girl was still in the van. Swiftly he went and fetched a tarpaulin from the garden shed. Bush wrapped the corpse of the once lovely light of his life in it, and struggled with it into the garden. Privacy in his home and garden was not a problem.

No-one could see over the high dense hedges and it was already dark. The threatened rain had not yet arrived. Rasping for breath he lay Sophia down. Without a backward glance he hurried back inside.

He took a deep breath and resumed his scrubbing. It was important Karen would not detect any sign of a previous prisoner. The floor finished, he changed the bedding and sat down.

It had all been hastily conceived and executed and Bush had the jitters. After he had brought in some food and water for his new captive, he would bring Karen to her new room.

After a final look around he went up to the kitchen, assembled some food and water, and took it into the basement.

A decision had to be finally made now. He was reluctant to wear that face mask but it obviously helped to protect his anonymity. Also it helped to maintain the deception that he would release the girl when he was ready. He remembered how well-disposed towards his demands Sophia had become, once he created the deception of that ransom note. That made up his mind. More of that would definitely be fruitful. The face mask was essential.

Today Bush had learned much about himself. He had known nothing like this – ever. It was terrifying when he acknowledged the risks he was taking but he was hooked now. The excitement he was experiencing was, he realised, only in part due to the thrill of the girls. Driving and enforcing himself into the danger of exposure and capture was stimulating him in a way that he had not experienced since years earlier as a boy taking on that swine of a teacher, Mr. Tapsill.

The effect on him of killing Sophia had been unexpectedly awful but he knew it was necessary, and would be again if he wanted a change of captive. He thought he might. Today Bush had learned much about himself. Already he knew that he could want more. Risking and winning was exhilarating.

A new, serious Bush strode up the basement steps to fetch his new girl.

CHAPTER 16

By Wednesday afternoon Francis Ulanski had realised he would be unable to discover the location of his relatives in the time available. It would be necessary to use a private investigation agency. The one he contacted was brisk and professional in its approach. The brief details he had available were taken, and the principal of the agency said he could make a start immediately. When Ulanski phoned his father and gave a progress report, the old man made an unexpected request. He asked him, that if he took any photographs of Magdalina and Ryszard Bushmanov, he must never show them to his father. He wanted to remember them as they were when he last saw them.

The hotel on that evening had arranged a six piece jazz band to play in the Wharton Suite where there was a hot buffet available. A jazz fan, Francis Ulanski eagerly made his way there.

At the very instant Ulanski had entered the Wharton Suite in London, one hundred and fifty miles north in Sheffield, Bush had been making the unsuspecting Sophia kneel on the floor with her back to him. By the time the jazz finished, Bush had acquired his second captive schoolgirl.

*****

When the agents had finished and Catalina lay sobbing through the wet gag, Tamayo fetched a camera out of a drawer. He photographed her. She was held in various positions by Rivera so that the camera captured shameless views of her.

After the photography they unshackled Catalina and allowed her to dress.

"You will say nothing to anyone about what happened in this room. Your papers will be kept for one week so that we can be sure you have said nothing. After that I will give your papers and the documents you need, to your brother-in law. I will make sure you have no problems with the Mexican side. Remember also, we know where you live and we can come for you whenever we want if you cause any trouble. These photographs would cause a lot of interest if we sell them to certain magazines, or put them on the internet, or send them through the post to your employers, friends, and family. Be a good girl and this is the end of the matter."

Catalina went home. She had been used by two men but was undeniably still a virgin in the strict sense.

*****

Carrying his new girl down to the basement had been the easy part. Once down in the cellar, even trussed the way she was Karen put up a mighty struggle to prevent her clothes being removed. It had taken a while, but when Bush had them on the floor, he was able to examine the naked girl. Her pretty face lacked the glorious symmetrical loveliness of her friend, but her figure was superb. The thin summer dress she had worn in that TV interview had provided more than a hint of a fine figure. Naked, Bush could see she was simply magnificent.

He fixed the manacle to one ankle and plonked Karen onto the bed. Muffled protests had been coming through the effective home-made hood all the while. Once Bush began his lascivious handling of her naked body on the bed, the noise increased dramatically. Unperturbed Bush continued. Before long he discovered that Karen, unlike Sophia, had been a virgin.

****

Now there was the matter of disposing of Sophia's corpse. Here was where luck would have to play a big part if he was to get away with it. He had given the problem some thought, on and off all day. Driving well out into the countryside late at night in a van, would run the risk of being stopped by the police. He almost never went out at night and so had no idea how numerous the patrols would be. The countryside was too risky. He needed to be where traffic was normal. It was already nearly 11.00 p.m. If he left now people would be going home after a night out. Then there was the CCTV problem. If he went where there were cameras there was the risk of being traced and questioned when the police found the body. So he had to avoid the City centre and main roads. There was nothing for it but to take a decision and get on with it.

The night was black, and the air was still and sultry. He retrieved the tarpaulin and was soon sweating profusely as he carried the tarpaulin-wrapped body from the garden. It was necessary to place the bundle on the drive whilst he rummaged for the keys to the van.

"Christ." A mistake already: the keys must be in the house. The thrill of excitement vanished in that instant. If he had forgotten a simple thing like those keys, what other mistakes was he making? It took him some minutes before he found them in the kitchen.

After hurriedly shoving his grim load into the van, Bush drove away. His destination was a countryside hill off the Rivelin Valley Road, on the outskirts of Sheffield near the Derbyshire border. The journey would be through built-up areas until he reached Rivelin Valley Road, and then it was not far to his intended drop-off spot.

It was the best he could think of.

His heart was in his mouth the whole time throughout the long hours of that endless journey. Panic had replaced excitement. It had, in fact, taken just twenty three minutes and had proved quite uneventful, but it had seemed a lifetime. There was light traffic in the area. He was in luck. He was in countryside and no other cars were near as he approached his objective. Driving anxiously up the unlit narrow hill, he knew he would be able to see the lights of any approaching vehicle. There were none. He stopped the van.

Rain had been threatening to start all evening, and now it did. The heavens opened. A brilliant flash of lightening was instantly followed by an ear-splitting clap of thunder. Accompanying the downpour came the arrival of high wind. The torrential rain straight away cut down his visibility to about fifty yards. If anything came it would be upon him before he knew it. Still, it was now or never. He raced out of the van, opened the rear doors and unwrapped the corpse from the tarpaulin. The rain made the girl's naked body slippery. Already staggering under the weight, the wind knocked him over. He dropped it on the road. The night was pitch black now, no moon, no stars; just teeming rain. Cursing, sweating, and panicking, he managed to lift the body and bundle it over the wall. Back in the van, soaked to the skin, it was all he could do to get the keys into the ignition. His hands were shaking like a madman and he was hyperventilating. When the van began to move he drove at first like a nutcase to put distance between him and the corpse.

It was the sight of oncoming headlights coming down the hill that brought him to his senses. Suddenly he regained a measure of control. Both drivers of the two vehicles were almost blinded by the driving rain, but they managed to pass slowly by each other in the narrow country lane.

A minute later and back on roads with street lighting, Bush calmed down a bit. It was still extremely dangerous because he had no legitimate reason to be out at this time. What time was it now? He checked his watch. It was not on his wrist. He remembered he took it off to scrub that floor. He must have forgotten to put it on – another mistake!

The rain was a godsend. No officer would volunteer to be out of his vehicle in this lot without a mighty good reason. There was nothing to be gained by worrying. Bush did worry – every inch of the way home.

CHAPTER 17

Thursday morning found DC Frank Cropper early for work and at his desk before any of his colleagues, or so he thought. He could not have explained it. A change had come over him this week. He looked forward to going to work. When she had kissed her husband and watched him walk to his car, Janet Cropper had noticed the change. Of late he had sauntered with a heavy tread. The difference was noticeable. It reminded her of his eager attitude in those early days when she had waved him goodbye and watched the train until it was out of site and clonking its way to Colchester to join his regiment. Janet Cropper stood quite still for a while deliberating about the reason for the change.

Cropper had his head down and was finishing off his report on his Wednesday afternoon interviews at the school. Today, Thursday, was the final day of term, and all interviews of the girls and staff at Sophia's school had been completed yesterday. He had been teamed with Sergeant Tate and they had worked with a methodical efficiency, and had finished just half an hour before the final bell had signalled the end of the school day.
For a moment he sat back reflecting on the event which had taken place on their way back to the station resulting in Philippa Tate saving the life of child.
It had been an astonishing act of bravery. Afterwards she had never given any hint of it. No-one knew of it except him. He was as impressed by the modesty of the girl, as by the instinctive courage of the deed. He was also chuffed to be the only one who knew.

"The Girl" was how he regarded her. She possessed both vitality and a guilelessness that was natural and easy. He admired this Philippa Tate. She had guts this girl. She had decency, spirit, and intelligence. Philippa Tate had won him over. Frank Cropper recognised that fact, and he knew she had done it without even trying. What was more, Frank was pleased. She was half his age and she was his superior; and he was glad to be working with her.
Frank Cropper completed the report. His reverie was ended when he was summoned to a meeting.

*****

Chief Inspector Mallard had been in the office of Detective Superintendent Shaw since 6.00 a.m. Also present had been a Detective Inspector, Brady. Events had moved swiftly during the night. A second sixteen year old girl, Karen Clayton had also now disappeared. The Superintendent and Mallard would look after both cases, whilst Detective Inspector Brady would primarily lead the investigation into the Karen Clayton disappearance. More than half of the existing team would be allocated to him.

"Flexibility and co-operation will be vital." Mallard had just finished updating Philippa Tate and told her to devote her main energies to the missing Sophia. "Leave Brady's lot to concentrate on Miss Clayton. Two girls go missing within a week of each other, from the same year, from the same school. Both of them were good friends and saw a lot of each other. There is a link. Any initial thoughts? I'm damned if I can understand young girls – any girls for that matter. You are a lot nearer their age than me."

He smiled at his own exaggerated inadequacy, but she could see he was glum.

"Girls like to act together. If they are going to do something naughty or something unusual, they prefer support. A week is too far apart for them to be acting together. Karen struck me, when I spoke to her, to be mystified at Sophia going missing. If Sophia did go voluntarily, and she is hiding, which I don't believe, then for Karen to become part of it, there must have been some contact between them very recently. I would concentrate on that, Chief. Sorry, that is all I have to offer at this stage."

"Obviously we are checking for any contact. She locked her things away in the locker at the Arena and we have them. Her phone is with young Higgs-Whitethorn. OK, Philippa - find Sophia for me."

Mallard left the Karen Clayton investigation in the hands of the Inspector for the time being and called a Briefing of his Sophia Pearson team.

Apart from the forensic item from Sophia's bed, which would only be useful if they apprehended a suspect, there was not one solid lead. None of the known offenders was a match. Using the familiar brainstorming technique of which he was a staunch advocate, Mallard tried to elicit constructive suggestions from the team. An hour later a whiteboard was full of their outpourings. There was nothing really new that looked promising. Mallard was at a loss. It had been necessary to already cut back his active Sophia team, from forty-five officers to nineteen, concentrating the other officers now, on the Karen Clayton disappearance. In truth there was little more to follow up. Every one of the usual perverts and paedos had been eliminated. He was about to end the meeting when news broke. Mallard had the phone to his ear and the watching officers could all see the hand gripping the device, becoming whiter. With an ashen face Mallard surveyed his officers.

"The body of a naked girl has been found. From the description, very brief at this stage, it sounds like our Sophia. It is definitely not Karen. She is blond. This girl is a definite brunette. It ten-to-one is Sophia."

"Where?" a simultaneous chorus of several officers called out.

"Hagg Hill."

"Hagg Hill, Crosspool, chief?" Cropper asked.

"Yes, I don't know any other one. There cannot be more than one with that name."

"I went down there last night."

"What time?"

"About 11.45. The rain was coming down in buckets."

"See anybody about, Frank?"

"I passed a van coming up the other way. It was a very tight squeeze but we managed."

"Better put it in a report straight away, Frank. It might well be significant. Right Frank, you do that report, Philippa you come with me to the scene. First I have to update Detective Inspector Brady. Also I need to know who is with Karen's parents."

*****

Exhausted but relieved his efforts had been successful; he had collapsed straight into bed and slept. When he awoke it was 5.30 a.m. on that Thursday, and after a rapid bathroom session he went naked down to the basement. Pulling on the half-mask which was hanging outside on its usual hook, Bush went inside. The hooded girl started screaming when she heard him open the door. She still had her hands tied behind her back. The girl had had nothing to eat or drink since leaving home last evening. Bush knelt beside the girl and began to talk quietly.

"Good morning, Karen. Please stop screaming because I have something to say and I want you to hear it. Good, good that's a little better but still too loud. Karen calm down. If you stop screaming I will take the hood off. You would like that Karen, yes? Shall I take off the hood?"

The girl nodded vigorously and went quiet. Bush slowly removed it. She stared at him, tears in her eyes. When she realised Bush was naked she screamed in terror. It took Bush some time to quieten the girl. Tears were streaming rapidly down her cheeks, her breathing came in short hurried gasps, and she stared wide-eyed at her captor horror-stricken.

"Don't hurt me please."

"Be quiet."

Bush said nothing more. He watched Karen, appreciating her desperation. He was in control. The girl must obey Silently he tilted his head onto one side as if considering her words. He did not touch her or make another sound. For perhaps half a minute there was silence except for the sound of Karen's stentorious breathing.

Then, "Please give me a drink. Please, please give me some water or anything."

After another silence, briefer this time, "Let me tell you Karen, this is how it works. You have just obeyed me. When I told you to be quiet, you went quiet, briefly anyway. That is good. That I like. Obedience gets you favours."

He reached for the plastic bottle of water under the bed, unscrewed the top and held it before her, but did not give it to her.

"You understand how it works, Karen? Obedience gets favours, right?"

Karen nodded, eyes on the bottle.

"Say it – obedience gets favours. Say it."

"Obedience gets favours. Please may I have the water?"

"Excellent, Karen."

Bush held the bottle to her mouth and she gulped down some and spilled more. He was patient and he held the water until it was she who moved away from the bottle.

He put down the bottle and held up a piece of cheese from the plate of food. Karen ate it, all the while looking at him. She had stopped crying.

"If you are a good girl you can have more water and food before I leave. I have to go to work soon so you will be alone all day. If you are very good I will untie your wrists. Have you remembered how it goes, Karen? Say it."

Karen nodded. "Obedience gets favours?"

"Exactly. Now we are going to lie on the bed and you are going to be a good girl, aren't you?"

The screaming started again. Quickly Bush grabbed the hood and forced it over her head. It was obvious she was not going to be good.

"No problem, girlie, no problem at all," he said as he lifted her, and he threw her harshly onto the bed. For an hour he entertained himself with the frantically screaming, resisting girl.

Finally, slaked, he went to his bathroom, took a refreshing shower, and during breakfast concentrated on what he needed to attend to in his shop. He went back upstairs and finished dressing. He reached for his watch but it was out of place. In a downstairs drawer he located an older spare watch.

The storm had raged during the night, but it was a beautiful morning. The birds were busy foraging in the already warm sunshine in the garden. Bush wandered around his garden, making sure there was no trace of what had occurred there the previous evening. Invigorated, content, and whistling, he locked the house and drove his van to work.

Bush was half way to work when he realised his head had been so full of the thrilling, blemish-less Karen, that he had not watched the morning TV. Had he done so he would have seen the lead story which was of another missing Sheffield schoolgirl - his girl, lovely Karen.

******

Throughout the night, officers had been examining the CCTV footage of the Skating Arena and surrounding area. Sheffield Transport Authority had made film available from the bus on which the three girls had travelled. Film from cameras on the roads leading to the Arena had been obtained. At 9.00 a.m. Detective Inspector Brady and his team assembled to review progress. There was nothing helpful from the bus. No-one had boarded the bus with the girls. No-one else had alighted at the same bus stop when the girls got off. The bus did not stop at the stop before theirs, and just two people got off at the stop after. The man and the young woman had only eyes for each other, and had hastened away from the Arena. The bus was out.

It was almost certain that a vehicle would be involved. Several hundred vehicles had used the roads leading to the Arena, during the time bracket specified by Brady. Most, but not all, of the number plates were recognisable. Their details were fed into a database. A team was tasked with checking them all.

Only limited information could be obtained from the car park because of the extraordinarily dark night. From 6.45 p.m. until the lights came on at 8.50 p.m. most number plates were indiscernible. Another team would quickly be able to investigate the identified registrations and their owners. The van which Joel Bush owned did not appear in that category and was never checked.

It was more promising inside the Arena. Footage was visible. Another team checked those films.

When they first saw him, they knew they had spotted their man.

Still photographs were captured from the film of the Ice Rink, and Detective Inspector Brady and three other detective officers began to contact the Arena manager and staff.

It was a frustrating business for them because the evening staff was mostly unavailable until they arrived for work at

6.00 p. m. They questioned those reachable, but just had to be patient until the arrival of the ones likely to be of real help.

*****

"Time of death, Anthony?"
Wiping his glasses thoroughly Anthony Pemberton stood up to his full height, five foot six and a half with his socks on. He looked at Mallard. What the pathologist may have lacked in stature was not displayed in his professional competence. The two men had a mutual respect for each other that stretched back to that first meeting four years earlier when Mallard had been a Detective Inspector.
"Some twelve hours ago plus or minus a couple: say 9.00 p.m. last night."
Most pathologists would not take a crap without filling out three sets of forms: not this one. Mallard waited. He knew AP would continue with the relevant details that he could be reasonably sure about.
Overhead, the police helicopter circled, filming the crime scene. SOCO specialists had already left with their paraphernalia and digital films.

"You will have observed perhaps that the girl was not killed here."
Mallard had, but he said nothing. Pemberton was alone in the field with the corpse, and the grass came up to the tops of his green Wellington boots.

Everyone else stood in the road waiting until the pathologist had finished. Already some of the officers were having to prevent pedestrians circumventing the barriers which had been swiftly positioned blocking off the length of Hagg Hill. It was important to be away before the Press arrived, zooming in, photographing and filming.

The field was below road level which meant that Mallard, looking over the wall from the road, was seeing more of Pemberton's bald patch than the man would have been comfortable with, had he realised. Like Mallard, Pemberton was single. Unlike Mallard he was fussy about his image and appearance. Mallard for once felt a hint of superiority. He still had a full head of hair.

"Cause of death likely to be the broken neck which is apparent. I will do the autopsy this afternoon and let you know for certain."

Mallard spoke in a voice louder than previously. "For the benefit of the rest of the team who will not be as bright as you or me, will you please explain how we know the girl was not killed here?"

"Instructing and coaching your team is one of your functions, Chief Inspector. You explain it and I will correct you where necessary."

Detective Sergeant Philippa Tate could hardly keep her face straight. "He thinks the Chief doesn't know; oh, how brilliant."

Mallard was miffed.

"The grass, Anthony, the grass. It was undisturbed except for the indentation made when her body fell into it. There was no sign of anybody else either jumping over the wall or walking through the field. Someone heaved her over that wall. She would not have climbed up onto the wall, and fallen into the field and broken her neck, because it is inconceivable that she would have come here stark naked. There is no sign of any clothing. If she had been larking about with a boyfriend, stripped naked, climbed up onto the wall looking for a spot to have a bit of nooky, and had accidentally fallen and broken her neck, he would have been over the wall like a shot. Anything I missed, Doctor Pemberton?"

Philippa Tate waited. Had the pathologist observed something that Mallard had missed? This was quite rare. Two highly competent senior officers pitting themselves against each other in the hearing of their juniors. She was fascinated.

"What about the wall, Detective Chief Inspector, the wall?"

Mallard stared at the wall and then looked at Philippa. She shook her head.

Pemberton was smiling now. He had him. Carefully, a good twenty yards down from where the corpse lay, he clambered over the wall.

"It would have to be a huge coincidence if it was unconnected with this incident. There is a wristwatch lodged in the wall, just where the body is. Looks like a man's. See you at the autopsy if you like. Fare thee well."

Mallard watched him walked sprightly to his car, then with a brusque flick of his left hand, motioned a detective constable into action. "Bag it, detective constable."

With the departure of the pathologist, two mortuary attendants stepped out of the black HM Coroners van. Mallard gave them the OK and they efficiently went about carefully placing the corpse into a body bag, and then lifted it into their vehicle. This was always an utterly sombre moment, watching the black van carrying its lifeless passenger on route to the morgue. When both the Coroners van and the helicopter had left, Mallard instructed two officers to collect soil samples.

"You do realise, Philippa, that it is impossible from up here in the road to see that wristwatch."

Sergeant Tate managed to keep a straight face. Mallard's friend, the pathologist, had unsportingly got the better of him and Mallard was piqued.

"Absolutely, sir."

"Please inform Sophia's parents a body has been found. They need to hear it from us first. Remember, we do not know the identity of the girl for sure. Choose someone to go with you and shoot up there straight away. I will see you back at the station for the autopsy."

*****

"So it's Sophia then. That is definitely an appendix scar, doctor?"

"Certainly. Appendectomy without a doubt. Done about seven years ago from the look of it, Chief Inspector."

Pemberton was about to begin the autopsy and had arranged the body lying face upward. Mallard hated the smell in that building. He slipped a Fishermans Friend lozenge into his mouth. D.S. Tate would have appreciated one; but she was going to have to learn to bring her own. The scar was clearly visible. There was a small birthmark just below the left buttock. Philippa Tate had the photographs and a note of the two distinguishing marks provided by the parents who had rushed back from holiday.

"Absolutely no doubt about it. Identical to the photographs, and two completely definitive DM's can leave no doubt."

Mallard stared down at the lifeless form.

"In the prime of life."

"Not now, John I regret to say. "Not, regrettably any more."

There was no humour or malice on the face of Pemberton. They both felt the sadness of such a tragic waste, such insane wickedness.

At that moment Mallard could cheerfully have broken somebody's neck.

"Sixteen years old with all her life before her, a beautiful healthy girl with everything to live for. What a terrible waste. What a terrible, awful, tragic, monstrosity."

The other two both felt it. Only Mallard voiced it.

Mallard regained his composure.

"So doctor, to summarise the main points before we go off and leave you to do what you have to do – Killed about 9.00 p.m. yesterday, neck deliberately broken somewhere, taken and dumped over the Hagg Hill wall later that night. Anything else you can tell me just now?"

"Nothing you cannot see for yourself, John. Looks extremely fit and in good muscular condition. Signs of some bruising especially around the knees. Looks like she has been on her knees quite a bit recently. There are definite signs of having been kept captive and chained I reckon. These marks around her right ankle suggest she has been shackled. Just supposition of course. If there is anything more it will come later – stomach contents etc."

He looked at Mallard and saw the tiredness in his face. "The other girl, I suppose this is not co-incidence?" "Bound to be connected. She will be in terrible danger."

Mallard and Tate left and entered the corridor to their department. Back in the main office most of the abduction team had assembled. They heard what they were expecting to hear.

"It is now a murder case. The body has not been formally identified and I do not want the press getting any information on this except from me. Nobody is to reveal about the watch being found. Understood?

Philippa and Frank come into my office. The rest of you carry on with the tasks I assigned before lunch. I am especially after CCTV information. Frank, I know it's a ball-aching job but it is totally vital. I have a feeling we will get sod-all from that field. The body was naked and it rained stair-rods all night. We are going to be up the creek without CCTV. He must have used a vehicle. The width of Hagg Hill means it would not be a very big vehicle. A Transit is possible but not a removal van – you get the idea.

Do your best man. This is a sixteen year old naked girl with her neck twisted. We all want this bastard. Get the Bosun and some others to help you."

DC Frank Cropper looked blank.

"The Bosun, chief?"

"P.C. Higgs-Whitethorn, Frank."

Frank looked at Philippa. She shook her head.

"Right, young Trevor. Trev Bosun. Right."

"Philippa, how did Sophia's parents take the news this morning?"

"It was dreadful of course but they are clinging to the hope it will not turn out to be Sophia."

"I am afraid you will have to go and see them now, straight away. We have to let them know we are pretty sure it is their daughter. They must come down and identify the body when they are able. Frank, go with her. You have seen this many times, Frank. I know it never gets easy but experience does help. Concentrate on the CCTV when you get back. Remember, Philippa, no false hope."

"Yes, sir."

Mallard knew this was the first time she would have had to do this. She left the office looking as though she was walking to the gallows.

Frank followed her like a mother hen, and then dashed in front of her to open the door, to let her through. The silently watching detectives, having seen Frank open the door for a superior, would not have been surprised if the heavens had parted, and angels playing harps had descended and sat singing sweetly at his desk.

CHAPTER 18

Two remembered him.

"We thought he looked shifty. Hadn't we said to each other? You can tell them. Perverts!"

Inspector Brady was encouraging the Cashier and the Cloakroom Attendant. The two middle-aged women were a bit flustered and delighted to be helpful to a Detective Inspector. They were staring at the still photographs.

"Always interested in the young ones. You know them that wear them short skirts and tease the fellas. Sometimes you can't really blame the blokes. He can't take his old eyes off them. Them with them short skirts and tight sweaters. Nearly poke your eyes out some of them lasses. We thought he was a wrong 'un. No, sorry, don't know his name. About three times a week he comes. Not Thursday, though. He won't come tonight. Never on a Thursday. Saturday will be next. If you come on Saturday you will nab him."

Brady groaned. "Where is the Membership Register?"

"Bloody hell, wait a minute. 'Course. The membership list. He will be on there. Members get a reduced price, twenty percent off admission and ten per cent off drinks and food. You can tell he's not rich. Bound to be a member. Wait, though, there is no photos. No, no photos. Don't know how you can tell him. I remember him though. He joined on 1st January. He waited for the New Year special offer. First of January not this year, last year. No photos so how you goin' to spot him."

Brady knew. They knew he was aged between fifty and seventy. Get the names and addresses of men in that age bracket who joined on that date.

Almost everybody joins at the beginning of January. The membership year runs from then and allows for no reduction for part-year membership. In that age group, there were fifty-three joined at the beginning of January. A quick examination revealed some of them had other family members with that same family name who were also members. Their man was a loner, so thirty-nine were out, for now. Narrow it down. Set the age bracket at fifty-five to sixty-five for now. That produced seven to check. The time was just past 6.30 p.m. Get cracking!

*****

Karen dreaded the opening of the door. By being a "good girl" she was free of the hood and that morning he had untied her arms. It was forty-eight hours now and she still did not know what he intended to do with her. Her parents did not have much money, so if that was what was needed for her release there was not much chance without selling the house. That could take ages. Maybe it was for sex alone. He never missed doing things when he came into the room. She had heard about some girls in America who had been kept for sex for years. "Oh, God."

****

Ten o'clock already, and just two left now to check. Sod's law was in full stride, and Detective Inspector Brady felt it was bound to be the last one on his list where they would catch the sod. He had a full team with him. The Armed Response lads were his insurance. He had no idea what to

110

expect once they arrived. This one was a terraced house. No door bell was fitted so the AR leader knocked loudly on the door. The others stood out of sight, and out of any line of fire.

"Who is it?"

"Christ! A female voice. Can it be Karen?" Brady's thoughts whirled.

"Police, madam – can we have a word?"

"Police? Just a minute. Dad, it's the police."

"Oh, Jesus not another abortive visit."

The girl who opened the door was nine years old and was in pyjamas. Her dad came quickly hopping to the door. He had just the one leg

"What's up?"

It was not their man. There was nothing for it but to check the last one on this list. If this proved not to be him Brady would have to widen the age bracket.

Before Brady left, the father told him the girl was indeed a member of the Ice Skating Club and she had joined at the same time as him. When pressed as to why she did not show up with him on the Members list, he explained belligerently that he was a sort of step-father. The girl's mother was his "partner", and both females had a different surname to him. He went to the Rink to make sure the girl came to no harm. You never knew these days. He did not skate because the club did not have one skate to fit his knee. The girl giggled. Brady did not.

No they had not been skating this week, not for three weeks. With a straight face, he said he was devoting his energies to training to be an Olympic gymnast.

He hopped back inside and the giggling girl closed the door.

"Right," Brady said, more to himself than the team, "the last one has to be the one!"

******

Ray Milton's bank account was virtually down to zero now that he had paid out nearly three thousand pounds for the new TV, computer and camera. But it was worth it. The Zoostorm Advanced Gaming PC had lightening fast graphics and produced wonderfully clear pictures.

The new camera had been bought five weeks earlier. It had a powerful zoom facility and full 3d HD video option. Even an amateur like him could get great footage with it. The camera could be connected to the computer, which in turn, was connected by an HDMI lead, to the smart TV in his lounge. The TV had a 60" backlit 3D screen and the thumping image was crystal clear.

He loved that TV. It took up most of one wall of the small room at the back of the house. It was more private there. Also the room's wall adjoined an unoccupied room of the next door neighbour. The old lady only used the front room. He could turn up the sound as much as he liked.

Ray Milton was economising now on his nights out. Thursdays was Quiz Night down at his local pub. He really enjoyed a few pints with the lads, some free chip butties in the thirty minute break, and a wander round the room to see if you could swap some answers with another team.

The team's captain was Bill. Bill took his drinking very steadily until their answers had been handed in. After that another four pints would be swiftly on their way into his gut; to be seen again when he took a leak before setting off home. A bit of a boozer was Bill; but clever. The stuff he knew amazed Ray Milton. The other two in the team were a husband, Frank, and his wife Immogen, both in their fifties. They seemed to spend all their time watching soaps because that was their value to the team. Any soap question was a given. Frank seemed a bit of a drip. Whether he noticed the innuendo that went on between his wife and some of the blokes in the pub was a puzzle. Immogen was lively. Ray had tried it on himself but got nowhere.

Ordinarily he would have been there, but not this night. Tonight he would drink his Homebrew. Tonight was to be spent with those beauties now flitting across his screen. His eyes were fixed on the TV. At the Skating rink on the previous evening Ray Milton had captured some brilliant footage.

With a pint of rocket fuel in the fist of one hand, and the computer mouse in the other, he leaned comfortably back in his reclining leather chair.

****

Karen was a smart girl. This might become a long term arrangement. He had just left her, and climbed the steps to his lounge. Tonight she had not cried at all. She was being surprisingly co-operative, although Bush had to admit he was learning how to manipulate these girls.

Now that he had allowed her the freedom of her arms, Karen was able to feed and wash herself and do some of those things he did not enjoy.

It was time for the local TV news which began at 10.30 p.m. He must watch this programme.

The new girl had gone missing last night, and a girl's body had been found that morning. His actions were bound to dominate the broadcast. Bush switched on the TV, opened a can of beer, and sat back in his leather chair.

The doorbell rang.

****

Detective Inspector Brady crouched in the drive and watched the Armed Response leader ring the doorbell. Rain was falling steadily and there was not a star to be seen through the heavy clouds. The sound of the doorbell could not be heard. Was it working? Brady nodded for the bell to be rung again. This time man's voice answered almost immediately but it took a full minute before door the opened. The air was electric. Brady and the others crouched low. Just audible in the distance, thunder softly rumbled. In the garden of a house nearby a dog howled. Brady knew how it felt. This must be the right house, surely.

Slowly the door opened. It was him. They had the bastard.

In they went mob-handed.

CHAPTER 19

On that warm sunny Friday in London in late July, there was an exhilaratingly lively confusion of humanity bustling, strolling, clicking cameras, or just standing and staring. In the streets, tourists outnumbered residents by a wide margin, for the residents who were not working or otherwise obliged to be out of sight, sensibly left the main attractions of the city to the tourists at that time of year. In a park in London, just after noon on that Friday, Francis Ulanski was grateful to have some time to be a tourist, and for the tracing work to be being carried out by the agency. Sitting relaxed on the grass he read again from the pamphlet.

The Albert Memorial is located in Kensington Gardens on Albert Memorial Road opposite the Royal Albert Hall.

It is one of London's most ornate monuments, designed by George Gilbert Scott.

Unveiled in 1872, The Albert Memorial commemorates the death of Prince Albert, Queen Victoria's husband, who died of typhoid fever at the age of 42.

Ulanski had been impressed with the splendour of the monument to Prince Albert, but as he sat now with his back to it, he contemplated the building he had travelled across London to see. The Albert Memorial is directly opposite the main entrance to the Royal Albert Hall. When he had seen concerts on American TV, several venues had impressed him, and this was one of them.

Opened by Queen Victoria in 1871, The Royal Albert Hall is one of the world's most famous stages.

Each year it hosts over 360 events which include classical music, jazz, world music, circus, rock, pop, opera, dance, comedy, tennis, dinners, award ceremonies and the Royal British Legion Festival of Remembrance.

It offers daytime tours, a shop, café, lunchtime jazz and world music in the Café Consort and a free exhibition series as well as a wide range of events from intimate comedy and jazz to classical recitals in the Elgar Room.

He was not disappointed with the view. With the sun shining down onto the impressive structure, it was an imposing sight. He was determined that one day soon he would spend at least one evening there. At the time the BBC Proms were in season. He could see the sign above the main entrance doors.

Looking above the building, Ulanski watched aircraft flying over it down an approach path to Heathrow, through the cloudless sky. A feeling of well-being washed over him. It was a relief to be geographically away from the problems he had been coping with for months in San Diego. Now that the agency was handling the tracing, the pressure was off him here in England. He realised that he was happy – well relatively anyway.

The sight of the aircraft though reminded him of home and his father, and he wondered how brief this feeling of content could last. He stood, and as he did so his mobile phone rang.

Swiftly he hurried up the slope and away from the traffic noise. The news was brilliant. The agency had traced his relatives. If he would transmit electronically the balance of the agreed fee, they would email the full details that he had requested. It could all be completed that Friday afternoon.

Ulanski set off for the hotel and his computer. He was savvy enough to avoid using his mobile phone for a banking transaction. It must be on his own computer. Tourism was now on hold.

*****

His lounge looked bare. The computer table top was as bare as his bank balance. The police had said he could have the TV, computer, camera, and his phone back "When we are finished with them."
They had kept him overnight, bastards! Knocked his beer over and made a right old mess, they had. No, Ray Milton had no intention of leaving town. His destination was the pub. First he had to visit his mother. It was Friday and he went every week to the Nursing Home.
Not so clever-dick are they, these coppers? They did not know about his mother's house three houses down. When he got back from the pub, he could call into his mother's and get his old computer and her TV. He would not see the Wednesday girls, but there was plenty on the old computer from before.
He was not daft. Before the coppers had come for him he had heard it on TV. That girl Karen, she was one of the Wednesday girls. Silly sods thought it was him.

Crapped his trousers though when they had him in that van, and had a go at him. Frightened him to death they had. Stuck that terrifying Kalashnikov or whatever in his mouth. Serves them right, the smell. Smiling at the way he had got just a little bit of his own back, Ray Milton went to see his mother.

****

Joel Bush knew who it was. He had looked through the window before bothering to open the door. He had seen them running away. The two lads were twins and they lived just down the road. It happened every year at this time when the school holidays started. They would sneak up to a house, ring the doorbell and run away. After a couple of weeks they get tired of the game. They would be off to the Bahamas soon anyway. That family has plenty of money.
"My dad's got a motor cruiser in Port St Charles."
Still, Bush remembered he used to ring doorbells with his pal Stuart. That was a few years ago now. He had lost all track of him.

Looking again through that same window, bathed in the summer sun on a warm Friday morning, Bush did not realise that a surprise was on its way, to further change his life.

****

Detective Inspector Brady was not a happy man, and it was the two officers most responsible for the can of worms of the previous night, that had felt the full force of his wrath. When they had seen the CCTV film of Ray Milton, with his camera exclusively on Karen and her two friends, and everyone had assumed he was the one responsible for her disappearance, the two officers had stopped looking. Unbelievably they had not checked the remainder of the footage. If they had, they would have seen Milton still filming after her two friends were running looking for the missing Karen.

To make matters worse, the two officers were watching the leader of the Armed Response Team, demonstrating to the full office, how he thought a one-legged man would perform at ice skating.

Those two were not the only ones to have received a tongue-lashing that morning. Brady had listened whilst the Superintendent had given him a right rocket. He knew that he himself should have checked the tape for longer. There really was no excuse. Mallard had been there and had stood quietly at first, whilst the unrestrained bollocking had been delivered. The tirade that had been quietly and vehemently delivered by the Superintendent had been the worst minutes of Brady's career. Then Mallard had started on Brady and that was just as bad.
It was a relief when the Superintendent merged the two teams. Detective Chief Inspector Mallard would have all of the officers working on the merged case. The decision was that one or more men had abducted both girls, and had killed one of them. The word "already" had remained unsaid, but had been in the heads of all three.

CHAPTER 20

Where on earth was Sheffield?

In front of him being attended to by the lone concierge, were two obese men covered in flowing white robes. Their two families, about twelve of them in all, sat nearby watching silently. The two men could apparently speak very little English. Two other staff were at lunch, or somewhere keeping out of the way, so the hapless concierge struggled on alone. It is imperative, as every man knows, in a situation where the other person does not understand what you first say, you shout. The shouting will cause the other to be suddenly enlightened and enable him to give a full and comprehensive answer to your query. If shouting does not work first time, you shout louder. Inexplicably, this did not seem to be cultivating the required illumination in the idiot concierge.

At one point the assistant hotel manager whizzed across to lend his expertise to the customer support service, for which the renowned and revered hotel has been admired since the nineteenth century, and attestations to which may be read at leisure in the hotel manager's office. Aged twenty-one years and five months, senior management unaccountably generated no improvement. For the first few minutes it had been amusing.

After ten minutes, Ulanski went to lunch in the restaurant. He would try again later.

After lunch, Ulanski was faced with the welcome sight of all three concierge stalwarts, now behind an empty counter. All three stopped trying to look busy, and smiled hopefully at him, willing him to relieve the monotony of having to be at their station, ignored for hours on end.

Walking up to the front, Ulanski chose the oldest, wisest looking individual. The man, who might well have been the grandfather of senior management, proved to be an ace. Armed with a map of England, an A to Z Street Map of Sheffield, and a telephone directory of that City, Ulanski waited whilst the man booked his train ticket to Sheffield for the following morning.

Back in his room he first chose a hotel in the City centre and booked a room. Then he assembled the information he already had.

It seemed the cousin of his father, Ryszard Bushmanov, once in England had changed his name to Richard Bush. The couple had had just one child, Joel. So Ulanski had a sort of cousin, who at age thirty-three was three years older than himself. The couple had died, but Joel Bush was still alive, or at least his death had not been registered. Ulanski had the address and Joel Bush had been registered as still there on the last Electoral Register. The chances were that he would find his cousin at that address.

Ulanski studied maps and consulted the telephone directory. He found J. Bush listed at the address the agency had given. This was terrific. He was nearly there.

He went to the room safe and took out the silver crucifix which lay on top of a letter. Fingering the crucifix he sat pondering its significance to his father. What tales could this have told, if it could? Why exactly was it so important to his father to return it now that he knew he would soon die?

He picked up the envelope addressed by his father to Magdalina Bushmanov. She was dead. What should he do? His father would not give him any details of the contents of the letter and had made him swear not to open it. The significance of the crucifix and how it came to be still in the possession of his father after all those years was a mystery. Should he open the letter?

He stared at both for a time, and then slowly put both back in the safe. He closed the safe and sat looking at it, tempted, yet circumspect.

From the internet he learned more about Sheffield and then went for a walk. He needed to think.

******

Two of the officers that had been assigned to the CCTV footage of road traffic in the Arena environs, were replaced by the two held responsible for the fiasco of the previous day. They were happy to lose the drudgery of that monotonous road traffic. Tasked now with scrutinising the footage of the inside ice rink, taken by Milton, they set about it with fresh enthusiasm.

The camera's focus was always on one or more of the three girls as they skated all around the rink. Additionally they could sometimes see all the other skaters and, crucially, the spectators.

At one point Karen had lost her footing and sprawled on the ice. The boy of a similar age, who had been trying to catch Karen's eye, skated immediately over, and helped Karen to get to her feet. Milton had zoomed in close and stayed zoomed in until Karen resumed normal skating. The boy's watch was clearly visible. One of the officers spotted the wristwatch and asked the technician to stop the film at that point, and zoom in onto the watch. It was digital and clearly showed 7.23. By synchronising both the film of the internal CCTV camera, with Milton's film, they could now view both the wide-angle from CCTV and the Milton camera's close-ups. They also had the exact time of any event.

There were only two unaccompanied men who watched the skating from the seating area. One man sat close to the lockers which were situated in the centre of the outer area. He was aged about twenty and seemed to be keenly watching a couple gliding expertly over the ice. The male skater was tall, slim and graceful. The girl also was slim, lithe and supple. She had legs which were extremely shapely as female ice skaters seem inevitably to have. As they were dancing, at one point, one of the lifts went wrong and the girl was dropped in a heap on the ice. The watching man stood at that point. It was subsequently discovered that the man skating was his brother.

The other lone watcher was seated near to the exit. He wore a woolly hat and was obviously watching the skating. He spent some time regarding the three girls. But so were many other people there. The three girls were obviously having a whale of a time. He did not seem to be taking an unusual amount of time on the girls alone. He actually kept looking around a lot as if he was waiting for someone.

When Karen's friends went to the toilet the CCTV captured both their departure and Karen sitting down. At that point, Milton had paused the filming. When it resumed, the girls were coming back onto the ice and they started looking for Karen. They resumed skating. Milton filmed it all. It clearly showed the girls skating for a few minutes, leave the ice, and begin looking all around for

Karen. Until the end of Milton's film there was no further sight of the missing girl.

Concentrating on the CCTV, the officers saw the seated Karen apparently reading something. Then she looked around, stood up, and hurried to the exit. Another camera caught her leaving through the car park exit, and then nothing. It was 7.46. She did not return.
The car park CCTV did not show the doorway, just the car park. It was too dark and the film was useless.

Of the two unaccompanied men, the younger man had left exactly seven minutes before Karen who had still been skating. They located him the following day. He did not have the use of a vehicle and was there because of his brother and his partner. They went every alternate night. The man himself was an accomplished skater. Currently he was resting a pulled muscle. He was dismissed from the reckoning.

The CCTV had shown the older man in the woolly hat leave just a minute before Karen. He clearly had a bad limp. He had tottered out and hardly looked the type to have the strength to tackle an unwilling healthy female. They watched the films until midnight. Dispirited they went home.

****

"My, my Karen, and I thought you were being such a good girl."

They were not there. Magazines were neatly stacked, and on top of them, the two novels were centrally positioned. They looked as though they had been geometrically arranged dead centre. Her plastic cup and water bottle were carefully arranged. A solicitous, precise girl is young Karen. Where they should have been, in the top corner of the bedside table, his condoms were gone.

Bush lifted the girl onto the bed and sat beside her.

He saw the slight smile. She really was lovely. Karen was without make-up and her eyes still showed signs of the heartfelt crying of those first hours. After only minimum and troubled sleep, still the natural beauty of that lovely face, overcame those conditions. Bush was not a tender-hearted soul, but this girl reached him in a way that Sophia had not. As he looked at her, he felt a kind of admiration. The girl was intelligent; she was beautiful; and she had substance. Karen had bottle.

"OK, we will manage without them Karen." He pushed Karen back and began.

Ten minutes later, Bush was walking to the door.

"You do realise now, that hiding the condoms has consequences. For your information, it is much better for a man to do it without them. The feeling is a lot better. You were a virgin until you came here, but I was not. A smart girl like you will know about SDT."

Karen laughed out loud. "SDT?"

"Yes, you know."

"Silly man, you mean STD, Sexually Transmitted Diseases."

"OK, clever sod, STD. Are you sure I do not have one? What if I've got AIDS, then?"

Karen had a serious face now. There was another terrible possibility.

"And what about babies, my sweet little Karen? How would like one with me? It is up to you."

The door closed behind him. It was Bush who had a smirk as he climbed the stairs.

CHAPTER 21

The Saturday morning first class carriage was sparsely occupied and Ulanski was able to stretch out his legs and leisurely enjoy the free coffee and biscuits which were surprisingly good. Passing by the train window, the green fields and hedges of England were a relaxing sight which somewhat eased his mood. He had begun to think about it during breakfast. As he watched the passing countryside Ulanski pondered the matter of his father's unopened letter. It was in all probability the final letter his father would ever write. Magdalina Bushmanov was deceased and would never know its contents. Should he give it to his cousin to open? What if the letter contained something his father would not want Joel Bush or anyone else to see? There must be a reason his father would not even give a hint of the contents to his own son. But, yet again, it might be something which needed some action to be taken. Perhaps it was news that would benefit the Bush family. Why then wait for so long to communicate it? Could it be advance notice of his will, or even a request to attend his funeral?

The few passengers in his coach were spending the journey time, mostly with their eyes focussed either on a book or an electronic device. He was in a Quiet Coach and so far no one was breaking the peace and quiet. One man who had a hideous red and white spotted handkerchief in one hand, worked on a laptop and was inputting desperately. Beads of perspiration stood out on his forehead and he kept dabbing his forehead with the handkerchief. A tight deadline was looming perhaps. Ulanski felt a twinge of sympathy for the man. A beautiful Saturday morning offered so many alternative ways to enjoy life; so many possibilities.

In contrast, a young man seemed to be in a blissful state as he was listening to something coming through his in-ear headphones: music, a lover's voice, religious text?

Whilst he allowed his subconscious mind to weigh his own situation, Ulanski let his thoughts wander and speculate on the respective circumstances of his fellow travellers. That did not last very long. His mind always returned to that letter. A decision was needed before he contacted his cousin.

Curiosity won. Ruefully he reached for the letter. He found himself looking over his shoulder to see if anyone was watching. Smiling at his own guilty paranoia, he carefully opened it.

It was written in Polish. Francis Ulanski knew almost nothing of the language.

He did know a lot about computing. Using the free WIFI available in first class compartments, Ulanski was quickly able to access the internet, and select a translation website. It took a little time to change the keyboard to polski characters and it took even longer to exactly type the contents of the letter. He struggled to read some of his father's handwriting, but he managed. Translations from free websites are rarely perfect. This one was no exception. With a bit of common sense he unravelled and improved the grammar and sense of it.

My darling Magdalina,
Please do not be offended at my calling you my
darling. To me that is what you have been since I fell

in love with you on that journey so long ago now. I have loved you ever since. I still do.

My son is bringing this letter to you, and returning the crucifix which belonged to your mother. I humbly beg your forgiveness for stealing your crucifix, and for depriving you of it for all these years. When I left, I was desperate to take something of you with me. This was something that was dear to you, and so for that reason, dear to me also. I have kept it by me all these years and have looked at it and thought of you every single day and night. I treasure this crucifix but am ashamed because it should be with you. Please take it back, Magdalina, and try to forgive me.

Francis is my only child and I love him dearly. I hope, Magdalina that you will not hold against him, this evil that I have done to you.

It was many years after I last saw you that I came to America and eventually married. My wife, who regrettably passed away some years ago, was a fine American woman. I tried to be a good husband to her and love her as best I could. We had a reasonable and happy life together, but Magdalina, she was not you. My feelings for you have never faded. They never will. The illness which has taken hold of me, leaves me now very little time on this earth. I will take my love for you with me to the other side, which my faith convinces me awaits. When I get there I will continue hoping that you have found it in your heart to allow me some portion of forgiveness.

Please tell Ryszard, my cousin that I am sorry, and that I love him.

Goodbye, my darling Magdalina.

Lucek Ulanski

For a long time, the stunned son stared unseeing, at the written outpouring of emotion, the confession from the soul, which the weak fingers of his mortally sick father had written.

Francis Ulanski cried.

Aloft in mid flight, the red spotted handkerchief paused. The perspiring keyboard maestro had noticed Ulanski's condition. In a reversal of mood, the direction of sympathy switched.

CHAPTER 22

Chief Inspector Mallard had assembled his full team at 8.30 a.m. and for two hours they had reviewed and assessed the crimes against the two schoolgirls. It was not encouraging.

In the case of Sophia Pearson, Mallard had expected a breakthrough with the watch, but no. It was a common one, about three years old, and could have been bought anywhere. The only DNA they had was from the bed sheets. A fingertip search of the field and a careful search of the whole of Hagg Hill had yielded nothing of use. The only possible item they had was the van Frank Cropper had passed. Other than it was a light coloured Ford Transit van they had nothing. It was clear that the motive was sex. They were looking for a man or even a boy, given her age. Whoever it was, drove, though not necessarily having a driving licence. It still could be a boy, in fact now that another sixteen year old had been abducted from the same school, a boy must certainly be high on the list.

With Karen Clayton there was little to work on. The Arena and especially the rink were the key. It must be. She was reading something and then went straight out. An assignation? Again, a boy or young man was favourite. There was nothing for it but to establish the whereabouts, on both nights of the disappearances, of every "eligible" boy, and all of the male personnel at Karen's school. Most of them were on holiday now, so this would take for ever. If the disappearance of Karen ran the same course as that of Sophia they probably had until next Wednesday to find her. That left four days after that day, Saturday.

The team was dejected and none more than Mallard.

"Can I make a suggestion, chief?"

"Please do, Philippa."

"Some of us, who have been solely concentrating on Sophia, have not seen the full details of the Karen disappearance. The other team is not completely up to date on Sophia. If we all have a look at what we have not yet seen, a fresh mind might spot something. I must admit that I find it puzzling that we have no clues, for example, from the arena. As you said a few minutes ago, it has to be pivotal. I do not mean any disrespect to those who have reviewed the events at the arena, but a fresh mind might just turn something up. Same thing with our Sophia investigation. We can have missed something."

"Anybody else have any suggestions?"

"I agree with Philippa."

"Thank you, Frank. Anybody else?"

"Right we will proceed like this. Detective Inspector Stan Brady will lead four of his original team and go over everything pertaining to Sophia. The others will come under my direct supervision to establish alibis, and hopefully the lack of one, of those males at the school. Only one stipulation though Stan, any contact with the Pearsons must be done by me or in my absence Philippa."

"Right sir."

"Philippa you will lead the Karen Clayton review with Frank and Trevor. I will look in as much as I can. Again consult Inspector Brady if any contact with the Claytons is required. The rest of that team will come under my direct supervision to establish lack of alibis. Do it your own way, Stan and Philippa, and we meet to review progress at 8.30 a.m. sharp on Monday."

"Sir, can I have a word in private, please?"

"In my office, then, Philippa."

The door to Mallard's office closed, Sergeant Philippa Tate began.

"I feel terrible asking you this, sir. I really am loving working here. I have never been happier and I feel I am serving a useful role in your team. I…….."

"For Christ's sake, Philippa. You know how precious time is for Karen. Please say what you need. I must get on.

"Sorry sir. It is the Christening of my brother's son, their first baby, next month, and I have had the arrangements made to go for five months."

"Good for you. Go. Please close the door on your way out."

"They live in America, sir."

"Oh, Jesus."

Sergeant Tate looked at the face of the Chief Inspector and saw his alarmed consternation. With a deep unhappiness, but a realistic understanding, she spoke.

"OK, sir I will cancel my flight. It is impossible I can appreciate that."

Mallard was torn between anger and sorrow. He could see the woman's face. The job must come first, was the mantra he had always tried to live by. Yet is she so vital? Can they manage? What were the chances that her absence would mean the difference between solving the case and not?

"When is the flight?"

"Not for another ten days, sir."

"How long?"

"Two weeks, sir."

"Go, but don't expect a present from me. Now sod off and let me work."

"Oh, thank you, sir."

"One more thing, sergeant. Don't come with any more shocks. My saintly-language resolution cannot stand it."

****

The condoms were back that evening. Bush picked up one of the packets whilst Karen watched him.

She had decided that her best option was to try to gain his affection. It might be hopeless, but what alternative was there?

Karen had gone over and over the situation in her own mind. The man had brought her here for sex. He had made no mention of ransom. It was not kidnap. She knew she was attractive. It had become obvious years earlier, even; how males paid more attention to her than any one of her friends; all of them. OK, so she was desirable then.

What about killing him? It might be possible. What then: she was chained and he never brought the key anywhere near her. With him dead and herself chained, she would starve to death. That was out.

It was sex, then. So how can this help her? Her only asset was her body, her looks, her usefulness. There was no alternative. So, how best can that help her?

Obedience gets favours, he had repeated. It had to be done. Step by step she would earn more favours. She must not give up hope. They might find her: and they might not. She had reasoned that her future was in her own hands. She had to take responsibility for, and manipulation of, her own fate.

"I knew you were big and strong, but I did not realise that you might be clever as well. I am much younger than you, so I suppose it is right that you know more. I must not have a baby. I have put the condoms back. I apologise for being stupid."

"Well done, Karen. You think I am big and strong do you, my lovely."

Bush was holding the girl close. She did not move away even when those hands began to follow a familiar path. "Well, this big strong man will teach you lots of things, Karen. For some of them we won't need condoms. Maybe tomorrow I will tell you what else I like. For now though, my lovely Karen, I want you to put this condom on me."

Karen tried to divert Bush.
"You know they will find me don't you?"
His hands never paused. It was as though she had never spoken.
"You shoved me in a van. They have CCTV cameras everywhere. They will have your number. If you let me go I will tell them I came with you because I wanted to."
"Yeh, right."
"Did you steal the van?"
"No: will you put that thing on me? Don't just twist it like that. It's not a balloon girl. You know what it is for. Come on Karen."
"So the CCTV will have you."
"They won't. It was dark; too dark; and I switched my lights off just before I went through the car park gate. Clever, eh? Come on, little beauty; put it on me for

Christ's sake. Look at me. You've got me bloody bursting here."

"The road then. That Queens Road is full of cameras, and you have to pass the football ground, Sheffield United. Can't move for cameras round there. They are always showing bits on TV from them, when there has been a punch-up or stabbing at the matches. My dad says there are nearly as many cameras as spectators. You are bound to be on some of those. Ow, don't do that, you are hurting me."

*****

Where the West Yorkshire Norfolk female had a cold heart, young Philippa Tate's was the opposite. It was not on open display, far from it, but a seasoned female-observer such as he, could see the signs. When she spoke to the aged or the infirm, it was there, and genuine; the feeling.

She had compassion and humanity. Breaking the news of the horrendous loss of a daughter was immensely difficult, even for battle-scarred old sods like him. When she had told Mr. and Mrs. Pearson that they had found Sophia, Philippa Tate had done it marvellously well. The tears in her eyes had not been contrived. He could see that Philippa's heart was being pierced by the twin daggers of sympathy and concern. After the three of them had sat for forty-five minutes of profound sincere grieving, and DC Frank Cropper had sat watching like a right royal gooseberry, the Pearsons had thanked her and seen her to the door, and Frank had had to squeeze by them to extract himself from the hall.

He had seen her courage, for he had been with her when that child had made a dash across the busy Abbey Lane, when it had spied that big huggable Saint Bernard dog. Without a thought for herself, Philippa had skipped in front of the lorry, which managed to swerve and miss her by a hair's breadth, pick up the unsuspecting child, and dash through the traffic across to the other side, by a miracle it had seemed, unscathed.

On some nights, when he got home, he would speak of her to his wife. Janet Cropper would listen attentively as she always had, for she loved her man. Twenty six years married now, and she well knew his strengths and his foibles. She had seen the brave man proudly wearing his red beret, had feared for him when he was overseas and in danger. She had welcomed him back and loved him in their happy bed when he came home. She knew of his weakness for females, and had had to watch his humiliating downfall, in the West Yorkshire police force. She had blessed him for his fortitude and support when they discovered she was barren.

Janet Cropper saw the look in the eyes of her man when he spoke of Philippa. She knew he was regaining some of the fire in his belly, and a renewed eagerness for work.
His wife recognised what her man had not yet fathomed. Frank Cropper had discovered the daughter he had never had.

*****

It was Sunday afternoon and he was tired. The week had been unbelievably eventful and it had taken its toll on him. He could hardly believe he had been capable of accomplishing what he had done.

With the shop locked until Monday, the week's records all passed to his accountant, and all the cash banked, he could rest all day, try to regain some energy, and hope to have a more restful week next week. He would put his feet up, have a drink or several, watch TV, and visit Karen for a session - then bed.

Bush felt he had done well. According to the news, the police were flummoxed. His new girl had settled in well and she had no scars to spoil her soft skin. He had visited her for a huddle, first thing.

What was it Karen had said last night? The CCTV cameras on those roads he had used going to and from the Arena? The route had taken him right past the football ground. He too had seen countless TV clips outside the ground. The girl had a point. Still, there were loads of vehicles up and down there all the time. What if they checked though? Where could he say he was going? He had the disguise but it was no earthly use if they had his registration number. Where could he have been? What was round there on a Wednesday night? There had been no match. Try the internet for some ideas.

Ten minutes later he had the answer. That would do nicely. Maybe they would never check, but better safe that sorry – awfully bloody sorry; for the rest of his life, for ever.

He thought for a minute. Yes, he would do that tomorrow. Thank God he had a smart girl down in the basement. She might just have cut her own throat, so to speak, but she might have saved his bacon. Feeling smug, he switched off the computer and sat down to relax.

He had a thought. Why not? Karen was the right size. Upstairs, he went into the bedroom that had been his parents. From the fitted wardrobe he took out two items. Moisture came into his eyes as he handled them. He had wanted to keep something of his mother, and these were just two of the few he had kept. He was not giving them away, they were on temporary loan. His increasing fondness for the young Karen made it seem fitting.

Proudly he entered the basement room where Karen sat reading. He handed over the nightdress and housecoat. "These belonged to someone very dear to me, Karen. You can wear them if you like; until you leave. Please take good care of them."

Karen noticed the sincerity in his eyes, and the serious look on Bush's face. After he had left, she had a good look at them. These were very good quality, very tastefully feminine, and exactly the right size. She slipped on the nightdress and it felt very pleasing to wear it. It was also a relief to be no longer naked. She would leave the housecoat until later when it would be cooler. Karen wondered who exactly it had belonged to.

Back in his lounge, Bush picked up the TV guide. Sunday afternoon usually meant there would be some films on BBC without all those adverts. That would do nicely. There was a decent film starting in ten minutes so better get organised. A can of beer from the fridge was poured into his pint glass. Crisps and nuts from the pantry were positioned on the table by his reclining chair.

His thoughts turned to Karen. Wouldn't it be great if the girl was a willing partner, a voluntary girlfriend who could share this at his side? The sex was superb, but he was still lonely at these times. He was thirty-three. A proper mate was all he wanted. It was not too much to ask, was it?

Still, you can't have everything. He was lucky to have Karen the way she was – little beauty: clever little beauty.

He switched on the TV. The doorbell rang before a picture appeared.

"Little bastards!"

Bush shot out of his chair. He was not having this again.

He flung open the front door. There was a man standing, smiling, on his doorstep.

"Joel? Joel Bush?"

"Who the f… , I mean   err,   yes."

"Sorry to call unannounced. It seems we are relatives. Can I come in and talk to you?

"No. I don't have any relatives, American or any other."

"Yes I am an American. Were your parents from Poland, Joel?

"Yes. How did you know?

"Your father used to be Ryszard Bushmanov, and your mother was Magdalina. Please let me come in and talk to you."

A staggered Joel Bush simply could not believe what he was hearing. He just stood there gaping at the visitor. Ulanski continued.

"My father and your father are, or rather were, cousins. You and I are the sons of cousins. We share some of the same blood. I am Francis Ulanski, son of Lucik Ulanski. My father's mother was the sister of your father. My grandmother's maiden name was Bushmanov. She married and took her husband's name, Ulanski. You see?"

Bush sized the stranger up. A similar age to himself, the man was clean-shaven and well dressed in a casual fashion. Bush could see that the short-sleeved shirt was a good one. He wore shorts and Adidas trainers. His hair was cut in a modern cut and his smile was natural and friendly. In short, the stranger looked neither threatening nor mad.
"I am confused. I don't believe it. Come in anyway."

As Ulanski followed Bush he realised he was a bit disappointed with his relative. Apart from the face, which Bush could do nothing to change, the man's whole appearance and bearing was, to put it kindly, unimpressive. He did not look dirty, not at all; it was unavailing. Also to Ulanski, primarily, his relative's appearance was sloppy. He himself was fairly meticulous in his appearance, not a dandy, but neat.
They went into the lounge. Bush turned off the TV and took a gulp of his beer.

"Sit down. Would you like a drink?"
"Love one. Do you have any red wine?"
Bush poured from a three litre box of supermarket Australian red wine. Not a connoisseur, then, thought Ulanski. Then Bush sat opposite his unexpected visitor. His posture was upright. He perched, rather than relaxed;

on the edge of the seat. His whole manner was attentive, guarded to the point of suspicion.

"So just go through that relations bit again slowly. I am not too bright. And another thing, how did you find me? Oh, and another, how do I know you are for real?"

****

It had taken some time and two more glasses of wine. The difficult part had been convincing Bush that he and his father were who he said they were. He had already decided not to give Bush the letter. Ulanski had left it in his hotel room. It was incredibly personal to his father, the woman to whom it was addressed was dead, and its effect on Joel Bush could not be anticipated. It might have damaging consequences.

He had decided, though, to return the silver object to where it apparently belonged – his cousin. Ulanski explained about the condition of his father in San Diego, and then handed over the box in which was the silver crucifix.

The crucifix was what had transformed Bush from being a wary sceptic to becoming an emotional relative.

The minute he had in his hand, something from his maternal grandmother, something which had been fashioned in his original homeland, something from the place where he had been conceived, Bush changed completely. Ulanski watched the tears well up in the man's eyes. The crucifix he held gently in his hand had hung around his grandmother's neck. It had been against his mother's breast, his mother's skin. It had been kissed and treasured by both of the women, before he was born. The two women, from whom he had sprung, had revered and worshipped the small silver article which he now held. They looked silently into each other's eyes. A bond formed. Bush saw sincerity in the other man's eyes. He was convinced. He really had a relative. It was what he had missed so much all his life. His parents had been wonderful. But he never had relatives. All the other kids had relatives. Joel Bush had none, ever - until now. Bush was holding the silver cross and chain delicately in his palm. He kept looking at his cousin, and then down at the crucifix, just staring at it.

Ulanski stood and wandered around the lounge giving Joel some privacy with his crucifix. There were some lovely feminine touches around the room. They would undoubtedly have been selected and placed there by Magdalina. There were two photographs on a shelf above the fireplace. The oldest was a black and white photograph of the couple on their wedding day. Ulanski assumed it would have been taken somewhere in Poland. They were both smiling happily, as one would expect, but although it was obviously a dull day the photograph still gave out a joyous image even after all those years. Magdalina had been truly beautiful. Ulanski could see why his father would have fallen for her. The man at her side, Ryszard, looked a good match for her. Pity, thought Ulanski, their son had not inherited the same quality of looks. The other photograph was of Joel aged about 10 years old, with his parents, and taken at some event in the countryside.

Ulanski turned the photograph over. *Bakewell Show, Joel 9 years old*, was all that was written.

There were some old long playing records in a bureau and he tried to read the titles without disturbing them. They were very varied, pop type albums.
On another shelf was a row of books. Some were on meat and butchery, but mainly there were war and crime novels.

Bush had ended his reverie and came up to join him.
"Sorry to hear about your dad, though, Francis."
Ulanski just nodded, "Thanks pal."

Bush could see it would be better to change the subject.
"You read much, Francis?" There was warmth in Bush's voice now. He was talking to a relative, a really welcome relative.
"Some. I spend a lot of time on computers so I have never bought too many actual printed books. I get most of what I want off the internet."
Bush refilled his glass with more wine and they sat down. There was silence for a while. It was not an awkward silence, much more a relaxed silence.

" I am over here in England because that is what my father wanted. He has not much longer to live and I want to be home with him for his last days so I cannot stay over here for long.
By the way, you coming to the funeral? Come to think of it, why don't you come over and visit him? He was over the moon when I told him yesterday I was actually coming

to meet you. He was upset about your parents dying, though."

Bush swallowed hard and his eyes clouded once again. "All my life I have only ever had my mother and dad. No brothers or sisters, no relatives, no close mates, and with my looks, girls just don't want to know. Now you are here. Now I have an uncle in America and a cousin here in this room with me, here and now. I not only have a cousin, he is prepared to be a mate, a close mate, a real one hundred percent close mate. I am choked. I don't know what to say."
Ulanski fancied that this was one of those significant moments in life that could be life changing.

So far, Ulanski acknowledged, he himself had had two really significant life-changing moments.
The first had been at college when he had discovered an aptitude for computer programming. It had absorbed him and thrilled him. When he had become proficient at it, and when he could control the computer and make it do his bidding, he had felt a profound joy of achievement. He strived to become expert, and he had succeeded. Even now, after so many successful projects, an intense pride always welled up in him when he saw his work run for the first complete, effective performance.

The second had been the sale of his Mobile App for smartphones. When his father had been diagnosed with Systemic Lupus Erythematosus, Francis had researched the disease and foresaw some of the problems he would be faced with in being responsible at home for his father's care. His mother was dead. Already working full time, his time then, was limited. He would need a lot of help. Hospitals in America are intense users of computers and he had previously worked on some medical projects. There was nothing currently, that he could discover, that could assist a Carer. An idea came to him whilst shaving one morning. Carers cannot be at the patients bedside one hundred percent of the time. Communication and feedback are essential. Responses need to be fast and most of the time speed is vital.

At first, the time needed to look after his father was light, so he was able to devote his spare time to developing his idea. He devised a system which would be non-specific. It would be a boon to Carers of patients with many different illnesses; serious life threatening ones, and also those ailments which are not.

Ulanski wanted his proposed software to operate on a vast number of devices around the world. Furthermore his software would be designed to help Carers at home or in communes, not just hospitals and organisations with expensive computer systems. Carers and patients can have their phones with them almost anywhere. He developed software for computerised systems and for inexpensive mobile phone functionality. It was a success. With the proceeds of the sale of the programs and the App, Ulanski's life changed significantly.

As Ulanski saw the emotional effect his recent words had just had, and as he looked into the eyes of his cousin, an unexpected feeling of warmth and affection mounted within him. Bush appreciated the look of genuineness which he saw in the other man. They both recognised that a foundation of real friendship was being laid.

Ulanski rose from his seat, and stretched out his hand. With an earnest purposefulness, Bush stood and took it.

"We are family."
Bush responded, "Glad to know you, cousin. From the bottom of my heart, welcome."
"I think we need a strong drink." Bush went across to the bureau. "What do you want to drink now, Francis?"

"You got any scotch, Joel?"
Bush nodded and poured big measures.
"Neat?"
"No, on the rocks Cus."
They drank and relaxed. An easy air of intimacy was in the room. The ice had been broken and they had bonded quickly. They chatted of life in their respective communities – the food, the laws, and the government. Bush wanted to know about San Diego.
The whiskey bottle was upended several times and conversation flowed easily.

It was 7.30 p.m. when Bush looked at his watch and stood. "Be back in ten minutes, Francis."
Karen had to be fed. Bush busied himself in the kitchen and went down to the basement with the tray and set it down for her. When he left the basement, the girl pounced on the food and ate rapidly.

Outside, Bush carefully locked and bolted the solid door and then stood unmoving for a full minute. A decision had to be made. Could he risk it?
"Family we may be, but how trustworthy can he really be? I would love a genuine mate, a partner-in-crime, in fact -

not bloody fiction. How would he react? What shall I do?"
The matter unresolved, Bush climbed the stairs.

"Fancy a snack, Francis?"
"Sounds good, Cus."
"Come through to the kitchen and see what we have got."
Six eggs made into omelets, a stack of frozen chips cooked
in the oven, and a tin of peas disappeared in quick time.
"Like to try a can of English beer."
"Surely."
The pair relaxed and leaned back in their chairs facing
each other.
"So what else do you do in your spare time, Francis? You
must have a lot of it."
"Baseball has always interested me, so I take in some
matches, go to some concerts, and spend a fair bit of time
on my computer. I can't travel at present because of dad,
but later I will. You much good on computers?"
"I can do what I need to do, but I only do the basics,
nothing fancy, nothing in your league I bet."

For two hours they relaxed in the lounge and told each
other something of their lives. There was no awkwardness,
or rivalry, or envy as they each spoke frankly of their
experiences and inclinations. Time passed easily. By the
time Ulanski stood and said he had better be off, they had
established an undeniable, substantial kinship.

Bush rang for a taxi and showed his cousin around the
house and garden whilst they wait for its arrival. The
basement was bypassed.

They agreed for Bush to make contact tomorrow.

Bush watched the taxi drive away and disappear out of sight. For several minutes he remained staring at the empty road without really seeing it. Before his cousin had arrived that afternoon, Bush was spending almost all his free time, either thinking about Karen or being actually with her. During his time with his cousin he had barely given her a thought. Like now, for instance it was not Karen that had his attention, but Francis and the prospect of a real friendship and close comradeship. If he had to choose between Karen and close kinship, he would choose the latter.

Whilst Karen spent another desperate night alone in the basement, and Mallard and his team became more disconsolate, Bush slept peacefully.

****

In San Diego, Lucek Ulanski stared at the empty wall, and the spot where he imagined his beloved crucifix still hung. He was happy. Into and out of his mind would come images from his past. Periodically he was lucid and knew where he was. When the phone call from Francis had arrived, with the wonderful news that the crucifix had been returned to its rightful place, he had wept with relief and deliverance. He was redeemed and could go to his Maker free of that guilt. He wept also for Magdalina. She was already there.

Now his reverie was again upon him. That beloved tiny silver object, that meant so much to him, was lighting up the room for him. Although it was pitch black in the depth of night, the room was shining with Holy incandescence. God was upon that crucifix. The crucifix was still there, as it should be: where it ever was.

CHAPTER 23

Monday morning found Joel Bush in a good frame of mind. His time spent before work with Karen had been energetic and fruitful for him. Whilst he had slept, his subconscious mind had been working on the answer to visiting San Diego. The decision was made.

When Francis Ulanski's voice answered the call from his cousin, he too sounded chirpy. His call home had found his father in a relative good disposition. When he had told him of Joel and that he had invited him to come to San Diego to visit, his father had enthusiastically agreed.
Yes Francis would see Joel at home that evening.

When Bush finished that call, he dialled the Big Yellow Storage Company. He made several enquiries and requested that their brochure and full details of their services, be posted to him at home.

His staff heard him begin a tuneless whistle as he worked in the rear of the shop. They liked that – that he wanted to whistle; but not the sound of it. He was happy so life could be more pleasant for them for a while. The tuneless whistle continued .

****

Philippa Tate was eager to see her Chief Inspector first thing on Monday. She arrived before the Briefing was to start, scheduled for 8.30 a.m.. Mallard had been called to see Superintendent Shaw and it was already 8.25 before he returned to his office.

"Yes Philippa."
"I think we have something from the Ice Rink. Frank thinks, and I agree with him, that there is a man there deliberately hiding his real appearance. What's more he left immediately before Karen did."
"Show me."
They entered the Major Incident Room and Mallard called out, "Briefing for 8.30 postponed. Stick around, we may have a development. Frank, over here with us."
The computer graphics technician was already at the equipment and the three of them sat waiting for him to begin. He had been briefed by Philippa Tate before they had left, late on the previous evening.

Two particular scenes from the video, taken by the released Milton, clearly showed the man in question. In one, the camera had zoomed in on Karen as she stopped for a minute holding the rail of the rink. She had been directly in front of the man. The man who sat on the front row could have touched Karen if he had reached out, because she was so close to him. They could clearly see the woolly hat and the moustache. As Karen stood there, he briefly removed the dark glasses. It was enough for the technician to zoom onto his face. Because the focus was centred on Karen, as she stood there breathing deeply, the image of the man's face was not too detailed. It appeared that there were only a few wrinkles on his forehead. His eyes appeared to be brown but that was not a certainty - dark anyway.

The second scene showed the man leaving. This was a distant shot because he was at the opposite end to where the two younger girls were skating. Karen was not visible .The camera had followed the youngsters. There was enough, though, to discern his limp.

A clip was then shown from the CCTV. It showed the man arriving alone. Again his limp was visible but from a distance. When zoomed in, the picture was grainy due to the limited pixels of the ten year old CCTV system. He clearly had a pronounced limp.

"I don't get it, sergeant."

Mallard's use of title rather that her Christian name indicated displeasure. Frank Cropper spoke up.

"It's altogether overdone, chief." He too had picked up on the Mallard's mood, and was trying, for once, to be careful.

"There are just two people in the area all night wearing hats. The other was a youth with a baseball cap. That woolly hat is neither smart nor necessary in that area where he is sitting.

The moustache is unfashionable. Nobody these days wears that style. Look at it. Vincent Price had one like that in the 1960's.

Then there is the limp. I think it is false. The man is a fraud."

Philippa took up the argument.

"Also he arrived just before Karen, and he left exactly ninety-three seconds before Karen was seen going through the exit. I believe he should be checked out ASAP, sir."

"OK, Philippa. We have naf all else. Start now. Forget the review meeting and give this top priority. Take Frank and the Bosun with you. At last we may have something. Did you check his wrist?"

"His wrist?"

"The wristwatch, sergeant. The wristwatch from the wall at Sophia's crime scene. Don't tell me you have forgotten that poor girl already."

He hurried out not waiting for a reply.

****

Approximately ten miles south-west of Sheffield, in the Peak District village of Hathersage, The Crown Inn was rarely busy at lunchtime, especially in midweek. In the Snug that afternoon sat three men. Two of them sat together as they invariably did, and the third was a stranger wearing a baseball cap, who sat silent and unaware, alone at a table positioned directly under the wall ornament. Nobody knew the age of that Elk's head which was attached to a gnarled wooden mounting. Its origin was forgotten for it had hung in that room since before any of the current locals had been born. A few though could, and indeed sometimes would, tell of the day when it had taken it upon itself to drop upon the head of young Eli Sykes. Young Eli was seventy-one years young at the time. He always had been known by that name because his only brother, Big Eli, was older by two years. When Eli was only one quarter of the way down his second half of mild that early afternoon, the Elk had dropped and ended Young Eli's drinking, permanently.

Young Eli had been a man careful with money all of his life. The wise locals sitting in their usual places the following afternoon agreed, and sagely observed, that it

154

was indisputably shrewd of Young Eli not to have ordered a full pint.

At present, though, that metaphorical Sword of Damocles was directly over the skull of the newcomer.

For ten minutes no-one had spoken. Silence enveloped the cheerless room. In a corner of the room above the bar, the wallpaper had begun to curl. On the floor, the carpet which had not been properly cleaned for a decade at least, had been trampled by countless feet. The only movement was that of someone's hand occasionally reaching for, delivering, and then releasing a glass containing the savoured ale. If the Elk fell again it would at least break the monotony.

"Stupid sod."
One of the pair had half-turned and uttered quietly to his companion beside him. The one who spoke was the elder by five years and unvaryingly considered himself to be superior.
"Eh?" The man beside him had been staring unseeing whilst he pondered upon a pressing dilemma, and was surprised to hear the voice.
"Stupid sod."
"Who?" He was alert now and beginning to feel uncomfortable. "Who?"
His companion nodded his head a fraction. It was indistinct and did nothing to aid his companion.
"Yon"
"Yon? What?"
There was a shuffling, signalling agitation.
"Him."

"Him?" Light began to dawn.

"Him."

"Baseball cap?"

A grunt conveyed success.

"What?"

"Look."

He would rather return to the matter of his beloved tomato plants, but he would indulge his friend first. Ern could be very touchy.

"What?"

"Tap tap tap."

Baffled, he shrugged. "Give us a clue."

"Mobile. Bloody mobile. Stupid sod just keeps tapping away on that contraption."

"Oh."

A minute went by.

"What should he do, Ern?"

The poor sod was on his own and a stranger. Ern looked at his companion with clear disdain.

"Should just sit here and enjoy himself like us, Fred."

Fifteen minutes later the excitement was broken by the sound of Wilfred, the landlord, calling time. Francis Ulanski stood, walked across to the bar, returned his empty pint glass, and walked towards the door. Two pairs of eyes followed his every movement. The door closed behind him.

"Silly sod's gone."

******

Cleaning the office, her colleagues had noticed. The sales girls at the supermarket were puzzled. A few had asked and none was the wiser. The reason for their friend's melancholy, uncharacteristic quiet, was unexplained. Why? She had only one relative, two if you count the sister's husband. Was that it? Was the sister ill? Surely it cannot be Catalina herself? She looks healthy enough, but it is clear she is not sleeping. Is it a man? No, she keeps to herself, no it cannot be. Can it? That must be it. It has to be. They had worked it out. Catalina had a secret boyfriend and he was giving the girl a hard time. Swine! Her colleagues watched Catalina as she cleaned.

Her papers had been returned to her already. A man had come to her room. The man had reminded her. They could come for her at any time. She was available for questioning whenever they wanted. It was obvious she would not talk. He had looked her up and down. Catalina could see he knew what had taken place. He had moved up close to Catalina, and stroked her hair. Petrified, she just stood there. He had groped her briefly. As he left the room he signalled what would be her fate if she talked. His fingers had made a slashing motion across his throat. Now she was desperate to get out of Mexico. If they took her to that room again she would die. She would kill herself. Never again! Never, never!

Her visa application had been handed in. How long before she knew? What if they said no?
Catalina dusted on autopilot whilst her insides churned. Every day was a year. Every hour was a week. Please, the visa must come. How long will it take?
"A few weeks, madam until it is processed."

"Madam!" I am not a madam. If it becomes known, I never will be a madam. Oh dear Holy Mother, help me. I will never sin again. I promise. I will be good. Please, please, let the visa come.

All I want is a good man for a husband, and to have babies for us both to love. Is it too much to ask? Holy Mother, I would be a wonderful mother. Please help me.

****

On a good day, if the sun was shining, if there were no supply problems, and if the till was pinging away regularly, then on such a day - not by any means all of them – never overdo it; on such a day, Bush might be heard whistling for a few seconds.
When the staff in the shop heard their lord and master, who was sorting paperwork in the back office, burst into song, there was a stunned paralysis. Singing was a first. Fortunately the shop was empty. Had it not been, a customer dash for the door could have been counted upon. His voice was, if anything, even less agreeable than his whistle.
Naturally it was Darryl who said it, spoke for them both, summed it up.
"The fucker's singin'."

*****

"What made you think the limp that man had was not real, Frank?"

"Experience son, experience."

"Would you tell me what experience?"

"After the food, son."

The Huntsman pub was busy and they were lucky to have snaffled a table straight away. Frank went first and came back with a plate piled high. Higgs-Whitethorn's food portion, when he returned, was more modest. Frank finished first. He downed his pint and fetched another.

"Right, lad it was like this. I was on a special training course somewhere in the north of Scotland. They never told us the name of the place but it was damn cold. My lot, 2 PARA, were being flown to Cyprus the following week. We couldn't wait to get away from the brass monkeys of where we were. Five of us were singled out for "special work". All they would say was that we might be needed to exfiltrate somebody. There was bother brewing in one of the Eastern block countries, this is 1989 by the way. If the shit hit the fan then we were to go in and get this bloke out, whoever he was. Why us? We worked it out. We would already be in Cyprus. The trouble areas looked like Albania or Bulgaria. We were just round the corner. Both are warmer than England so we were laughing. Except for the Scottish sergeant bastard who we got for our special training. Campbell was his name.

Remember, lad, that we were paras - 2 PARA. We were all of us twenty-two years old and fully trained. We were bloody fit. Not fit enough for this Scottish bastard, though."

Frank could see he had the lad's rapt attention. He swallowed another half pint and continued.

"It was tough. I won't go into details, but a couple of the lads, when we finally got in one night, actually bloody cried.

To spur us on he had a favourite screech in his high-pitched Scottish voice.

"Imagine the Macleods are after ye laddie. The Macleods are behind ye with their kilts lifted, coming for your bare arses. Built like Priapus laddie. The Macleods are behind ye."

Stupid sod!

At the very end of the day, when we were already knackered, he had us running up and down this high snow-covered hill in full kit. If anybody had upset him the day before, they got a thirty second penalty. Otherwise we all set off together. Five times up and down the bleeding hill. Last one home got Jankers.

Jankers was easy. Just up and down the fucker twice before breakfast. Nobody gave us a wake-up call. The Scots had deliberately shoved us out of the way where we could not hear Reveille. If you were late for breakfast, tough shit. You missed it. One lad would never have woken up without a good shake. If the roof fell in on his soddin bed he would have slept on. For a laugh one day we left him asleep."

Trevor sat smiling, occasionally sipping his beer. Frank could see Trevor was right with him in Scotland.

"Bet you didn't hear tales like this at Cambridge, son."

The young man just smiled. "What about the limp, Frank?"
"Right, the limp. When we finally got to wave a fond two-finger bye-bye to Sergeant Campbell, we got an officer called McCorquodale. Posh bloke he was. Probably been to a good university - like Oxford."
Just a smile from Trevor. He didn't mind it from Frank.
"This one was OK. His job was to teach us, in three days, enough to help us survive in the streets, of wherever it was we were going. Remember, we were young and fit. Everybody else our age was in the army. One of the tricks he taught us, was to put a stone in your boot and cause a limp.
He said to us that not even Robert DeNiro could feign a limp like somebody in real pain. We didn't know what feign meant then, but we got the idea. If Robert DeNiro couldn't do it, what chance did we have? We liked McCorquodale and we hobbled about for the best part of three days.
We had no time then, but after, in Cyprus, we watched the injured lads, and the locals, the cripples. With the stones, we limped different to them. Right enough, our bloody heels hurt because of them stones in the boots. But I reckon that after a while your body adapts. It copes with pain. Also your body finds the easiest way to walk. We all watched because you never know if you're going to have to stake your life on something like that.
That man in the rink was new to pain. He didn't know how to walk, proper."

"And did you exfiltrate the person OK?"
"Never had to do it. Nobody ever said why. Never mentioned again. Scotland - just a fond memory, full of

Campbells, Macleods, McCorquodales, and bleeding bagpipes. Never been back. Never will – bloody place! We weren't bothered. We were swanning it in Cyprus. Stayed there six months doing virtually sod-all then came home to Colchester in the summer."

He nodded and Higgs-Whitethorn fetched him pint and brought a half for himself.

There was silence for a minute.

"Trevor, tell me something. Are you into sailing?"

"No, never been sailing, why."

"Something Mallard said. He said to me 'Take Bosun with you.' He was talking about you. What is he talking about?"

Higgs-Whitethorn smiled.

"You didn't get it, Frank?"

"Get what?"

Trevor shook his head.

"Here goes. You did ask me. You will not know a lot about particle physics, Frank. Not many people are very interested.

The boson is a fundamental component of the Standard Model of elementary particles. The Standard Model is a widely used and accepted theory, which attempts to conceptualise and categorise particles. Until recently one particular particle existed in theory, but had never been proved by being detected experimentally. That particle has often been called the God particle. One distinguished founder researcher in that aspect of particle physics is a man called Peter Higgs. That particle has become known as the Higgs boson. In 2013 Peter Higgs and Francois Englert, won the Nobel Prize in physics for their work on the theory of the Higgs boson. See the connection Mallard must have made, Frank? Higgs-Whitethorn, Higgs boson. Some wits at university did the same."

"I felt a right nut when I had no idea what he meant. Thanks for that, son"

"Frank do you mind me asking you something a bit personal, now?"

"Depends."

"Tell me to buzz off if you like, but why are you still a Detective Constable? You are just as smart as most people in CID who are above you. Loads of experience, like spotting this limp. Why?"

Cropper's expression never changed.

Fools rush in …… Trevor had unknowingly mouthed the question that most of them at the station had pondered at length, and frequently, and feared to tread.

Trevor watched him, waiting patiently. Obviously DC Cropper was gathering his thoughts.

Eventually, having now marshalled the words to begin, "I won't tell you to buzz off, Bosun. That would be uncharitable of me. I will just say two words."

P.C. Higgs-Whitethorn sat expectantly.

"Yes?"

"Fuck off."

When Philippa Tate walked in and looked around for them, Frank saw her first and stood up to get her attention. Whilst she ambled across Frank rearranged the chairs and held one ready for her. Trevor felt he ought to stand since Frank was being so gallant. They both stood until Philippa was seated. Mystified, the woman just smiled hello.

"What you having, Philippa?"

"Just a tonic water with ice and lemon, please Frank."

"Bosun, get the sergeant her drink, son."

"Any joy with the Ice Rink?"

"Typical office lot, Frank. Finally got through to the manager and he is phoning round the staff who were on duty last Wednesday. When he can get them there, he will ring me. We will just have to wait: again."

"Are you going to eat here?"

"I am. Carvery any good?"

"Not bad at all. It will be getting a bit stale if you leave it too long."

"Say no more."

Frank watched her glide her way through the tables and up to the carvery.

CHAPTER 24

He rang the doorbell and Bush greeted him and took him inside. Earlier when Bush had arrived home he had gone straight down to the basement. He quickly cleaned the room and then changed the bed linen. A silent Karen watched him as he bustled wordlessly about. Then he went to the kitchen.

Thirty minutes later, when Karen had finished picking at the unappetising food, he removed the food tray. He left drinks and a packet of crisps for the girl. Karen had pestered him for information but he had just told her he would see her later.

Bush had just finished his own meal, another microwave delight, when the bell rang.

"Had a good day then?"

"Yep, been on one of your buses out to Hathersage and had lunch in a great pub called The Crown, built in the sixteenth century - only two locals and me in the place. Went for a walk in that beautiful countryside and breathed in deep lungfuls of country air. Gonna see more of this area before I go back down to London. Your little country is impressive. What about your day?"

Your little country indeed!

Resisting the urge to speak up for the achievements of Great Britain compared to the big new boy on the block, Bush simply said, "OK."

For several minutes they went through a ritual of small-talk that interested neither of them.

"Oh, how's your dad by the way, should have asked earlier?"

"Pa's hanging on. I told him you might come visit, and he was over the moon."

"Truthfully?"

"Absolutely. If you're going to come, though, it had better be soon. Don't know how long we've got him for."

"This is not bullshit? You mean it? I can come, for sure?"

"One hundred percent, man. You can stay at my place in S.D. and I can show you around. We can have a terrific time."

"Right. I want to come. I am definitely coming, one million percent."

"I have an open air ticket in case I have to rush back, but in any case I don't want him to spend his last few days on earth alone. If all is well, I plan to stay in Sheffield until Sunday, have a week in London until the next Sunday and then I will fly home. If I need to go before that, so be it."

"I could book a ticket and fly with you on that Sunday, all being well with your dad."

"That'd be great, Cus."

*****

The investigation was floundering.

Fifteen male officers had been assigned to re-interviewing the boys at school and the male teachers. A further thirteen female officers were talking again to Sophia's known friends, all of the girls in the same year, and the female

166

teachers. It was proving a nightmare due to the school holidays.

The forensic report and post mortem had turned up nothing helpful. After the parents had identified Sophia's body, they immediately began to agitate for its' release in order to arrange burial. Moreover, the Press was out for blood.

A list had been compiled of all the Ford Transit vans in Sheffield. Another list recorded all others within a fifty mile radius. The first showed two hundred and twenty-six, and the other, eight hundred and ninety-one. The lists were scrutinised to check if there were any names on a van list, who were connected with the school, friends or relatives. That proved negative. A decision was taken, to put checking those vehicles in abeyance, until resources allowed.

Considerable progress had been achieved in checking the vehicles in the vicinity of the body. All of them, that had been identifiable by CCTV on that atrocious night, had been checked. Three had looked promising. Initially they had no believable alibis. Persistent questioning had discovered reasons why two of them had been reluctant to be honest.
The first was simply a married man coming home "late from work" by way of the house, and probably bedroom, of his lady friend. The second had resulted in a conviction for theft. The officers had spooked the man into confessing to a theft, rather than be arrested on suspicion of murder. When the officers had related their success to Inspector Brady he quickly brought them down to earth.

"The murder is the target. Everything else is misery. Stop smiling, get miserable, and find me the murderer. Out!"

The third and final identified vehicle looked more promising.
"Out for drive" was not a reason that inspired anyone at the station with its credibility.
The two officers had initially questioned the man at his home. Straight away they knew he was being evasive and unhelpful. His early smile had quickly vanished and he had become belligerent. That had been Sunday evening. He had been taken into the station and questioned again. He had not asked for a solicitor. He had made only one phone call and that was to his place of work. He was sick and hoped to be back tomorrow.

When Inspector Brady reported to Mallard he informed him of a man still being questioned because of lack of a believable alibi. He had been caught on CCTV coming down Stannington Road, just before the rain had started. It was not clear where he went after that, because there were so few cameras and the weather had been so bad. Hagg Hill is just five minutes away at the most. The problem was he just did not fit the physical image. The type able to do the heavy lifting required to manhandle the dead weight of a corpse was not a puny five foot seven, and weighing an estimated sub eleven stones.

"If he could lift a nine stone motionless mass, Chief, I am Oprah Winfrey."
Brady confessed they had unearthed nothing else new on the Sophia Pearson case.

"Get to the bottom of it anyway. Let's either put him behind us or charge him. Sort it!"

Brady decided it was time to straighten it out personally. Successful interrogation of suspects was one of the attributes which had brought Brady promotion. His technique was "enthusiastic". It was a trait which a succession of superiors had judged, made him a promotion risk. They welcomed the results and had managed to keep a lid on the methods. He was an asset in difficult situations. Thousands of miles away, and ignorant of Brady's existence, federal agent Rufino Rivera would have been an interested observer.

His first action was to summon two officers who had shared some of his previous successes. For several minutes they listened attentively to his plan of action. The female was a trim twenty-nine years old, fit looking, young woman. She looked friendly with an easy smile. People liked her. The male constable was the opposite. He would have made an imposing bouncer. It was not simply for his physique that Brady had first chosen him. His manner and attitude matched his looks. At school he had taken a fancy to a girl in his class. After George Mitchell had been seeing the girl for less than three weeks, her parson father had been heard to call the boy, a bastard.

In Interview Room Three, the suspect had sat alone since lunch. Unmoving, he watched the three of them enter. Two of them sat opposite him whilst Inspector Brady stood leaning on the wall behind them.

"Right Alan, my name is Detective Sergeant Val Irwin and my colleague here is Detective Constable George Mitchell."

His eyes flicked to the recording equipment and back to them. He said nothing.

"Have you had enough to eat, Alan? Would you like a drink of water?"

"I'm OK."

Again his eyes moved to the equipment. It was definitely not switched on, but he made no remark.

"I understand Alan…."

"My name is Williams, mister Williams. I am not your friend. I do not wish to be friends. Stop calling me Alan. It is mister Williams to you."

Unperturbed, Sergeant Irwin continued.

"I understand Alan that you like to go for a drive on a bad night. Were you upset about something, Alan? Or were you perhaps hoping to meet someone Alan. Prostitutes might well be out working even on a bad night. I am understanding here, Alan. I know lonely men like a little female company once in a while. Was that it, Alan? Don't be embarrassed. I will understand."

If the man had had any presence of mind, his intelligence would have recognised a way out. All he had to say was yes, that was it. I was horny and I needed a woman. The chances are the police would have accepted that and it could have ended there.

"I don't use prostitutes."

"A married lady then; were you off to see a married lady?"

"No!"

"Alan, what was it then? Why were you out?"

"Piss off."

"Is your hobby playing the violin, Alan."
"Yes."
"Can I see your hands? You need very supple hands to play that instrument."

Surprisingly, he showed her.
"Oh yes. Delicate fingers, slim and flexible aren't they? Have you seen the hands of Nigel Kennedy? I saw him on TV playing The Lark Ascending. His fingers are beautiful, Alan."

"He's a great virtuoso violinist, quite brilliant."
"You obviously look after your hands, Alan."
He said nothing.
"Will you be honest with me, Alan? What were you doing that night?"
"Bollocks."

There was a look exchanged between the two male officers. Sergeant Val Irwin had seen it.
"Oh, Alan. I am trying to help you."
"I've got nothing to say. Except, why is the machine not on?"
"Oh, Alan love. If you won't tell me, my two colleagues here will have to have a word with you. The machine is off because, oh well, you will see for yourself very soon."

She leaned back. Inspector Brady moved away from the wall, produced a pair of handcuffs, and sauntered slowly behind the man. Constable Mitchell stood and closed up behind him. Val Irwin sat still. Mitchell grabbed the man's arms and held them behind, whilst Brady slipped on the handcuffs. From his belt Constable Mitchell took out a truncheon and gave it to the Inspector.

Mitchell pulled the man around so that his back was to the table. Mitchell forced the man's handcuffed hands down onto the table and held them there. Brady moved up close to the man's face and showed him the truncheon.

Williams was shaking with fear now. Brady took hold of his face and turned it so that he could see the table and his hands which were pressed firmly down onto it. Brady raised the truncheon and brought it crashing down with all the force he could muster. The table resounded with the impact as the truncheon slammed down, inches away from the man's fingers. Williams screamed.

"Oh, Alan. Let me help you. These men are going to make sure you never play the violin again. You see now why the machine is not switched on. They will break all of your fingers on both hands. They will take about an hour doing it. They actually enjoy that: doing it slowly to prolong the pain. I hate it but they make me sit here with you, and watch it. It is a nightmare. The last man they did it to, was in hospital under sedation for days. The only thing that will stop them, Alan is if you be honest with me. Tell the truth, Alan. I want to help you."

The man had overcome his initial fright. They could not do this to him. This was Sheffield. Things like this did not happen in England, did they?

"You wouldn't do it. You daren't."

"Hold him really still, George. Keep your own hands out of the way. We don't want any accidents."

Up went the truncheon, and then down it came. The scream was louder this time. It had missed his fingers by less than an inch.

"OK, Val."

Detective Sergeant Val Irwin walked to the telephone on the wall by the door.

"Jack, this is Val. I'm in Interview Room Three. Please ask the Police Surgeon to shoot down here ASAP. He will need a supply of those finger splints again. There is a prisoner here. The surgeon will need to fix his terribly mangled fingers."

CHAPTER 25

"The surgeon will need to fix his terribly mangled fingers."
When Alan Williams had heard those words, he believed them.

This was England, yes. But was not this the police force that had covered up the true record of the Hillsborough football tragedy in 1989? This was the South Yorkshire police force which had falsified official police log books to hide its conduct.
Was this also not the police force which was primarily involved in attacking protesting miners during the miners strike of the 1980's, and then tried to falsely incriminate them? Again, it was South Yorkshire police who had knowingly, allowed dozens of girls to be sexually exploited for years in Rotherham, just next door to where Williams was now about to be mutilated. It had taken many years for a glimmer of light to reveal just some of the earlier illegality. Some good that would do Williams if it ever came to light!
Those responsible had continued in their careers, thrived, and retired on full police pensions. This lot were their successors.

Williams had always been fascinated by history, from medieval history and battles, to the present day. He knew that deep down in human nature, there is a base element which recurrently begets appalling behaviour. Throughout history and often in the name of "a righteous cause", acts of extreme savagery have taken place, committed by men who, like these, were part of a force.

Frequently in the name of religion, thousands have been massacred, mutilated and tortured. Ostensibly in the name of Christianity, or Islam, campaigns were mounted and thousands, who up to then did not subscribe to the view that only in their Deity was the one true belief, were slaughtered by the believing faction. Belief in the only Good God, brought death and suffering in his name, to masses.

The Ottomans attempted to eradicate Christianity and created more decimation. Latterly in the War on Terror, or for self preservation or other advantage, countries have been invaded and thousands killed by those acting for governments. Individual acts of sadism and depravity are rife in those circumstances.

Men who believe they can act with impunity risk giving vent to their underlying baseness. Under the umbrella of government and officialdom the risk is highest. These people, who had Williams in that room, were personifications of that condition.

There was no recording machine to back up Williams' account of this ordeal. True, he would have his useless fingers as evidence of the "alleged" crime. He knew that acceptance of his word against a shedload of lying police would be precarious. Even if the court believed him, that would not bring his fingers back.

He saw the light. He folded.

****

"It turns out it was about an injustice at work."

Early morning and Brady was reporting the disappointing outcome to Mallard.
"Williams felt he should have been given the promotion, when his immediate boss was transferred to head office. Instead the job went to a younger man, in another department. This man is the brother, of the live-in lover, of the female Branch Manager, and if Williams is to be believed, he is a right wanker. Plain and simple nepotism."
"Get to the point, man."
"Williams had produced a report, a policy proposal, on the future strategy of the firm, to survive the threat posed by a new entrant company into their business. The firm supplies high-tech precision machine tools. The report had been judged, by the bloke who had transferred to head office, his recent boss, to be brilliant. There was one original copy which had been placed in the safe of his boss, and a photocopy that Williams had made and kept: no others. There was a copy on his own office desk computer, the one on which he had produced the said report."
"For God's sake Brady."
"Sorry, boss. Anyway, Williams had swiped the original report out of the safe, taken his own photocopy home, and deleted the file on his own office computer. From the safe, he had also taken the back-up disks for the computer used by his boss. When we caught him on CCTV he had already taken the report and computer disks, and dumped them in the council tip. From there he had called in on a friend of his, to find out the best way to spike the office computer that his new boss was inheriting upon his arrival the next Monday: last Monday, now. That computer held all the specifications of the next generation of products. With no

back-up, and his vital computer knackered, the man would not have a pleasant beginning to his new department. Also the man was due to go to head office with that female Branch Manager, to outline branch strategy.
Williams was on his way home when he was filmed."
"So, another waste of time."
"Do you want me to pursue Williams for criminal industrial activity?"
"Come and ask me again, Inspector when you have solved both the murder and the abduction cases you are currently nowhere near, yet solving. Close the door after you."

CHAPTER 26

The three of them were in the house where Craig had lived all of his life. His single mother was out at work and it had become their regular meeting place, somewhere reasonably comfortable where they could have privacy. None of them was employed and they usually had nothing better to do in their afternoons than to hang out there.
Glen had his head out of the kitchen window. Craig's mother would go bananas if she smelled smoke in her house. The other two were non-smokers and continued talking.

"Say it again, Vic. I didn't hear that."
The undisputed leader, looked across at the window, and bellowed.
"If you shut the sodding window, half the street that's copping our gab will not be able to hear either. Come in or sod off home."

Vic had not been the brightest, but he had developed physically, quicker than most of the boys in their class, and had used that advantage to get his own way. The pattern had stuck: he led, they followed. They were all the same age and had been to the same school, a Church of England school a hundred yards from where they sat. Glen flicked the half-smoked Park Drive into the back yard and closed the widow.

With Social Security benefits as their main source of income, times would have been hard if they had not been able to make money elsewhere. This they managed to do sporadically, in a variety of illegal ways. Only Glen had been caught, arrested, charged with theft, and had served six months inside. It had been an opportunistic solo effort of which Vic and Craig had known nothing until he had been arrested.

"Old man Swift takes the cash to the bank every Monday and Friday morning. He goes alone in his own car and comes straight back home to open up."
Vic looked at the other two. He had their undivided attention.
"So how do we get the money off him?"
"He always parks in the bank car park, at the back. He gets out of his car, walks across the car park, and goes into the back door of the bank. We snatch the bag in the car park."
"On his way in?"
Craig and Vic looked at each other. Vic leaned forward and patted Glen on the cheek. Gently as if playfully toying with a baby, he squeezed one of Glen's cheeks between his thumb and forefinger.
"No, Glen. We snatch the empty bag on his way out."
Glen thought about it for a few seconds. "Yeh, right then. Better on the way in."

Craig asked, "Which bank, Glen?"
"I've been watching him for a month. Nat West, Sheffield Road is where he banks. We pinch a car Thursday night and use that for the snatch Friday morning. Me and Glen do the snatch. Craig, you drive my car early to Asda, I'll show you where. You park there and wait for me and Glen to turn up in the pinched car. We leave the pinched one in Asda car park, and you drive all of us straight to the train station. We will put our cases in my car first thing Friday before we do the business. Do the job, then onto the train,

and next stop Heathrow. With Swifties' takings, we've got our spending money for a right ball over there. Like it?"

"How much do you reckon will be in the bag?"
"Look at it this way. The Lion does meals, right? The place is heaving every night. Monday, Tuesday, Wednesday, Thursday; that's four days since he last banked. Say fifty meals a day, with drinks, at about ten quid each. Then you get the boozers who don't eat, say another fifty at ten quid each every day. Work it out, it will be plenty of spending money for three of us."

Craig fetched his calculator.
"That's four thousand."
"Then you've got the pool table, slot machines, fag machines, raffles, and quizzes; all cash. He won't pay it all in. He will want some spending money for him and the missies, plus he might pay some bills and wages in cash. We should get a thousand each. A thou for three weeks over there should help a bit, right? You both in?"

They were.

******

Having had time to consider the practicalities, Bush had decided not to fly on the same flight as Francis. Bush did not want to fly on the Sunday. There was his shop to consider. His accountants would "manage" the business in his absence. The accountants main concern would be cash and the banking of takings, but they would also ensure that all other primary functions were running smoothly. It had worked well in the past. The cost was considerable, but Bush had no alternative if he was to be away on holiday or off sick. They always kept in touch over the internet, giving him daily reports of income and expenditure. It had never been necessary, but they had his mobile phone number in case of emergency. Bush had no qualms about leaving them in charge, but it would be best to hand over to them on the Monday morning at the shop.

He walked out of the shop and made the short journey to the local travel agency.
There were direct flights both ways with BA from Heathrow on the Tuesday. He took an option on flights and returned, whistling, to the shop.
Francis was coming that night and Bush could confirm the flights tomorrow.

******

The Friday morning was a dry morning. Vic, Craig, and Glen were nervy and irritable as they loaded their suitcases into the boot of Vic's Ford Mondeo car. They then fitted false number plates onto it and stored the genuine ones, wrapped in a supermarket bag inside the car.
Paid for from their illegal success of one month earlier, a holiday abroad would be a first for all three. There was the imminent prospect of some easy spending money coming their way within an hour.
But for the present, nerves and anxiety showed on all three. The good times were just around the corner.

The routine slogging work of the case of the schoolgirls had eased substantially and Detective Constables David White and Tony Barton had been permitted to go ahead with their prearranged two weeks foreign holiday. There was some necessary last minute packing to be done before meeting at the Midland station for the start of their journey to Thailand. It was a good life.

In his bar, Ray Swift was a happy man as he finished counting the takings for the previous night. The Lion had been exceptionally busy and he had kept the bar open long after normal closing time. He carefully made out the bank paying-in slip, and filled in the amounts on each row. His hand shook a little as he first confirmed he would be taking nearly five thousand pounds to the bank, and then he entered the total.

His breakfast was already on the dining table. As he began to cut into the bacon and arrange a chunk of fried egg onto the fork with it, his mind wandered to Christmas, the following year. He would retire in the middle of December next year, and by Christmas Day they would be sailing away somewhere on a five star cruise to a place warm, sunny, and peaceful. They were fortunate indeed, his wife, and he. Both enjoyed good health, and in the past four years since the Red Lion had been extended to include a restaurant section, business had boomed, the money had rolled in, and they were very comfortably off, thank you very much.

Times were good.

There was much to be done that day, so with breakfast over, Ray Swift checked his watch and walked out to his car carrying his bag containing the cash. Unwisely, he possessed a personalised number plate on his red Jaguar which ensured he was recognised whenever he drove around his home area. He drove down the narrow driveway beside his pub and carefully turned onto the main road. The journey normally took eight minutes but the traffic was thick that morning and it took almost an extra five minutes.

It was just a few minutes since the bank had opened for business and there was ample space in the car park. There was no reason for him to notice a black Honda Civic already parked near to the back doorway of the bank. Inside the stolen Honda with its darkened, tinted windows, Vic saw the expression on Glen's face.

"What?"

"I forgot the cosh, Vic."

It was the sole thing Glen had been given to do; bring a large old potato inside a thick sock. Glen would cosh the landlord with the sock containing the potato whist Vic snatched the bag from Swift's grasp.

Vic rummaged in the Honda's glove compartment and found a torch. The point about a potato was that whilst firm enough, it would have some give, some pliancy. The potato would stun but should not permanently damage. The torch was a heavy, solid, expensive type. It would have to do.

"To hell with the cosh. Use this in your hand. Put your gloves on, moron. We're not taking the torch with us. Don't hit the bastard too hard."

"No problem. Sorry Vic."

"Bastard's coming; ready. Now!

Swift might be the name that Ray had, but by nature he was the opposite. When he had the car settled to his satisfaction he locked the car and walked steadily towards the door of the bank gripping his bag tightly. Vic and Glen got out of their stolen Honda they had already donned balaclavas. They had only a few yards to cover to intercept the unsuspecting Ray Swift. Glen hit him with the improvised cosh and Vic grabbed the bag.

Seconds later the bag of money and the assailants were in the Honda, which was driven by Vic quickly but in a controlled manner, out onto the main Sheffield Road. In five more minutes the Honda had been parked in the designated Asda supermarket car park. As it parked, Vic's own car with Craig driving drew up alongside. Hastily the pair transferred cars and Craig drove Vic's Mondeo away. Four hundred yards down the Sheffield Road they drove into side-street, removed the false number plates they had fitted that morning and refitted Vic's authentic plates. When they continued to the Midland Railway Station it was just twelve minutes after Ray Swift had pulled into the car park at the bank.

By the time the Mondeo reached the railway station fifteen minutes later, the unconscious Ray Swift was on his way to the Hallamshire hospital. The ambulance was in full emergency mode. With siren blaring and blue light flashing, it shot through road junctions, traffic lights, and queues of vehicles. Inside, the medical team had a drip fitted and oxygen in place. The team was concerned. They signalled the Emergency team at the hospital and asked that a Consultant Emergency Surgeon be available. Ray Swift was in trouble.

*****

It was an unhappy Inspector Brady who shut himself up in his office to review matters. His career was in trouble.

He had left Leeds University with a 2-1 degree in European languages. His first choice of career was to be politics, but the more he had learned whilst at university, about politics and the people who were its leading lights, the more he had realised that his intended career in politics was not for him. A man of action, he had realised that, that particular attribute would not be an advantage. It was not to be politics, then.

Additionally, he knew he was not cut out for either a lifetime of academia, or for the city. By the time he had graduated he had decided that the police service was where he could make difference.

Progression in the force had come rapidly. With a little bit of luck helping him along, he had moved into his intended CID without trouble. It had been pure good fortunate that a girl he had met by chance in a restaurant one day, and genuinely fallen in love with, had been the daughter of a Detective Chief Superintendent.

That good fortune did not continue. She had left him, for a lawyer, after six years. She was now in Ashford with their two children. She had married the man after divorcing Brady, and appeared to be happy. The children had settled into their new life. Brady saw them when he could, but his job made definite arrangements difficult to keep, and the distance involved was an added hindrance.

Brady had spent the first eighteen months trying to get her back. His performance at work had suffered dramatically, and the fact that her father was ever-present at work, had added to his distress. A year after the decree absolute he had managed to transfer away from Lancashire. After two years in Sheffield, he had regained some of his self-confidence and equilibrium. Brady knew he was leading an unfulfilled life. He needed a partner, a lover, someone to share his life with.

He knew that now, but in those early years it had been the last thing he had wanted. Perversely, it was then that there would have been several available females. More than one was angling to catch his eye. A few friends of him and his wife, turned out to be papering over their own marriage cracks. When later he thought back over those early months, he recognised what he had been ignorant of then. Two of those women had been extraordinarily supportive: and, through no conniving of his, he had found himself alone with them on several occasions. A nod and a wink were just as useless to the blind mule that he then was. He knew though, that even if he had recognised the signs, he would have walked away from them. Problems with one marriage were more than enough to cope with. Add another set, the problems of someone else's marriage, and it would have been unbearable.

Brady pulled himself together, swore out loud, and picked up the file of the Sophia Pearson murder. After reading for several minutes, he had an idea. He replaced the file and looked through his office window and out into the Major Incident Room.

P.C. Higgs-Whitethorn replaced the telephone and looked for the next number on the list. This was the second day that he had been making appointments for a team to re-visit the boys in the same year as Sophia and Karen. He was about to dial another when Inspector Brady arrived. "I want you to leave what you are on with for now, and do something for me."

The young man's eager response confirmed to Brady that he had a willing gofer.

"DC Cropper reported he passed a light-coloured Transit van in Hagg Hill. I want you to identify all Transits on the lists of vehicles in the vicinity of the Skating Arena and/or Hagg Hill. Then, I want to know if any of those vans on those lists, are registered within a fifteen minute drive of Sophia Pearson, and/or, which are registered within a fifteen minute drive of Karen Clayton. Got that?"

"Yes Inspector."

"Give this top priority, and do it right, for God's sake."

Before Brady had resumed his seat back in his office, P.C. Higgs-Whitethorn had swept away the lists of schoolboys, reached for his computer, and begun tapping away at its keyboard. At nearby desks, Detectives Frank Cropper and Philippa Tate had overheard the exchange.

"You will have observed, Bosun, intelligent lad that you are, the appropriate initials that belong to our beloved Inspector, Stanley Olwyn Brady."

Philippa Tate looked up and saw Frank wink at her.

Higgs-Whitethorn stopped for a moment, considered the remark, and then, smiling, he resumed the flying fingers. Without pausing his input, he said, "It seems that his parents may have been psychic, Frank."

"His mother might well have been, but not the father. I am given to understand they are still looking for one."

The three laughed out loud.

Frank watched Higgs-Whitethorn working. The lad had his teeth into something he enjoyed, and his mind and body were in top gear. Frank pictured the boy, at home learning in his room, at college finding his way through the advanced technical exercises, and finally in the examinations. The lad had, to Frank, the demeanour and appearance of a winner. He handled the computer with virtuoso ease, and lists tumbled out of the printer.

If there was anything to be found, the Bosun would nail it.

Two hours later the mood of all in the room lifted.

"I say, sergeant, look at this." Higgs-Whitethorn was leaning over her shoulder, pointing to an item on the print-out he had generated.

"A white transit van appeared at 6.56 p.m. on the road to the Skating Arena. It is registered to a man named Bush with an address four miles, as the crow flies, from the Pearson home. It is five miles from that of the Clayton family. This is what "Son of" is looking for, sergeant."

"Well done Trevor. Come on."

Miserably, Brady was writing a detailed report of no progress. It was being adroitly massaged and wrapped up in circular logic. The content was bullshit and he knew it. His report was almost finished, when his door opened, and the untouchable but appealing Sergeant Tate, and the Clever Devil hurried straight in. With a sigh, he stopped writing and looked up. One look at their faces told him it was good news. At last, he might be onto a winner.

One minute later, "Frank, in here."

He was there like a shot.

"Frank find out who the Community coppers are for both the Pearsons and the Claytons, and get them both in here, in my office, like yesterday. I want to see what they know about our man.

After that, you two, find out all you can about this man Bush. Get Trevor to do the computer bit, Electoral Roles etc. you know the drill. Get Brownose to help you with ideas.

Philippa, pick two constables, two people who look like they could be romantically compatible, get them in plain clothes and send them up to speak to Bush's neighbours. They are not to go to the Bush house.

They are house-hunting. What is the area like; who lives round here; who lives at number 137 and what are they like, etc. etc.? Use your and their initiative. Everybody back her at 8.30 p.m. I want the full team in. I am going to see the Chief.

Go on, chop chop!"

"Just on thing, sir."

"What is it, Philippa?"

"The couple that I send, I think they should call at the Bush house. If he is in, they could give us a first impression. If he is out they could have a good look around. There might be outhouses or a detached building in the garden. The houses up there are definitely big enough for structures in their back gardens. Is there a van there, a Transit?"

"No! Definitely not. If we do that with a couple, that couple will be you and me, sergeant. That will be, if we do it, between about 9.30 and 10.00 p.m. tonight. Be dressed appropriately, just in case."

CHAPTER 27

"What should I call you? Now that we are speaking to each other quite a lot, may I know your name, or at least a name that I can use for you?"

"I'll think about it, Karen."

Bush was clearing away the food remains and the empty bottles.

"For now, I will call you Henry. Can I ask you something, Henry?

"What's special about Henry?"

"You know, Henry the Eighth. Locked his women in the Tower. Can I ask you, I am going to anyway? The food here is awful. "Can I have a take-away sometimes, pretty please?"

"You know the deal."

 "Henry, please, don't I mean anything to you? I am a person, like you. Sometimes with me you are really gentle; not often, but sometimes. Do you like me? As a person I mean. Please treat me with some feeling, some humanity."

The door closed and he was gone.

******

The trio parked in the station car park and Vic phoned his sister to tell her from exactly where to retrieve the car. Kylie was as thick as they came but she could legitimately drive. She had failed the driving test four times. At the fifth attempt she had managed to beguile a driving examiner, possibly with the help of a seriously short skirt, to award her a pass. Slow-witted or not, those legs were world class.

Kylie was at work at the time. Vic made Kylie write down the car's registration number. She might manage to recognise the colour but expecting her to identify his car was out of the question.

The three were elated as they stood fidgeting on the platform, their suitcases beside them. Vic had the bag with the money inside his backpack. They did not yet know how much it contained but once on the train they would soon count it and find out. On platform 1A they had only ten minutes to wait for their train. It was Craig who noticed the label on the suitcases of two men waiting near to where the three stood.

"You off to Thailand, then lads?"

"Us? Yes." DC David White looked down at his luggage label. That was how this fellow knew.

"Same here. Been before?"

"I have, but it will be his first time." Tony Barton watched them but seemed disinterested.

"First time for all of us. OK is it?"

"Depends what you like."

From the way the three were dressed it did not look as if they would have a lot of money. All wore trainers and jeans which looked to have come from a market. Their luggage was ancient. They did not look much like seasoned travellers. Tony Barton chipped in.

"You lads into museums and art galleries?" Tony winked at David.

"Fuck no. Why?"

"Might not be your sort of place then, lads."

"Bollocks!"

Detective Constable Tony Barton turned to DC David White and kept his voice low. "Got a feeling about those three, Dave."

The train to St. Pancras came into view.

"Patience, Tony. Control your feelings for one more day, if fancying young men is your thing. Thailand is full of *katoeys*."

Tony thumped him.

There was a whispering among the three men and after a few furtive glances at the two detectives the trio walked further along the platform.

"Look at that, Dave. Those three are up to something."

David White stayed silent but watched the men cautiously.

On the operating theatre table the situation was serious. Ray Swift lived for just fifty minutes after being attacked. A murder investigation was launched with Detective Chief Inspector Mallard was given the role of Senior Investigating Officer.

******

After a brief and hurried discussion on the platform Tony Barton had persuaded David White to ignore their seat reservations, and instead follow the three men into their carriage. The three of them all stored their cases in the luggage area at the front of the carriage. One of them clutched a backpack and kept it firmly on his knee. The two detectives kept the three men under discreet observation. Once the train pulled away from the station, the one with the backpack rose and went swiftly along the carriage to the toilet. His two companions kept their eyes constantly on the door of the toilet.

"See Dave, they are watching that toilet door as if it is going to fly off its hinges or something. There is something suspicious about the behaviour of those three."

"If he comes out without that backpack we have to act. I hope to Christ there is not a bomb in it."

Tony Barton checked his mobile phone for messages from the Control Centre. He found none. He rang in for an update, on crimes that morning. One was of interest.

"A pub landlord has been robbed and killed on his way to the bank with his takings. Do you think there might be a connection with these three? I would love to know what's in that backpack. Why didn't he leave it with his mates, Dave? There is not room to swing a cat in those toilets. If he's having a crap he must be sitting on the bog with the bloody thing on his knee."

"I'd rather it be money in his bag than Semtex."

It was fully five minutes before he re-emerged and he was clutching the backpack.

"Unless it's a suicide job it's not a bomb, Tony."

Vic was bursting with excitement. He was speaking before he sat down. It was intended to be a quiet whisper but his excitement boosted the sound and it came out in an audible rush. "Five and a half fabulous grand, that's all boys. Five and a half smackers all in beautiful used notes. How's that for a morning's sweat? How's that for some lucre for Thailand, then?"

"Jesus, Vic. Keep your bloody foghorn down."

The two detectives had heard but remained impassive, and they were both looking through the widow as the train sped by green fields. They could see the trio by the reflection in the window. After a minute, David White stood and walked down the corridor in the direction of the Buffet Car which was several carriages down from theirs. After walking two carriages down the train he went into the toilet and phoned the Sheffield Control Centre.

When the train neared London it branched off the high-speed inter-city line and onto a service line. Slowly it came to rest some half a mile short of St. Pancras station. In a service carriage on the adjacent line nine uniformed policemen and one plain-clothes officer waited. When the Sheffield train halted they boarded the carriage using the doors at either end, five through each. The two Sheffield detectives made themselves known to the police and pointed out the three suspects. The men were arrested and taken away.

Four and a half hours after the robbery and murder, Detective Chief Inspector John Mallard sat at a press conference and announced the capture of the criminals. For once it had been an excellent morning, and it would briefly take some of the heat off the Force over the schoolgirl case.

Later that day there were three empty seats on the direct BA flight that would have taken the three yobs to Bangkok. By the time the flight departed, Kylie had been arrested in the car park of Sheffield Midland Station as she opened the door of the car which belonged to her brother. It was later established that the girl had known nothing of the robbery and she was released without charge. Some months later Vic was sentenced to twenty-one years imprisonment, Glen had struck the fatal blow and got twenty-five years, and Craig who had not actually been at the scene was given fourteen years.

CHAPTER 28

"So is that OK with you?"

"No problem, Joel. Who are you flying with?"

"BA."

"Where do they fly to?"

"Lindbergh Field. Direct flights."

"Brilliant. I will pick you up from the airport. We will be home in forty-five minutes from the airport."

"Is your dad OK, my uncle? I hope I can meet him."

"Yep. He is still doing OK. He has something else to look forward to now. He wants to meet Ryszard and Magdalina's boy. You have never been to the US, have you?

"No. I have not been far at all, just Spain and two Greek islands. The shop has always come first: first with my parents and now with me. Three weeks will be the longest….."

The doorbell rang. Bush went to the window, half expecting to see the lads scampering down his drive. A man and a woman stood there. Bush half opened the front door.

"Sorry to bother you, sir. My name is Detective Inspector Brady and this is Detective Sergeant Tate of the South Yorkshire police. May we come in for a minute?"

"No. I am busy."

"We really would like to speak to you. It won't take long, sir."

Bush's mind was racing. "Christ, they've got me! Is it the cameras?"

There were only the two of them.

"It is not convenient. What is it about?"

"May we come in, sir? It is not very hospitable out here. We will be very quick," the woman sergeant spoke this time.

"OK, but be quick. Come through here."

Bush led them through to the dining room which he very rarely used.

"Thank you, sir. May we sit down?"

"No. Wait there, I have a visitor. I'll be straight back."

Bush went to the lounge and told Francis he would be a few minutes with two visitors, then hurried back to the dining room.

Both of the officers were going round the room looking for anything suspicious or unusual.

It was obvious this man was on his own. There was not the slightest trace of femininity, nor were there any photographs. There was one picture, a print of a single boat on an otherwise empty sandy beach.

"Right, what is it?"

"May we sit down, sir?"

"No."

"Very well, sir. Do you live here alone?"

"Yes."

"How long have you lived here?"

"Nearly all my life. What is it you want?"

"Do you own a vehicle, sir?"

"Yes."

"Just the one, is it, sir?"

"Yes."

"Can you tell me the registration number of the vehicle, sir?"

"Yes.

There was a pause as the detectives waited in vain.

"Righto, sir. What is the registration number of the vehicle, sir?"

He told them

"Are you the sole driver of the vehicle, sir?"

"I am not answering any more questions."

"Just a few more, sir. Does anyone else drive the vehicle?"

"Are you deaf, man?"

The female started.

"Do you go out in the evenings in the car sir?"

Silence.

The man resumed, more menacing now.

"You can either answer us here or down at the station. It is more comfortable down there for us. We can sit down at the station. Do you want to go there instead……..sir?"

Bush was not over-bright; he was not the sharpest knife in the drawer. Bush, though, did not come from a line of cowards. His size at six feet two inches had been advantageous in some tricky situations. He was known to stand his ground.

He remembered that time at school: that P.T. teacher who had a down on him, the one that always made a joke about him in front of the class, because he could not keep his balance on that narrow bench they made you walk along sometimes. That day the bastard tried to get him to skip along it. All the boys were laughing at him. Bush knew the teacher expected him to go arse over tit, and they could all have hysterics. Bush had refused to do it. The teacher, Mr. (tiddling) Tapsill – because of his half-pint size- gave Bush detention and 100 lines. What the teacher had not known, was that Bush, two days earlier, had been up at the

Hare and Hounds pub at High Storrs with his parents. They had sat outside on that sunny June evening and had drinks and crisps. It had been a happy little family outing and he remembered that his mother had kept trying to keep the table umbrella positioned to keep her out of the sun. They had joked and laughed about it; and Bush had nearly missed it. But he had not missed it, had he? He had seen the bastard.

Given 100 lines to write out 'I must obey my teachers instructions at all times and remember that it is for my benefit', he changed the script.
He had also changed the place upon which the lines were to be written. In his schooldays, blackboards were still used. On each of the blackboards, in five separate classrooms, Bush had written just twenty-four words - 'Ask Mr. Tapsill what he was doing hand-in-hand with Lucy Sutton at the Hare and Hounds pub, High Storrs on Monday night.'
Lucy was fourteen and in the same year, Tapsill was married, the headmaster was mortified when he saw the five classrooms. Tapsill never took another class in any school in the UK.

Bush was now annoyed. He was not moving. He said nothing.
The female had another try.
"We could arrest you, sir and take you down to the station."

"Do it! Arrest me or piss off."

The man again, "Look, sir, all we need is the answer to just a few more questions. It is much better for you to answer them here."

"Fuck off!"

The two officers looked at each other. All they had was a glimpse of him driving down a road one evening. His was one of hundreds of vehicles. Was he just unlucky that he lived where he did? They were hoping not.

He had led a completely innocent life as far as they knew. To arrest him was not really an option. His neighbours knew very little about him. They thought he lived alone, and said he kept himself to himself. He was always polite, quiet and an ideal neighbour in that he caused absolutely no trouble. They saw him chase those naughty boys away some times. That was it. Nothing bad or wrong was even hinted at.

"Thank you, sir. We will leave it at that for now, but we will be back."

When they had gone, Bush leaned against the door for a full minute. Gradually his heart returned to its more normal pace. That had been a bad few minutes. He needed a drink.

"What was that all about, Joel?"

"Oh, just some noises one of the neighbours heard. We heard nothing did we? I am having a scotch, want one?"

CHAPTER 29

Attila, what date is it?"

"Eh?"

"What is the date today?"

Bush got up off the bed.

"Why? What is this Attila?"

"Attila the Hun, you know. Attila is my new name for you. So, is it the 3rd today?

"4th August, why?"

"Do you have any feminine hygiene things in the house?"

"Any what?"

"You know, feminine hygiene."

"You mean deodorant stuff?"

"No!"

"Look I've got to go to work."

"Don't make this too hard for me, please. You know – girl things. We need them once a month."

There was a pause whilst Bush worked it out.

"Do you have any in the house?"

"Don't be bloody stupid, course not. Why?"

"I am due tomorrow. It could start today, or the day after tomorrow. It will definitely be one of those three for sure. Will you buy me some?"

"Write down what you want and I will get it. Do supermarkets sell it?"

Karen was writing. "Yes they do, best place I suppose really if you don't want to feel too embarrassed. Please will you get me some knickers; seven pairs?"

Bush took the note and opened the door.

"OK, Karen. Just for you. I hope you will appreciate this."

He winked at the girl. He could see she understood his meaning.

"Of course, it means you will have to leave me alone for a week."

He turned.

"That's what you think!"

Bush closed and locked the door behind him. He was smiling.

"Cheeky little devil this Karen: Attila the Hun."

This girl, he really liked. She had wit and personality. Shame she was not here of her own accord.

Laughing out loud, he was just able to hear the click of the letter box. That had been quick. The flyers from BT, three of them, and another from Sky, he dropped into the small waste basket he kept in the hall. The invoice from his gardener would have to wait. He opened the one he had hoped would arrive quickly. Opening the envelope, he took out the documents he had requested from The Big Yellow Storage Company. That would do nicely! Right, they could come again if they wanted. He was ready. The brochures placed on a coffee table in the dining room, he ran upstairs to get ready for work. The note from Karen was placed with his car keys. He would not forget that important personal item. She was a joy just to talk with, that girl; a real pleasure just to have at his home.

"Attila the Hun."

****

"To summaries then, another foul up."

"I don't think that is fair."

"You have eliminated him then from our enquiries, have you? Or are you going to arrest him on suspicion?"

"We need to speak to him again. He is not out of the frame by any means."

"We certainly need to speak to him again, but not you, Detective Inspector. I will do it personally. Today, in case it has passed you by, is Wednesday. If the abductor only keeps Karen Clayton for the same length of time as Sophia Pearson, he will kill the girl today. You and Sergeant Tate goofed about last night, and came away with the conclusion, that we need to speak to him again. Tell Frank Cropper I want him. Good day Stan."

CHAPTER 30

"Senorita, can I have a word with you?"
He had quietly sidled up to the door.
"Senorita, it is me."

The shower was running and Catalina had not heard.

He knew she was home. There was no response. Was that the sound of the shower? He pressed his ear to the door panel.
Yes!

This was what he had been hoping for these eight months since the young woman had arrived.

His neighbour next door had sent the girl round. Senora Hadas had no rooms spare. It was his good fortune; and since then he had been able to watch Catalina come and go. The girl kept regular hours. He knew when she would be coming and when she would be leaving. His favourite was watching the girl climb the stairs. Mexico was a marvellous country for admiring females. Not only were many of them shapely, but the climate encouraged them to wear clothing, that left men able to survey and appreciate the feminine form. This girl had a superb form.

The shower was still running. As quickly as he was able, he took out his master key and, with trembling fingers, slipped it into the keyhole. Once inside he left the door ajar and kept one hand on it, as if he was just entering. In his other hand he clutched the large envelope that had just been delivered. The shower was simply fitted into a corner of the main room. There was a curtain to shield the room from water spraying into it. The landlord knew that the curtain had hung there for twenty-two years. It had been a cheap one. His eyes were fixed on that curtain for the outline of the girl could be seen through the thin poly nylon.

Catalina turned off the water, and the man dare not breathe. It was obvious what was coming. The thin curtains opened. With her back to the landlord, Catalina wrapped the towel skilfully around her head, then turned and stepped into the room. Water slowly ran down her face, causing Catalina to keep her eyes partly closed as she continued slowly into the room. She turned and the landlord had a view of his shapely nineteen year old tenant, that in many magazines around the world, would be described as full-frontal.

The first indication that she was not alone was when she heard the thud.

******

This was better, much better. It had taken many days it seemed, but she was back to her normal self again. They all laughed with her and the dusting and polishing was really no effort when the atmosphere was like this.

"The first thing, I swear I saw was the envelope. A big brown envelope was what they said it would be. Nobody else sends me big brown envelopes; it just had to be from the embassy. I yelled with delight. Then I realised that the awful landlord was in my room. I swear it was the envelope I saw first. You believe me don't you, Elvira? The man was on the floor face down holding my envelope. How long had he been there? What had he seen? Had he died while I was in the shower? No. I had heard him fall. I tripped out of the shower and into the room and there was this big clout of a noise. It was him hitting the ground."

"Catalina, when you walked into the room, were you naked?"
"Yes. I had just had my shower."
"Catalina, darling. Imagine: you are a landlord, maybe a thousand years old, and you see a nineteen year old girl walk towards you. She is beautiful. You have been spying on her for all these months. Now, right in front of you so you can almost touch her, she is as naked as the day she was born. Do you think that had anything to do with him dropping dead?"
They all screamed with laughter. This was the third time Catalina had taken them through her story. It was so good to see her laughing again. And the good news! The interview was at the embassy next week; so soon. It was so good she was happy again.

*****

207

"I want you to come with me, Frank. We are going to see this man Bush, Joel Bush at his shop. Philippa has briefed you on her interview with Stan last night?"

"Yes, gov. I was here when they got back from his house. Apparently he's the right sort of weight and age as the bloke on the video. No limp, but we would not expect the culprit normally to have one."

"You will go in his shop and I will stay in the car. As discretely as possible, you will invite him to come and talk to me. I think you have been around long enough, Frank, to be successfully persuasive when you make up your mind. If he won't come, we will arrest him and we will grill him down at the station. Remember, Frank, if Karen is still alive, she is running out of time; fast! Come on. You drive."

Whilst Cropper walked into the butchers, Mallard changed seats and sat in the back of the Lexus LS460. The terraced shop was located on a main road in an affluent suburb of Sheffield. Within walking distance were greengrocers, bakers, an up-market general store, a small supermarket-type store, an off-licence, a newsagent, a chemist and several others. It was a busy little, almost self-contained area, where those with enough money could chose to shop more pleasantly than at a big supermarket. Mallard imagined that prices here would reflect the convenience and personal attention afforded by this locality.

Inside the butchers shop were two assistants and eight customers. Frank joined the queue. He could not see Bush. When his turn came, the young man, Bradley, smiled his usual lop-sided grin and waited for Frank to order.

The grin was lop-sided due to the attention of a dentist when Bradley was thirteen. At that age he had been a bit handy with his fists. His family lived in Pitsmoor, a district of Sheffield which had, for some unaccountable reason, over several decades, attracted more than its fair share of mainly Commonwealth immigrants. In that area, being handy with the fists, and also if possible, for good measure his "plates of meat", was not only an advantage, if you were white, as Bradley was, it was essential. On one particular day at school, a big lad whose family originated from India, had "done" Bradley. They had fought in the asphalt playground: and Bradley had come off a poor second.

Bradley knew this boy's sister was in a class two years below his. That night after school, Bradley had caught up with the girl and given her a kicking whilst she was waiting, as she did every night, for her brother so that they could walk home together. What Bradley had not known, was that their father was a dentist: the same dentist used by Bradley's family. The father had forbidden his son to take revenge on Bradley. He would deal with it. In due course, in fact eight months later, Bradley went to the dentist with a tooth abscess.

"No problem, young ladka" I will soon fix that for you. Just a small injection and it will come out like a fig from a tree."

It did - and with it a severed facial nerve.

Loppy Bradley, as he became known from then onwards, left the pair alone after that.

Frank spoke very quietly to Bradley, asking to see Mr Bush. Loppy went into the back and re-emerged with Bush.

Frank Cropper leaned very close and said softly, "My name is Detective Cropper of the South Yorkshire police. Can we go somewhere we can have a word in private, Mister Bush?"

"I've told your lot, no."

Both Darryl and Loppy were watching as they served other customers, puzzled at the aggression of their boss.

Cropper removed his wrist watch.

"You see this watch, sir? My wife gave me this on our twenty-fifth wedding anniversary. If I go home without this I am in big trouble. Take it. What I have to say to you will take no more than three minutes. If it takes longer, you can keep the watch. Here."

Bush took it.

"I will keep it you know?"

Darryl cut his finger and blood dripped onto the wooden block. Bush had not seen it. Loppy had, and his grin was wide, if somewhat lop-sided.

"Keep your eyes on your work, clown."

It was not often he got one up on Darryl.

In the back, Frank began straight away. It was true; he must not go home without the watch.

"My boss is outside in the car, sir. We are doing this as discretely as we can, for your sake. He wants to talk to you in the car."

"No chance."

Cropper took out his mobile phone, tapped into it and displayed a phone number.

"You see this number, sir. This is a journalist on the Sun newspaper, Maggie Morgan. If you are not outside this shop in twenty seconds with me, my boss and I are going to come back in here and arrest you on suspicion of the murder of Sophia Pearson, and the abduction of Karen Clayton. We will do it loudly out in the shop. You will come with us to the station. On the way I will telephone my Sun contact, Maggie, and leak the information that we have got the man, Bush, for the crimes. End of speech. I want my watch back."

Frank Cropper strode briskly out of the shop fastening his watch as he went. Bush hurried to catch him.

Mallard knew Frank would not come out of the shop alone. The change that had occurred in Frank had made him one of his most effective officers. Mallard wondered what had caused it.

****

"Mama, it is not fair. You go for me and tell them I am sick."
"It is no good, Yazmin. They will not have me. It is you they want."
"They have had me. It is only a few days since I was there. It is not fair."
"Yazmin, my darling, if they would have me I would take your place. It is not possible."
"It is father that should pay not me. I have done nothing. Why don't you stop my father?"

"Can you stop a waterfall?"

"You must try. It is not fair!"

"Tell me how, my darling. All these years I have tried but there is no stopping your father. He will never stop. It is a sickness."

"It is all the fault of my father, not mine. What can I do, mama? I have to go to the Policía Federal again this afternoon because of my father."

"You must be brave, my darling."

****

Not a word had been spoken on the journey. A worried man, Bush had sat in the back of the comfortable car as it purred almost silently through familiar streets. He had realised they were not heading for the police station, but he said nothing. The route was almost identical to the one he normally took.

Had they brought a search warrant? If they had the game was up. Would they make him empty his pockets? If they did they would find the note for sanitary towels and want an explanation. What did they know? Did they have him near Hagg Hill? Had she escaped?

They were in the dining room. Both men had seated themselves without being invited. These two were intimidating, not at all like the fairly courteous pair the night before.

"I have a business to run."
She had not escaped. There were no police cars in his drive. Nobody was searching his house.

"On the night of 28th July where were you."
No "sir";   no "would you mind;   this was going to be awkward.

"Probably here: what day was that?"
He knew what day it was. It was last Wednesday. This could be about Karen, or about Sophia, or both. Try to keep calm.

"Last Wednesday, where were you? Did you go out?"
It was the older, junior officer asking the questions. He was looking at Bush as though he wanted already to strangle him. Bush saw the hands of the man. They were huge; strangler's hands if ever he saw any.
A shiver went through Bush; better be helpful, here.
It was the only night he had been out - twice. He knew exactly where he had been. What time were they talking about? Was it about Karen or Sophia?
"What time are you referring to?"
As soon as he had said it, he knew it was a mistake.
Disaster was on its way. Say something to put them off!
"I mean I went to work and came home like I always do? Is that what you mean?"
"After work, in the evening. Where did you go and what time?"
"Wednesday night, just a minute, was that the night I went, yes it must have been. I know I went into town. What time? About 7.00, I think."
"Where in town?"

"Queens Road."
Bush saw him glance at his boss.

"Were you alone?"
"Yes, why?"
"What were you doing on Queens Road? Why did you go there?"
"I went to look at the Big Yellow Storage site."

The two officers looked at each other. There was disappointment beginning to appear on both of their faces. The Big Yellow site was within spitting distance of the Arena. He would have to drive up Queens Road to get there. There was no other way.

"Where is that then, sir?"
That is better; "sir" now.
"It's on Queens Road, officer."
Careful, don't gloat.
The head honcho took up the questioning.
"Why did you go there, sir?"
Bush had rehearsed this, in front of the bathroom mirror. Just that morning, after the brochure had arrived; he had concocted his story.
"I wanted to get a sight of exactly where it is, and to get an impression of the place. Brochures are all very well, but until you see a place you don't know if it is what you want."

"Did you go inside? Did you speak to anyone there?"
Crafty sod! He must know they are not open at that time.
"They close at 6.00 p.m., officer. I knew that. I have not been inside yet, but I have their brochure. Nearer the time,

when I am going to need it, I will go there in the daytime and arrange for what I want."

"What do need to store, sir."

"I am planning to open another butchery shop. I have not selected a site yet, but when I do, I will need used equipment. Shops are closing everyday. You can get some real bargains when you know what you are looking for. As I buy the stuff, I will need somewhere to store it until I am ready to open the new shop."

Pick the flies off that – clever bastards!

"Where did you go after that?"

"I came home."

"What time would that be, sir?"

"Somewhere between 7 and 8.00, I suppose.

"Did you go out again?"

Now then, what to say to this? If they have me on Queens Road at 7.00, and then later at 11.00 or midnight, I have had it. I can only deny it: bluff it out.

"No."

"When my colleague asked you at the beginning, if you went out last Wednesday night, you asked what time. You went out more than once did you not?"

"No."

They were stumped. Bush could see it. He tried to keep his face expressionless, but inside he was cheering. It looks as if he had got away with it. If Karen had not reminded him of all those cameras around the football ground, his goose would have been cooked.

Oh, what a real little beauty she was!

Bush stood up. Their faces told him, they were outwitted.
Bush was almost relaxed.
He was unaware of the golden rule. As all good salesmen
know, there is the first sales commandment. "When thou
hast the sale, thou keepeth thy mouth shut."

He walked over to the table and picked up the brochure
from the Big Yellow Storage Company.
Sitting down he began to fan out the pages so that they
could see them. They paid very little attention to those
pages, but both officers knew their business. They knew
people. They knew criminals, and they had seen the
reactions of many men who thought they had outsmarted
the police. They behaved just like this man Bush now.
Fearful at first; suddenly he had relaxed. He was almost
gloating.

"Sorry, sir I need a pee. Can I use your bathroom?
"No you can't. I want you to go.
"It will only take a minute, sir. I really need to go"
"You should have gone before you set off. No!"
Cropper had to accept it.

The Chief Inspector had a try.
"Do you mind if we have a look around while we are here,
sir?"
Bush got to his feet. "Yes I do. Look, I have to get back to
the shop. I have answered your questions. Please, can we
go now? I have a business to run."

Both men stood.
"Where is your van, sir?"
"Parked on the road near my shop."

"Can we look at your van, sir?"

"No. And I want to get back to work. Can we go?"

"Righto, sir. We will be off then now."

"Wait for me."

"Sorry, sir. We are not going your way. You are not planning on leaving town, are you, sir?"

"I am going to the USA for a holiday soon."

"When is that, sir?

"17th August, I think."

"And before then?"

"No."

"Good day, sir."

They left. Bush watched the door close and he leaned with his back to the wall in the hallway. That had been a nasty time. His ebullient mood of the morning had disappeared and had been replaced by fear. Now as he waited for his heartbeat to get back to near normal, he was grateful that he did not have to get back into the car with them. Would they want another go at him? Would they come with a search warrant?

He stood up and went to the telephone. It would have to be a taxi. Better that though, than a police car.

Outside, Mallard and Cropper drove down the drive, out into the road, and went up the slight incline in the opposite direction to the way back into Sheffield. Frank Cropper did a three point turn, and parked at the kerbside, in a spot which gave them a clear view of the Bush drive.

"Did you notice, Frank? He never once asked us what this was all about."

"I did. That bugger is guilty of something. There is nothing I could see to definitely prove that he is our man, but he is up to no good, for sure. Shame I couldn't get into the bathroom and snaffle some of his DNA."

"They will never let me have a search warrant either, damn it. All we have, is that he was in the vicinity; and our professional instincts. No chance will we get a warrant. I cannot support grounds for a twenty-four hour watch on him either. To hell with my no swearing rule for a minute. Frank, we are fucked."

"Boss, you can ask for volunteers."
"What do you mean, Frank?"
"To keep watch on him. Some of us will be willing, I will, to watch him in our off-duty hours, some of those hours anyway, gov."
"Good man. I am calling a Briefing for 3.00 p.m. this afternoon. I will ask for volunteers then. I will phone through in a minute, to send someone up to sniff around his van. You never know he might have left it unlocked.

"There is his taxi. Follow it. I want to see if he does go back to work."

He rang for someone to check Bush's van.

CHAPTER 31

He had seen this girl before. When was it? Yes, two weeks ago.

"Please sit down, senorita Gonzales."

The desk officer picked up the phone, spoke briefly, and replaced it. Yazmin saw him looking at her as he pretended to write. She knew what was coming. It was unavoidable again. Her father could not help himself. This should be the duty of her mother, but no – oh no. These men did not want middle-aged women. It was girls they preferred. So it fell upon her to keep them from putting her father into of one of their cells below. If they had him down there for more than a couple of days he would die. The old man was sickly, but he could never keep away from his gambling.

Sergeant Tamayo owned the gambling den closest to the shack that was their home. It was up to the girl to wipe clean the record of the debt run up by her father. This was the third time she had been made to come there. She was quickly up onto her feet the second that agent Rivera appeared.

The officer at the desk watched the girl walk behind Rivera towards the staircase. Her trim figure was worth a little of a man's time to contemplate.

The girl was engaged to be married. Perhaps when she lived across the river with her husband, she would be free of this burden. It was unlikely, but it gave the teenager hope.

****

An hour or so later, and the two men were still in the basement "office". There was a lingering aroma of the teenager's perfume. Both men sat and smoked, and both of their chairs seemed to almost defy gravity, as they leaned perilously backwards, with their feet up on top of the desk.

"Most enjoyable our little Yazmin, eh amigo?"
"Si senor. She always is. God bless her father."

They smoked for a time in silence.

"Javier Flores comes at what time tomorrow?"
"8.30 in the morning."
"Now that his visa has arrived and his papers are all in order, and the time is near when we will double our income, we will take him with us first to the Federal Centre For Social Rehabilitation. He can see where his family will go if he is foolish."

"Si senor. Flores will not want them there. Perhaps we can call in, and have lunch with his wife Maria and son on the way home, just to remind him of his own family?"
"That will not be necessary. Keep your hands off that wife of his as long as he behaves. What is necessary, is for me to arrange for our own journey this month. Quiet now, amigo: let me think."

****

220

"What do think of our famous Federal Centre For Social Rehabilitation, eh Javier?"

Javier Flores knew why they had taken him there. On the journey Sergeant Tamayo had summarised his life to be, in the USA. He would work at the same company as Luis Vasquez, and he would make the same journeys back to Mexico, but midweek not weekend. Their would be different supplier, not Alfred Walberg , so the two agents would need to go to San Diego to finalise arrangements. In San Diego, all would be arranged for Javier their new "pigeon" to make much money. When he was in the USA, Flores would see how happy and wealthy Luis Vasquez had become. Life was going to be very good for everybody. Javier Flores sat in the back seat of the vehicle with agent Rufino Rivera. In the front, Sergeant Tamayo had finished his spiel and was quiet. Rivera had been quiet all the way. When they had reached the remote spot in which the prison had been sited, the vehicle was parked just before the entrance to the complex. Built of grey concrete it was a depressing sight. The three men stood, two of them were relaxed and accustomed to the sight. The other, a now very nervous Flores did not want to be anywhere near the FCDR.

"Sergeant Tamayo, I will do everything you say. There will be no need for this place."

"I know you will, Javier. I know. When you arrive in San Diego tomorrow you will meet with Vasquez as early as possible. He has instructions. You will do what he tells you."

Without waiting for a response, Tamayo walked briskly back to the Hummer. Flores scuttled to keep up. Rivera, who had not spoken a word since leaving the Policía Federal, opened the door for Tamayo.

*****

Bush had gone straight back to work. Seeing him enter the shop, Frank Cropper parked the Lexus down the road, where he could see the shop. For ten minutes, he and Mallard waited to see if Bush would come out again. He did not. They were about to drive back to the station when a detective constable drove up, and parked his car nearby. They watched the detective for five minutes. He was the one sent to take a look at Bush's van, and he examined it as best he could. He tried to open all the doors, including the back double doors, but they had been locked. Without authority to gain entry, he could only peer inside through the windows.

The detective constable had not noticed Mallard's Lexus, although it was the most distinctive car in the vicinity. "Some detective, this," Mallard thought as they drove off.

****

Bush worked in the shop until lunch time. On some days he would drive to a pub a little way from his shop, and have their pub lunch. That was what he did on that Wednesday afternoon.

The detective constable had spent ten minutes inspecting the van and then left. When Bush came out there were no police to see Bush leave.

Whilst he ate, he reflected on his encounters with the police. It must be the case that they had caught him on CCTV, in or around Queens Road in that early evening. They had neither mentioned the Arena, nor his later journey with Sophia's body. He had thought up a good story; one they could never challenge. He felt fairly safe.

He switched his attention to the items requested by Karen. A supermarket that sold everything should have her requirements. He would avoid the one he usually went in. He did not want to be seen buying those girls' things. Wednesday afternoon was bound to be quiet. Better go now when it would not be busy. He finished his coffee and went to his van.

At the supermarket, he spent as little time as possible in it. He bought just those items for Karen. He paid in cash and left the store straight away.

From there, he drove to his normal supermarket and bought groceries and provisions to last a few days. Finally, on his way back to the shop he called into the travel agency and confirmed his USA fights. Then he returned to work and stayed until closing the shop at the normal time. When he drove home that night, he was followed by two policemen in an unmarked car. The two volunteers had taken up position thirty minutes before he closed his shop.

They congratulated themselves on their timing. If they had arrived before lunch, and if they had followed him into that first supermarket, and had seen what he bought, they would have had him. They had not; and they did not.

In spells, all that night, teams of officers kept watch on the Bush house. Francis Ulanski did not come that night and Bush stayed home. Three teams of bleary-eyed officers appreciated the sight of an occasional rabbit searching for food. One male and female team was witness to two cats doing what they could to ensure the continuance of the feline species. For a few minutes, the comments of PC "Noddy" Allen and PC Pamela Cook livened up the dreary duty hours. No team saw anything useful to the case.

Neither did the watchers see what Bush was up to with the captive Karen. No one saw her bravery and strength, as the demands of Bush that night reached a new level. He was trying to erase the memory of his encounters with the police. They had frightened him. With Karen, he was in charge. He was master.

CHAPTER 32

All four of the officers had arrived, and Mallard had bought each of them a drink on their way in. He had deliberately arrived first. He liked to observe the interaction of his colleagues when he had the opportunity. Although this was not the purpose of this gathering, Mallard watched them as they settled themselves around a table in a corner of the pub. The intention was to get away from the Major Incident Room in the hope that it might spark a new idea to take the case forward.

The four of them now seated, were his "inner circle" as he liked to think of them. Inspector Brady had been the last to arrive. He was there, in spite of Mallard's lack of confidence in the man, because he was his senior subordinate. Half Brady's pint had been downed by the time Mallard took his seat. Mallard knew the man had had a tough personal life in recent times, and correctly deduced that Brady's alcohol intake had risen as a result. Nobody would be permitted to have more than one alcoholic drink, so the man could drink it as quickly as he liked. He would have no more.
The Bosun had arrived first and had asked for an orange juice. Mallard doubted that this choice was designed to impress. The young man had sensibly chosen an appropriate table where they would be able to talk in confidence. There were plenty of other tables available as it was not yet midday on that Thursday lunchtime.
Philippa had arrived with Frank. Mallard was beginning to notice how Frank was frequently near to his sergeant. The Chief Inspector had seen no signs of anything in the behaviour of the pair that had suggested that anything

irregular was occurring; but it was noticeable. He would check the pairing of the volunteer watchers. It was best that Frank was teamed with another male.

"At least no new body has been reported found. We will continue with the hope that Karen is still alive." Mallard was only repeating what he had said at the full Briefing of his team earlier that morning.
"Shame there been nothing at all from the public appeal?" Philippa remarked.
"Nothing promising. We are still checking some, but it is clear, as always, that the enthusiasm of members of the public is greater than their specific knowledge. The truth is, apart from this man Bush, we are no nearer to finding Karen than we were the morning after the snatch. Right, as I said at the Briefing, for now it is Bush we concentrate on. OK, let's eat."

The Huntsman had been built in the nineteenth century and still retained a few of the original ceiling beams. Nearby, were several buildings which were over a century newer, and housed various departments of the Sheffield University. During term time, students and their lecturers used the Huntsman as a welcome retreat from the brick and glass exterior of their hotbeds of toil. It was currently quiet and there was no delay in being served.

"I wonder if this used to be open countryside? This pub, the Huntsman, seems to suggest it did."
"I doubt it, Philippa. It was probably named after Benjamin Huntsman who introduced steel to the existing cutlery business in Sheffield. That was a long time ago

now. I suppose it is interesting that pubs seem to retain their original names."

"Being a Sheffield lad, our Trevor is probably right. Time changes a lot but not pubs, it seems."
Inspector Brady had continued to look at his empty glass whilst he spoke. He though better of trying to order another. "Go on then young Bosun, you say it was a long time ago. At your age what do you know about the passing of time,"
Brady was looking at the young man with a severe expression on his face.

Mallard was not impressed with that comment,
"True in one sense, Stan, but I bet he knows a lot more about the nature of time, and the way to measure it, than any of us sitting at this table."

"Do tell, Bosun." Brady's invitation was an undisguised test.
"Oh, Boy. It is much too big a subject to do justice to, sitting here today. What I will say, is that if you want to measure time passing, you don't just use a sundial any more. You use physics."
"Have you not heard, Bosun, that somebody invented a thing called a clock?"
"Yes, Inspector, I did hear something about that now you mention it. Does your wristwatch there need winding up with a key, or does it use this new fangled electricity thing?"
"It is quartz watch: the most accurate kind. It keeps perfect time, constable."
"Not so, on both counts."

"Bollocks. It does."

"For a start, the accuracy of your quartz watch varies with temperature. For every one degree Celsius change in temperate above or below twenty-eight C, your watch loses one second per year. The watch casing helps to insulate it, but it is cannot prevent it completely."

"What's the second thing, Trevor?" Philippa had been keeping out of the pissing contest, but she tried to intervene by introducing a lighter tone with a smile on her face.

"The most accurate method we have….." They all noticed the "we have" and not a "there is". The young man had temporarily left the team, and moved back to the lecture theatre.

"….is the Caesium atomic clock. It is accurate to 1 second in 138 million years."

"Is that what you are wearing CONSTABLE?"

Mallard saw that events were turning into just the opposite of his intended team forging aim. He intervened.

"OK so that sorts watches out. But is it true, Trevor, that if our Philippa here wants to remain young and beautiful for as long as possible, what she needs to do is to jump in a spaceship, or on a fast bike, and tootle off into the cosmos like rat up a drainpipe, and she will come back younger than us lot who just stay here?"

Brady was bristly and jumped in quickly. "You never know, she might come back younger than Boy Wonder here. You go in any fast spaceships at Cambridge, Robin?"

Higgs-Whitethorn did not like Inspector Brady. He was not going to hide it. If it meant his career suffered, then it would have to suffer.

"Yes that is true, chief. Philippa travelling faster relative to us observers, time goes slower for her than it would for we observers.

Speaking of drainpipes and rats, where did you buy your watch, INSPECTOR?"

"OK you two. That is quite enough of that. Stan, Trevor, pack it up now! If you two cannot work harmoniously together I will have to do something about it. Come on, it's time we were getting back."

They all stood and walked to the door. The station being within easy walking distance, they had all come on foot.

Outside the front door, Frank stood erect on the pavement and removed his trilby hat. A fairly long funeral procession was approaching, bedecked with wreaths and flowers. Inside the vehicles, the sad faces of the mourners could just be seen. Most people ignored it, but Philippa and the others took Frank's lead, and stood solemnly watching its approach. In stark contrast to the gloomy procession, the summer sun was shining, and people attended busily to their daily interests.

Looking up at the blue sky, Trevor Higgs-Whitethorn remarked, "Nice day for a funeral."

"Not if it's yours, son." Inspector Brady responded.

******

Although, now regarded by his Chief Inspector as a valued officer, it was Detective Constable Frank Cropper who inadvertently alerted Bush that he was being watched. He had known full well since his years, that drinking coffee had a diuretic effect on him. It was best avoided when he was in situations when convenience facilities were difficult. Once, on patrol on a housing estate in Northern Ireland for six hours continuously, he had almost been unable to control his bladder. That had taught him a lesson he would never forget. It was sheer bad luck that one of the officers who was due to undertake the watching duty on Bush that afternoon had been called away due to a medical emergency. Coffee drinker Cropper had been next on the list and replaced him.

At the very the time that Cropper came back to the car from an enforced visit to improvised facilities, Bush was idly gazing through his shop window.

He spotted the man that had frightened him in his home. The man with the strangler's hands was just reaching his car. Bush watched the car. This could not be a coincidence. The car stayed parked across the road, on the opposite side, and with a clear view of his shop. Bush went back to his duties but looked out of the window from time to time. It was still there. It was just ten minutes to closing time, would the car follow him home?

The driver was good. He had the advantage of knowing where Bush was likely to be going. He was able to keep traffic between their unmarked car and his target. Bush would never have known he was being followed, had he not known which car to look for. From time to time he spotted it as it turned a corner behind him.

He decided to make sure. He turned off his route and went along a side street. There was a newsagents shop near the end of the road.

Years earlier, when Bush was at school, the shop had been owned by the parents of a boy in his class. At that time the shop had sold a wide variety of items, but of particular interest to the schoolboys, was the fact that it stocked sweets and chocolates. Sunday afternoon was the only time the shop closed. On some Sundays, the family would go out into the country, or visit relatives and friends. Occasionally, the son would manage to obtain permission to play with his friends instead of going with the family. The shop would be completely locked up, but it had no burglar alarm. What it did have, was a bedroom window which was left open to air the house. The boys saw an opportunity. One lad who was fearless, some would say imbecilic, would climb up a drainpipe which led to the flat roof of a kitchen extension. From there he could reach the house roof gutter. Using a hand over hand technique, which would have been an asset in a circus, the lad would reach the steep roof with the unlocked window. It was then a simple matter to swing his legs up onto the gutter, and roll up onto that roof; easy! The "Squirrel" was there. Then, he would manoeuvre the handle on the window with a penknife, crawl inside it, walk through the bedroom, down the stairs, into the shop, unlock the front door, and let the lads in – job done!

The boys enjoyed scrumptious chocolate and sweets for two months at their free tuck shop. When a neighbour saw the Squirrel one day and told the owner, the shindig ended.

Bush pulled into a parking spot near the shop. Slowly he got out of the van, locked it, and walked into the shop.

Without looking directly at the police vehicle, he was just able to see it finding a parking space much further down the road. He studied the magazines on sale. There was nothing he particularly wanted. As he perused the choice, a man entered. Straight away Bush knew it was the other officer. He ignored him, and the man studied which chocolate to buy. Eventually Bush bought a computer magazine and returned to his van.

After Bush started his car, the officer exited the shop and hurried down the street to the police vehicle. Smiling grimly, Bush did a three-point turn, and drove back up the road to rejoin his usual route. The unmarked police car did the same. Watching it through his mirror, enabled Bush to establish beyond doubt that he was a suspect. Forewarned was forearmed. He must be ultra careful.

At home he went straight down to see Karen. He was deep in thought and almost forgot to don his face mask. The girl was reading when he entered. His mood soared when he saw her. She looked terrific in the housecoat that his mother used to wear.

"I have brought your shopping, Karen. Hope these are what you wanted. Is this thing in time?"
"Yes, I have not started yet. This is what I need; but are these the best pants you could find?"
She snatched them from Bush and put on a pair.

"Karen, my little lovely, it is uncomfortable for a bloke to stand around choosing women's knickers. You should be grateful I brought these. See they fit great."
"OK, thank you. Don't stand there staring though."

"I've got things to do. I will get you some food."

"Genghis, can I have a take-away, please?"

"Maybe tomorrow. Another flattering name now, eh?"

"Please can I have a decent meal? The rubbish you are giving me is bad for me. It is bad for anybody."

"Tomorrow maybe. Now I am busy."

Upstairs in the kitchen Bush put another frozen meal in the microwave. He could see her point. This stuff was no good long term. He should have brought some pizzas.

****

Outside in the unmarked police car, PC "Noddy" Allen fiddled with the car radio and tried to find the frequency of the live European football match soon to start. Detective Constable Cropper leaned back with his eyes closed. They were due to be relieved in two hours. There was no discernable movement in the Bush house, and nothing to see on the road. It was a road which contained expensive houses set well apart. Nobody came along that road unless they were specifically bound for an address on it. It was a boring road to sit and stare at with nothing to do. Although it was a very pleasant summer evening, nobody was visible. No one exercised a dog. No one was just out for a stroll. Time would pass very slowly for the two officers.

Noddy had found what he wanted, so he was relaxed with his cherished football. He hoped he was gaining some Brownie points in his quest for one day transferring to CID and, hopefully, Mallard's team. Cropper just wanted to collar Bush and was prepared to do the hard miles to catch him.

"Let me know if you see the two lovebirds again, son."
"Lovebirds, Frank?"
"The two you saw the other night: those two fucking cats, fucking. I could do with a few pointers."

*****

In the bar were two couples who were talking quietly together. The TV was on, and Ulanski asked for the sound to be turned up. The evening news was just finishing and the weather forecast was on. When that finished, the local news started.

There was a sensational development in the Karen Clayton case. A body had been found in the early evening. It had been discovered in some woods not far from the same school attended by the two schoolgirls. It was not known whether it was the body of Karen Clayton. The corpse was badly burned. The reporter was hoping to interview someone from the police in the very near future.

*****

The house coat did look good on Karen.
"OK, Karen love?"
"I suppose so Genghis. Can I have a TV?"

"No."

"Why?"

Bush did not want the girl seeing the news. It still made reference to the murder enquiry.

"Can't get reception down here."

"Can I come upstairs, please?"

"No, sorry love."

Bush finished putting Karen's breakfast out and collecting the residue of the previous evening's meal. She had hardly eaten any.

"If I had a TV maybe you could get me some films or recordings to watch. I am fed up with just reading these stupid magazines."

It had never occurred to him. Why not? Then again, he was going to America in less than two weeks.

"I bet you have more than one TV already. At home we have four. Can I, please. Brad?"

"Brad now is it? Who is this Brad then? Brad the butcher; Brad the Impaler, Brad the bastard?"

"Brad Pitt, stupid. Let me have a TV and I will call you Brad if you like. Please can I have a TV?"

"Yes."

******

After his breakfast Bush went into his own bedroom. She could have this one for now. Beneath the flat screen TV was a DVD player with a few videos of popular films nearby. Bush had other videos tucked away in a drawer. He decided to leave them for now. If he took some of those down into her room he would watch them with her. The thought excited him.

When he took the equipment in to her, he was delighted with her reaction. She rushed to help him get the things into position. Grinning he went back into the kitchen. The morning news was about to start.
Bush saw the headline item. Another body found! This time it was near to the school. Police were investigating and would issue a statement later in the day. The parents of Karen Clayton had been notified but there was no confirmation that it was the abducted girl's body. There followed a few minutes of footage with what little film and information they had on Karen Clayton. The bulletin would leave little doubt in the minds of their viewers that it would be Karen.

A stunned Bush did not know whether he should be pleased. It might get the police off his back though. In a quandary, Bush went to the window. He could not see a parked car. Had they gone? Was he free of them?

Driving slowly out of his drive and into the street Bush confirmed that there was no car. No one was about. He put his foot down and hurried to take a different route to work.

CHAPTER 33

With parliament on holiday and almost deserted, the outpourings of misinformation, deceit and lies, by politicians was negligible; footballers were on holiday and no matches of the fancifully named, beautiful game were taking place in England; members of the royal family were apparently, if not in fact, behaving themselves. As a result, the media attention was almost solely focussed on the South Yorkshire police.

Although the Home Secretary was agitating, it was the Caribbean mosquitoes that were her primary irritation in the grounds of her hotel.

Her mandarins, though, enjoying cherished freedom from her usual guidance, were bending the ears of the bigwigs in Sheffield.

At 5.30 a.m. Detective Superintendent John Shaw and Detective Chief Inspector John Mallard had been summoned to his office. His main immediate concern, was what to tell the outside world, that would lessen the arse-kicking he was getting from all quarters. That they had worked all night cut no ice with Fisher. After an hour, he summed it up.

"We have fuck all then."

He was right.

"Doctor Pemberton has graciously agreed to favour us with his attendance at 9.00 a.m. sharp. Until he can tell us something helpful we are stymied. We know the charred corpse is female: that's it. How long dead? We don't know. How did she die? We don't know. How old is she, is she a schoolgirl? We don't bloody know!"

The two officers thought it wise to keep silent. Let him get it out of his system.

As was usual, like Macavity the Mystery Cat, he was not there.
Chief Constable Thomas Noel Tomkin was on a fact-finding mission to the Bahamas, that well-known apotheosis of criminal investigation and detection. It had fallen, and fallen heavily, upon Assistant Chief Constable Fisher to steer the ship. The shoulders of Assistant Chief Constable James Fisher were broad. That morning his smile was not.

"You have pulled your volunteers off Bush, and are insisting they work 25 hours a day on the mainstream enquiry, Chief Inspector?"

"If you insist, sir."
"When Macavity comes back after divining the entire wisdom of the Bahamas, or to attend my bleeding funeral, whichever comes first; you can check with him. In the meantime they stick to the mainstream investigation."

CHAPTER 34

He had expected some problems but there had been none.
He had met with Luis Vasquez who had taken him to his
room and then left. Javier Flores sat on his bed and
reflected. His wife and child were still in Mexico. They
were the insurance policy. The agents could reach them
whenever they liked. Flores had no intention of
misbehaving. The money they had promised him was
motivation enough. His loyalty was not in question.

Why, then, was he feeling so nervous? There was always
the possibility that something could go wrong, but Luis
had been doing the same thing for months, and said it was
a cinch. He knew that his nervousness was not the risk of a
foul-up.
It was Rivera who was the source of his unease. They had
both noticed it; indeed his wife had cried on his shoulder
and begged him not to go. When Rivera looked at his wife,
his hunger was evident. He was not a man to hide his
feelings. His desire for her was unmistakable.

Javier Flores sighed, shrugged his shoulders, and lay back
on the single bed. He closed his eyes. That was beyond his
control. Maybe everything would be fine. It had been a
tense and tiring day. He was soon asleep.

In his torpor he saw a stream begin to flow gently down a
grassy hillside. The water was clear and the sun, which
was high overhead, shone down into the water.
The river-bed was not rocky, but what was that on the
bottom? Yes, could it be? Yes, it was. It was lined with
bank notes. Sometimes the notes rose out of the water.

Then, what had been clear water had become yellow – no golden. The water was flowing liquid gold. It ran quicker. And the bank notes were larger. They jumped high out of the water, and then disappeared. He was rich. A flowing river of gold was before him. Huge jumping bank notes were his for the grasping. He was laughing. This was wonderland. He must tell his wife. She must see this. Where are you Maria? Maria, look!

Maria came. Sightless eye sockets were stuffed with notes. In her mouth was something that belonged to Rivera. Javier Flores screamed in his sleep.

*****

Jose Malona had known all week that something was wrong. He had been seeing Yazmin Gonzales for two years before they had become engaged. He knew that they must wait another two years to marry because that fool of a useless father of hers had refused them permission. Yazmin said she would marry Jose anyway when she was twenty-one. Jose was eight years older than Yazmin and was desperate to take her as his wife: still, he would wait. When he had gone to her house the previous night only Yazmin was in the house and had left Jose waiting alone when she went to her room to finish getting ready. Loudly the old man had staggered in, drunk as he habitually was, and had flopped into a chair grinning his gormless grin the whole time. At first Jose just ignored him but the father was having none of it. He wanted the man who wanted to take his daughter away, out of his house. The old man knew his daughter was the only thing that was keeping him out of jail. Words were exchanged.

"You want to marry a virgin I expect Senor Malona. Well have you asked my little Yazmin if she is a virgin? Have you? Did she say yes of course, amore? Did she lie to you Senor Malona? Go on, ask her. Ask her about her policemen lovers. Did you know my little girl likes big policemen?"

Jose Malona would have ignored the drunken old fool. With his back to the door, Jose had been so gripped by his contempt for the drunkard and the far-fetched words he was hearing, that he had not noticed Yazmin hurry into the room. She arrived just as the old man was finishing his betrayal. She had heard her father tell her fiancé she had been with policemen.
When the scornful Jose turned and saw the stricken face of his beloved, he could see it might be true. He would have killed the old man then and there, without any compunction. His dislike of the messenger had already been intense. The incredible and inexplicable message was so diabolical that Jose was immediately filled with a rising overwhelming hatred for the man. Yazmin managed to jump in front of her father who had ceased laughing and had been overcome by a fit of tubercular coughing. She managed to wrestle and plead with Jose until he turned away and slammed his fist into the panel of the door which Yazmin had not closed.

The girl managed to persuade her fiancé to go with her to her own room. For a long time Jose listened to Yazmin as she explained the events that she had been compelled to experience. The clincher was that she was still technically a virgin.

By the time Jose left, after soft sweet words and a few kisses, after his damaged hand had been bathed and bandaged, and after a promise of an early marriage if he still wanted her, he was so confused he thought his head would explode. They parted, and neither knew whether it would be a final parting.

*****

The negative results just came one after the other. The re-questioning of the teachers and pupils had yielded nothing. Some were still out of reach but there would be little hope of success from that direction. Friends, neighbours, and relatives of the two girls had tried their utmost to be helpful, but had only provided blind alleys. Constant watch at the Arena had proved similarly negative.

Bush was now off-limits.

The only area of current unfinished enquiry was in respect of the hordes of vehicles shown on the dozens of CCTV cameras. One driver of a transit van was being obstinate. Clive Wheway would offer no explanation of where he was going, where he had been, or the reason for his journey. It was a long shot. The radius of transits with a registered address within a fifty mile radius of the Arena to be checked, had been extensive. This one was forty-six miles. An unhelpful individual often indicated someone with something to hide. He had to be checked. Mallard sent for Inspector Brady.

"Stan, we are struggling. Do not take no for an answer."

****

It took Inspector Brady and his two helpers the rest of the day, and half into the night before they had the entire story. Within an hour they knew they were onto a winner of some sort.

This chap was not a violinist. He was a man who took pride in his appearance. His watch was expensive; the bracelet on his right wrist was solid gold; and his clothes were designer clothes. When he saw Detective Sergeant Val Irwin for the first time his eyes gave him away. This was a ladies man. Wheway was not the first. The team had come across his kind before. The area of special vulnerability had been quickly established.

"Right." Brady was about to confirm what the other two already knew.
"Fingers out; bollocks in."

CHAPTER 35

An unusually hot day in Sanorias City was coming to a close. Most people had dined on mats outside their homes, and stayed there hoping for a breeze to waft their perspiring bodies. Gradually, those with children had been drifting reluctantly indoors to settle their offspring down for the night. Several remained. Senora Francisca Valdez was one. The widow did not have anyone left to share her house. Her husband had fallen foul of a gang one night coming home from work, and he had been carried home with his throat slashed and bleeding to death. The Senora had watched him die lying on their floor. Her home had been her prized possession, but since that day, she could never look at that spot without seeing the blood and the grief on his dying face. Outdoors was a far better place. Her fingers knitted automatically; the muscle memory forged as a young woman who had knitted, as they all had, out of necessity. Nothing moved in Ynez Rd that the Senora did not see.

When it appeared, people hurried inside their homes and closed and locked the doors. All but one. The fingers moved patiently guiding her needles, but her rheumy eyes watched the Hummer approach. Upon which house would the trouble fall?

It stopped at the house next door. Unusually, only one agent got out, stretched, looked up and down the street, and then straight at her. The needles never faltered. The Senora looked straight down now at those clicking needles. My eyes see nothing, senor agent: you are invisible. Agent Rivera sensed no danger, certainly not from an old woman.

There was no one else now on the street. Even in that heat he wore his full uniform. That would be important to make his mission more easily and more quickly achievable. Inside her house the baby was asleep. Maria Flores had stopped clearing away the food remnants when she had heard the closing of a vehicle's door. Her door opened. He walked straight in.

Senora Valdez decided it was none of her business. The husband, Javier, everyone knew was in America, may the Virgin protect him! They never went about in less than twos. The wife, now alone, had a visit from an agent – one agent. Everybody knew, one alone meant it was personal. The Senora could not help the girl. She went indoors.

By the time the old woman had taken her seat in her usual chair, the noises coming from Maria next door were breaking the usual silence of her own house. The sounds were clear and distinct through the thin walls. The girl was pleading with the agent. Her pleas and his laughter went on for a while. The Senora's clicking needles continued, but the sounds changed. Pleading turned to wailing; laughter to grunts.
The knitting had lengthened by a dozen or more rows before the crying ceased. What he had come for had been done; that was obvious. Then his voice could be heard, speaking at first, and then shouting. They were arguing. The Senora expected to hear the door as the agent left. She heard no door. Was he staying the night?

After some time, there was movement outside. Senora Valdez went to the window. She saw Maria and her brother. He lived in the next street and worked on a building site as a labourer. When there was trouble the brother was a good man to have on your side. His muscles rippled. Would there be a fight? Maria had summoned him to help, had she? Silly woman. She would get him killed.

Across the street figures had appeared in other windows. Neighbours were curious.

Senora Valdez saw Maria open the passenger door of the Hummer, and her brother went into the house. The girl went to meet him. He was dragging something. Maria bent, and together they managed to lift and manoeuvre the frame of the uniformed agent. It was clear that uniform was splattered with blood. As the pair shoved him into the passenger seat, the back of the agent was turned towards the street. His back was a mass of blood.

"Holy Mother of God." Senora Valdez crossed herself. "Maria has killed the federal agent. Oh dear God. Now we will all have terrible trouble. Dear Mother of God, help us."
Senora Valdez was down on her knees as the brother drove the Hummer up the road. She stayed there praying for a very long time.

CHAPTER 36

In all probability she had been a teenage girl. The results
of the DNA would take hours more to become available. It
might well be Karen Clayton. It might well not be Karen
Clayton. The M.O. was totally different. This time the
body had been burnt, and it had been done fairly
thoroughly. Perhaps the killer had had more time on this
second occasion to further destroy any trace of his contact
with the girl. She must have been completely naked when
set alight. There was no metal or traces of any substance
other than the human corpse. From the posture of the
corpse, it was clear she had been dead or unconscious
when put to the fire.
The DNA would tell them if it was Karen; but again, there
were no other clues. The burnt corpse had been taken, and
placed carefully in the woods after the event. The careful
placing suggested a degree of affection, or concern, or
possibly regret.

Chief Inspector Mallard was finishing reading the report
when Inspector Brady knocked and entered.

"You sent for me, Chief?"
"Sit down Stan. Have you read this?"
"No, it was rushed straight in to you. Our copies have not
been printed yet. Anything useful?"
"Not really. I wanted to congratulate you on the work you
and your interrogation team did on Wheway. I won't ask
how you talked him into volunteering the information.
Have you heard we got five Iranians from that lock-up?
"Yes. A good day's work there for once."

"There are rumblings of interest from the National Crime Agency about you. Well done, Stan."

"Thank you, John. What's this about NCA? Can you tell me any more?"

"I don't know any more. You could ask the Super, he told me."

"Bloody shame, though. Another White Van Man turns out to be guilty of something not to do with our own case. All the glory will go to the NCA. I would love to get stuck into tracking down gangs involved in smuggling drugs or foreign illegals" to our so-called green and pleasant land."

"Me too. To get actively involved in a wider operation than you get as a regional copper comes our way only once in a blue moon. A bit of foreign travel and involvement with other regions and even countries would be most welcome once in a while. Having said that though, Stan, there is nowhere else I would prefer to live."

Brady said nothing. He could think of places.

"Do you think I might get a chance with NCA?"

"I really don't know."

Mallard could see Brady was really keen.

"I might go and have a word with the Super, John."

"Yes, I would. Good luck, Stan."

"Anyway, for now let's look on the bright side. It's nice to know the Oxbridge lot at the Home Office are having kittens. With the White Queen still in the Caribbean, they don't know whether to have a shit or a haircut. If they crow about how clever they are to have bagged Wheway and his lot, they will face another media frenzy on Immigration. If they keep stum, when it leaks out, they will be crucified for covering up the crime. They have even eased up on ACC Fisher. They know all he has to do is drop an off-the-record word to the Sun, and the balloon goes up. He nearly smiled this morning, Stan. Thank God for small mercies. Keep it up, Stan. Ask Philippa to come in would you on your way out?"

*****

"When is it you fly to see your brother?"
"I fly out there next week on Saturday night. The train will get me to Heathrow in plenty of time early Saturday afternoon, so next Friday I will be at work as normal."

"Right, now listen. I have been told to keep off Bush and concentrate on mainstream. The problem, Philippa, is we have not enough lines of fruitful investigation to keep everybody usefully active. Will you agree to do something for me that you keep to yourself, and I mean to yourself? I can't risk the ACC finding out what I have asked you to do?"
"You can count on me, sir."

"On the road where Bush lives, every house is likely to have outdoor CCTV fitted as part of their household security measures. There is a lot of wealth in that district. I want you to go there looking like an Avon lady or something. You will have to identify yourself as a police officer to the occupants, there is no getting round that. I will just have to hope that no pals or relatives of the ACC are amongst the people you will see. Make up some story like, say, we have had a report of a prowler, or something unconnected with this case. Check the CCTV from the

249

date of Sophia's disappearance, to now. Record every movement of Bush you see. Is that OK, sergeant?"
"This is going to take quite some time. Shall I phone in sick to explain my absence from the office?"
"Precisely."
"Just one more thing. I will need to borrow their CCTV tapes. Where do I watch and record them if I am to keep my activities secret?"
"Come with me, sergeant."

The Chief Inspector took Philippa to a building across the city. It was now simply a local police station. It was there that Constable John Mallard, as a bright-eyed keen young man straight out of Durham University, and with a good degree in Chemistry, had reported for his first day at work. There he had first met Constable Cyril Higton who was also starting on that morning. They had remained friends. Inspector Higton had listened to his friend on the phone early that morning, and was more than willing to help. A room containing the necessary equipment had been organised for Detective Sergeant Tate. The coppers at that station could not be told the reason for the Detective Sergeant's mission. An oblique reference though, had slipped out that very morning, about a visit to Sheffield next month. The Princess Royal was due to make some presentations at the renowned Sheffield Children's Hospital. The incumbent aces at the station effortlessly made the connection. After all, they were detectives! Proudly they continued about their duties, party now to royal security.

*****

Maria Flores had raced back into the house after her brother had driven the body away. The house had to be cleaned of the all the blood and signs of Rivera's presence. It was long after she had finished that her brother returned. He told her he had stripped the body in case there was any trace of Maria on Rivera's clothes. He had stuffed the clothes, and the knife, and everything else, together with some rocks, into a plastic bag into which he had pierced a few holes, and thrown them out into a lake. Then he had driven to a remote spot and left the naked body and the car. He had walked all the way back.

All they could do now was wait. Their entire street knew the body of an agent had been lifted into a government Hummer. The Policia and all the authorities were hated, so the pair had nothing to fear. Nothing, that is, until the first one was questioned. Everyone knew better, than to be caught lying to the Policia. If the Policia came, it would be better for both Maria and her brother to be dead.

CHAPTER 37

Jose Malona was missing Yazmin but had made no contact. Deep within himself he knew he loved her and must marry the girl: but the thought of two men having taken her and slaked their desire on her, not only once but several times, was breaking his heart. It was consuming him. The senior was Tamayo. He must take revenge on Tamayo first. Then he would seek out the other bigger man. He was ignorant of the fact that another had beaten him and taken retribution on Riviera. Malona needed to act before he could look into the eyes of his childhood sweetheart again. Only then he would feel like a superior man when he told Yazmin how he had avenged her. There was no other way.

*****

Very few witnessed the proceedings. There were no relatives at the service on that cloudy Tuesday morning. Rufino Rivera had had only one friend in the world and he, Tamayo, had arrived minus enthusiasm and with an absence of grief; but he was there. The Chief of the Policía Federal had felt it necessary to attend. Consequently, on instruction, a few colleagues had been there. It was not from choice, because he had not been popular. It was a pleasant day and they were happy enough to be away from the station.

His naked body had been found on the outskirts of Sanorias City. It was obvious that the knife wound in his back would have dispatched him swiftly. There were just a few small scratch marks on his face and hands, but no sign of a battle. Another unsolved murder went onto the official record.

It was officially unsolved; officially.
Sitting alone at a bar after the funeral, Sergeant Tamayo knew who had done it. In the afternoon of his murder, Rufino Rivera had made an excuse to miss their usual collection, on the grounds of feeling unwell. Always on that same evening every week without fail, the two of them visited the businesses that were under their "protection". A benefaction was received from each of those businesses.

Tamayo had known his colleague long enough to be able to read him like a book. He would not normally leave his share of the proceeds, to be at hazard to Tamayo's honesty. It was a woman! He knew the signs. Throughout the day Rivera had been glancing at his watch. His uniform was pressed and clean. That alone would have been a dead give-away.
Twice that week Rivera had enquired about Javier Flores, to ascertain that he really was still in San Diego; and on each occasion Tamayo had warned him to stay away from Maria Flores.

His lust for the woman had apparently got him killed. Exactly how and why, was of little consequence to Tamayo. If he arrested Maria or any member of her circle, her husband would be bound to return home. That would be the end of the new, potentially lucrative, racket.

Tamayo had not hesitated - to do nothing. It was Rivera's own stupid fault he had got himself killed. Javier Flores was in position, and would earn Tamayo a lot of money. The crime would have to remain unsolved. To do anything else would scupper the new business.

He sipped his beer. Tamayo needed a new partner. There was a man, Emiliano Jara, who had joined the Policía Federal, at the same time as Tamayo all those years past. One year ago, his son, Gelsen, had started. The young man seemed to have similar characteristics to his father: he would likely make a suitable partner for Tamayo. In any case, Tamayo had enough dirt on his old man to ensure a degree of assurance. He had another sip of his beer and took out his phone. It was still afternoon and Tamayo was the sole customer. The barman, as all experienced barmen habitually did, had made himself absent. The sound of a TV could be heard; a much better prospect for the barman than standing bored to death at the bar, or listening to a morose customer moaning about the state of his life. The solitude suited Tamayo on that occasion. Better start the ball rolling. He dialled Emiliano Jara.

*****

He had been following Tamayo all day. The bastard was alone now. He would do it now.

How long would the barman be away from the bar? Jose Malona knew they always kept some sort of weapon handy. It might be gun. Anyway he did not want to be recognised later. His intention was to kill Tamayo so it did not matter if he saw him or not; but not the barman. There was no noise as he crept slowly in through the open door. Bending low to avoid Tamayo seeing him in the mirror, he silently approached the unprotected back of his target. From the deep front pocket of his overalls he withdrew a hefty metal spanner. If he stood, he would be visible in the bar mirror which faced Tamayo. That would be a risk too far. Jose could see the police pistol in its holster and one mistake would certainly be fatal for him. The legs then; it would be the legs, first. He struck. The scream was instant. The left tibia had taken the first blow. Tamayo would not reach for his gun now. His two hands were on his left leg trying to ease the unbearable pain. With a grim determined smile of success on his face, the avenging Jose Malona stood, and prepared to deliver the killer blow to the skull.

He would never know where his mistake had been made. No one took the trouble to explain, that placed close beside the TV which the barman had been watching, was the CCTV monitor of the bar's interior. The barman had seen on that CCTV screen, a crouching man in blue overalls slowly creep in through the open main door. He had left by the side door of the back room, and crept silently inside the bar through the main door. He stood behind the unsuspecting culprit who was preparing for another blow, and cracked his skull with the cosh he always kept dangling from his trouser belt. Down went the interloper, out for the count. When he regained consciousness he had been handcuffed to a bar-rail with Tamayo's handcuffs.

A police vehicle and an ambulance arrived almost simultaneously. The two men went their separate ways.

Tamayo was given a morphine injection and stretchered into the ambulance, whilst Jose Malona was pistol-whipped and bundled into the Hummer.

******

A happy man that morning was standing on the pavement outside the Royal Albert Hall. In his hands was a ticket for a seat in the stalls for the concert the next evening. The Bavarian Radio Symphony Orchestra was appearing. Ulanski knew how good the orchestra was. What was more, it was to be led by the man who was currently possibly the world's finest conductor, the Latvian, Mariss Jansons.

Back in his hotel he decided he would lunch in their dining room again. The news of his father was that he was stable and in no immediate danger. The signs were promising that his stay in London would not need to be cut short. After a leisurely lunch Ulanski went to seek out the wise old concierge who had done him so proudly on his previous stay. A hopeful pair of younger ones spied him approaching and aimed their winning smiles at him. The sage just stood there. Whether he recognised him or not, Ulanski saw no sign.

Nearly an enjoyable hour later, the itinerary was organised, booklets and maps produced, and limousines arranged. Additionally, a complementary seat for him was reserved at the table of senior management, the twenty-one year old Peter Pan, who was organising a musical extravaganza on Friday evening.

The hopeful pair, again with no punters, looked on wistfully as they watched Ulanski stroll away.

*****

Although he had not a fresh mark on him, they had the full story. He was suspended. A rope which was wrapped around his ankles ran upwards to a hook in the ceiling. Swinging slowly to and fro, his head would be at knee height to a standing interrogator, and his hands were handcuffed behind his back. They no longer stood. With their primary purpose achieved, both lazed easily in chairs watching Jose Malona dangling in misery. They had already informed him that he himself would never leave the room alive, but the promise that the girl would not be punished for his crime if he told all, had been enough for him to gush out the simple story. That they already knew about his girl had surprised him. He was unaware that in his semi-conscious state from the pistol-whipping, on the way to the police station in their vehicle, he had repeatedly mumbled her name. After that it had been so easy for them. They taunted him now.

"Let me tell you about what we have planned for your little Yazmin, senor. There is a room on the next floor down from here. Little Yazmin knows the way, she goes there regularly. Your girlfriend is an entertainer. Did you know that senor? A very good entertainer they tell us. Regrettably senor, so far only two of our colleagues know exactly how good that little performer is. But oh dear, she seems to bring bad luck, your girlfriend. One of those two colleagues is now dead, and the other is for now in hospital. Your girlfriend was instructed to keep her entertaining recreations confidential. But no; she has chosen to share her joyfulness with you, senor. But senor, as a result you have been very wicked. So she has great blame, you see. My colleagues and I have a duty to point out the error of her actions. It is only right and proper that we fulfil our obligations to the full, is it not, senor? So we will invite little Yazmin to that downstairs place and teach her a few things in the privacy she will surely welcome. It will probably take quite some time. However, senor, you should not worry. You have an appointment to meet someone yourself. He resides in a place which is located on a level which is much lower than the room of entertainment downstairs – and it is also much warmer."

As the agent stood he removed a thin clear plastic bag from a uniform pocket. Crouching, he deftly slipped the bag over the head of the dangling Malona, pulled the drawstring tight, and stood back. Violent swinging and jerking as it was wildly agitated by the suffocating prisoner in his frantic attempt to release himself. It was brief. Soon the rope became free of the forces which had interrupted its resolute assignment to obey the instruction of gravity, to seek the centre of the earth.

******

News broadcasts had confirmed that the burnt corpse was not that of Karen Clayton. Since that disclosure, newscasts had come and gone, and the Sheffield schoolgirl enquiry, featured later and briefer in each subsequent one. The journalists were tired of having nothing substantial to convey. They could only retain the interests of their customers by flagellating the police, for so long. Some had tried to blame the school but had been forced to back off. Inconveniently, both girls had gone missing after school hours.

If not crime and police incompetence, then what for the media headlines? Showbiz!
Fortunately, an American actress seemed from photographs, to have gained about half a stone in weight. Was she pregnant? Who was the father? Photographs taken of the actress with various men over the past eighteen months were pulled from the archives. Since most of those men were "in relationships" with other women, additional fruitful reactions from those women were being canvassed. All good summer fun in the press.

At a meeting with his accountants that afternoon, Bush finalised details of supervisory cover for his shop during his USA holiday. Back at work, the drawer of his shop's till opened, closed and steadily became fuller throughout the afternoon.
Everything was as he had hoped it would be; the police had lost interest in him, Ulanski senior was stable, and the main thing left to do was to pack his suitcase in a few days time.
Bush had shelved, for the time being, deciding the arrangements for the exit of Karen. He still had nearly a week to enjoy her company.

"Tonight I will liven things up. How will my little dove react when we watch the sex films together for the first time? He locked the shop and hurried home.

As Bush negotiated the traffic, Philippa Tate began watching yet another of his neighbour's CCTV recordings. After that one, there was just one more remaining.

This was similar to all the rest. Very little of Beech Street could be seen on them. Predominantly they captured the houses and their own drives. This was proving a complete waste of time. As she watched, her mind kept switching to thoughts of seeing her brother again and her new nephew. Only three more working days left and she was off across the pond. She looked at her watch and decided to finish for the night.

****

It was evening of the third day and still Yazmin Gonzales waited for Jose to come. When he had left her he was desolate. She had begged his understanding. It was she who was the real victim, was it not?

Jose might well feel betrayed but it was not of her own doing. She, a girl, a daughter, was the victim of men. Not just those evil police agents; her aberrant father also. How she hated her father!

She crossed herself and went to her knees. She prayed for forgiveness for the sinful thoughts about her own father. She prayed her father would change. For Jose, Yazmin asked for his understanding. The health of her mother was almost an afterthought.

She rose from her knees and sat at the bare wooden table. Her father was comatose, drunk in his chair, and her mother was out. Yazmin stared despondently at the picture on the wall. The white light of hope which shone behind the head of the saint had faded over the years. It seemed appropriate for that house.

Whilst the engine was still running the Hummer parked directly outside her house, but Yazmin was unaware of it. She was also unaware, that wrapped in the back of the vehicle, was the body of the man for whom she had just finished a prayer. When she opened the door to the bold knocking she was confronted by the two officers. They had heard from the desk officer that the girl was a tasty morsel, but they had been eager to see for themselves. Each looked carefully at the girl. Both men were satisfied.

"Senorita Yazmin Gonzales?"
"Yes, officer."
"Senorita Gonzales I have to inform you that this afternoon your boyfriend Jose Malona committed a very serious crime. He made an unprovoked and vicious attack and he injured our Sergeant Tamayo. We arrested him of course and took him to the station. Stupidly he tried to escape from the police station. Regrettably Senorita I have to inform you that your boyfriend is dead.
In order that certain formalities can be completed you are required to report to the police station tomorrow at 8.00 a.m.

Goodnight, senorita. Do not be late."

*****

A worried Inspector Brady had been required to hurry that morning to the office of Detective Superintendent Shaw. His past sins and remissions weighed heavily on him. His nervousness soon disappeared when he discovered the explanation.

The Superintendent for once had a task that was not distasteful. Progress on all his current cases was virtually zero. A string of petrol station robberies which had been under investigation for several months had produced a variety of suspects. Subsequently they had been arrested: and subsequently released. Currently they had not one suspect.
A Post Office raid which had left one employee severely injured, and upon which he had reported that "it was proving difficult", had been a mastery of euphemism.
Top of his hate list, were the tragedies of the two schoolgirls, and the other female teenager. Two of them dead, and one missing and quite possibly dead.

In a rare pleasant interlude, Superintendent Shaw passed on the message to Brady and saw that had been so obviously well received.

When Brady left he was beaming. That was what he had been hoping to hear. Tomorrow he was to report to an address in London. There he would be interviewed, at the National Crime Agency, by a specific division of the UK Human Trafficking Centre. His ability to speak several European languages was in his favour, as was his remarkably high success rate in suspect interviews. Immigration and human trafficking had been the flavour of the month in England for two decades, and the taste for it in the media was rising. Consequently the UKHTC had a very short direct organisational line to the apex of the Home Office. Career prospects in that field were bright: so, to Brady, was the attraction of the work.

After leaving the office of Detective Superintendent Shaw Brady went straight to talk to Detective Sergeants Val Irwin and George Mitchell. He wanted to know if they would be interested in a transfer, if it was at all possible. They had played a huge part in his success. Both would think the matter over. It would obviously depend where in the country they would be based. At that point it was fairly academic anyway. As a matter of principle though, they were definitely interested. The two of them were proud of the results they had produced.

Brady was a happy man. The ability to pick the right team was an even greater asset than individual talent. His father had drummed that into him when he had first started. Stanley Olwyn Brady worshipped his dad. The man had brought the three of them up single-handedly after the death of their mother.

Brady hoped the pair would want to come with him. It was likely that he would be based somewhere in, or close to, London or Dover. That would give him more opportunity to see his children in Ashford.

CHAPTER 38

Simply by holding the hair of the girl Estella Hernandez in a viciously tight grip, she was controlled enough to have no option but to climb the four flights of the tiled staircase. Crying piteously all the way, she was pulled along the corridor, past five rooms on either side, to the end room. It was not locked.

That part of the building was located in the middle of a side road, in the midst of town. Black paint had been peeling off the stout metal gates that had been slid just open just enough by two burly men to admit them. Immediately they were through, those very heavy gates were slid back firmly into place to be secured. No one person would have the strength to slide those gates: certainly not one lone female. By the time the big padlock clicked, the girl had been dragged well into the far corner where the stairs to the upper floors were located. This was the rear entrance; grubby, seedy, inconspicuous. The public walked along that road and gave it not a second glance. Anonymous, it served its purpose well. There was no indication that it had any connection with the glitzy, brassy façade of the emporium onto which it backed; the *El Retiro*.

The girl had not been blindfolded; they were unconcerned that she knew where the car had driven, or that their features were exposed. The woman opened the door to the end room whilst the man shoved the girl inside. Kept unlocked and prepared at all times, this was the room for "Recruits".

A normal hot and humid afternoon in Sanorias City, the day would be humdrum for most of the population. The day would be anything but unexceptional for Estella Hernandez. Her Parents had been slain that morning by a hand grenade thrown through the open door of their home. Their crime was that they had been coerced into doing certain favours for a rival gang.
Estella had been informed at school of "an accident", and had rushed home and seen the outcome of the "accident".

One of the agents on the scene of the crime had been Sergeant Tamayo. Although now with a pronounced limp he had returned to work. When he saw the girl he had made a phone call. The heartbroken girl was in due course led to his police vehicle, and Tamayo had driven it to this place.

Whereas Tamayo looked base, the woman, Alegria, did not. Encountered in different circumstances she could easily become notable in friendly well-meaning company. At a religious fete one could imagine the priest smiling benevolently at her. In a classroom children could sit upon her knee and listen with wide-eyed absorption as she read to them, their parents observing her charisma.
Dressed with casual unconcern in a simple cotton dress, Alegria looked cool and composed. The solid gold jewellery she wore glistened.

It was by no means disinterest that gave Alegria an air of detachment. It was familiarity. A girl like this Estella was brought to her frequently. Although in her early thirties and old enough to be the mother of the girl before her, Alegria had a quality to which the girl, lovely as she was, would never attain. It was a rare, singular, physical and personal quality, that was the reason that she had prospered to be the proprietor of *El Retiro*, and become exceedingly wealthy in the process. How she herself had started was a story she told to but a tiny few; and then she would likely only tell it, if it was to gain her some advantage. She could adapt easily. As an actress she would have been a success. That ability, and superlative beauty, combined with intelligence and ruthlessness had led her to her current status. Once, briefly in another place, she had been the wife of a very wealthy man. It was not known what had happened to him. He had vanished. Soon, so had Alegria; with his wealth.

Tamayo released the hair of the girl and smiled a broad smile at the woman.

"Suitable, yes?"

"The female will do very well here, Sergeant Tamayo. You too as usual have done well. Will you introduce yourself to her right now or later?"

"I will return tonight and I may bring a colleague with me, Senora Proprietor."

"You sound like my lawyer. I keep telling you, call me Alegria." She smiled her little girl smile sweetly at him: but Tamayo knew her well enough.

"No, Senora. We have a business arrangement you and me, not a love affair. I shall want my commission as usual."

"You always get your commission, sergeant: same as you always have first go at the girls you recruit. Will your colleague be likely to want her as well?" She nodded in the direction of Estella without looking at her.

"I imagine so. If not this one, then another one of your *El Retiro* flowers."

Tamayo stepped away from Estella and moved towards the door. He looked intently at the girl. A little over five feet tall, the girl wore expensive shoes and clothes. Reaching the shoulders, her shiny hair was not completely black. The sunlight which was shining through the window, caught it and revealed an auburn tint. A subdued trace, it was uncommon in those parts and most enhancing. The girl stood bewildered with her back to the window. She was still in school uniform. That her figure had developed was obvious. Her complexion was clear and so very smooth. She apparently kept well out of the sun to avoid the hue that it brought. Girls with sense, her mother had informed her, need to look as white-skinned as possible to better succeed in life.

Estella had ambition, brains and white-skinned delicacy. Her lips were generous; a passionate mouth Tamayo thought. He would enjoy tonight. Tamayo knew she would be extremely popular in that establishment; for a time anyway. They always kept the new girls dressed in their school gear for as long as they could, but with the addition of very high heels: no make-up. Once the schoolgirl clothing became damaged, it inevitably became damaged quite quickly in that place; they would be exhibited in something far more skimpy: and then, with suitable make-up and guile, they would patrol the entertainment areas, in time eager for punters. It was a tried and tested sequence. The new girls assimilated swiftly. Why? Naive Estella was on the threshold of discovering.

The girl listened to the two of them. She did not comprehend what they were talking about. She came from a very good home and had had no idea that her father had been involved in crime.

Abruptly Tamayo turned and limped out of the door, followed by the woman.

Estella heard the key turn in the lock and the drawing of two bolts. She sat bewildered on the huge bed, and looked at the bars on the single widow. There was an empty bucket in a corner with a single unopened toilet roll. A single light-bulb with no shade hung from the ceiling. An ancient ceiling fan was fitted but was not switched on. As she looked around the Spartan room, she took in the well worn settee, a table and two chairs, and the washbasin with no soap or towel. Opposite the bed upon which she sat, was a very large-screen TV with a DVD player beneath. There were clean white cotton sheets on the bed. When she noticed the stout leather restraining straps attached to each of the four corners of the bed, her mounting suspicions were strengthened. The innocent schoolgirl, burst into another torrent of tears.

******

The large woman scarcely glanced at Estella as she entered the room an hour later. On the tray she carried was a plastic bottle of water, a bowl of soup, and a thick chunk of bread. Estella watched as she placed the tray on the table. She wore an expensive looking dress and plenty of jewellery. Neither lessened the appearance of a buffalo. The animal looked carefully around the room, turned and spoke.

"I am Mama. That is what you will call me. Say it!"

"Mama."

The woman was the permanent overseer.

"I am not your friend. Here you will have no friends. I am Mama, the Big Cheese, the Boss. I tell you what to do, how to behave. If you are stupid, if you make mistakes, if you are defiant, I have you punished. On my say-so you will be punished very badly. Try my patience too long I will have you killed – painfully. Do you understand?"

"I think so, but why?"

The woman moved slowly over to Estella and smacked her hard across the face. Three times she repeated the blows.

"You call me Mama. Say, yes Mama."

"Yes, Mama."

"Do you understand?"

"Yes, Mama."

"Tonight you will receive some visitors. There may be many. This is your room for tonight. I will come for you tomorrow and will show you the ropes. Say, yes Mama. Goodnight Mama."

"Yes Mama. Goodnight Mama."

The buffalo left.

*****

The soup had been surprisingly good and the bread fresh and crispy. Since then Estella had been trying to come to terms with her predicament. In summary – parents dead, held captive, probably going to be used for sex. She had cried continuously for hours. It was growing dark but she had not turned on the light.

Estella had formed an idea. She must try to escape. The bolts outside on the door made a noise when they were slid. That would give her time. She placed one of the chairs close to the door. In the darkening room, Estella sat herself on that chair and waited. Who would it be who came? Would they be alone? She must be brave. How could she stop them? Was there a weapon? There was nothing really easy to use, no knife or anything sharp. There was the spoon in the soup bowl. That was no good.

If she could get outside she knew there were other buildings. Someone would help her. It would have to be a chair. She went over to the other chair. She could lift it, and she could lift it quite high. That would have to do. She placed that chair near the door.

All Estella could do for now was to wait and pray.

CHAPTER 39

Yazmin's tears were drying on pale cheeks. It was the end. Life was not worth living. On her knees once more, but not for praying: she had lost all strength in her limbs. She looked across at her father, the source of all her troubles throughout her life. He had not moved in the twenty minutes since she had managed to close the door. Tomorrow she must go again to that evil place - to two more men. It must not happen. It would not – never again. A calmness had taken the place of anguished confusion. Control had supplanted tremors since she had made her decision. But first there must be some justice. If the Holy Mother had chosen not to look down on her thus far, then she could just keep on not looking down. It was proper: it was rectitude. It was justice, of a sort anyway. She even knew how.

Yazmin fetched it. Her eyes watched it wrap around her wrists, and her mind took her back to that fateful day when she was seven years old.
The baby rabbit had been her pet. She had first seen it when her aunt had taken it from her and was about to put it into the bucket with the others. She had begged and had succeeded. Her aunt had stopped, turned, and handed the two-week old bundle to her niece; and then turned immediately back and placed the lid firmly onto the bucket. All the other baby rabbits drowned in the bucket, but Yazmin had not stopped whilst they drowned. In the evening she would not eat the rabbit soup.

She remembered vividly. It was the earliest clear memory of her life, she remembered that frantic run home; so fearful in case her aunt changed her mind. Yazmin had loved the tiny animal. It was the only thing of value to her she possessed: the only thing she could call her own that meant anything to her. Holding it, and stroking the softness of that new baby fur brought her such joy. Its long pointed ears enchanted her own little hand as she would fold them neatly along its back. Part of the joyfulness came from knowing that it depended upon her. It was weaker and younger and needed her. How the seven year old loved her aunt for that gift.

The bliss lasted five days.
It was him again. Drunk, he had lurched into the room, knocking over a table as he had tried to reach his chair. The miniature bundle was curled up, on his chair: his chair!
Dropping her skipping rope in the process, Yazmin tried to reach it and snatch it out of harms way. He held her off, and made her pick up and hand him the skipping rope. Yazmin could see it now, through adult eyes. Her memory rolled away the intervening twelve years. She watched him pick up the sleeping bundle, wind the rope twice around the neck of the little rabbit, and then he simply held it out, at arms length, and let it hang there by its neck.
Yazmin could see again the kicking of its little legs, the trembling begin throughout its body, then increase frantically

Then the awful stillness as it dangled in death. For the tiny animal, life had begun and ended in the space of less than three weeks. Her father had taken away from his daughter, by his own hand, deliberately, the one thing that was giving meaning to her life then.

And this week he had done it again. There must be a reckoning.

Since that foul day, Yazmin had never touched the skipping rope. It had only been retained in the house for its usefulness as a washing line, in the small space above the sink.
There was a sensation of pleasure, of retribution, as Yazmin looked at her rope, wound now around her own wrists. The malignant man had caused the death of her beloved Jose whom she would have married.

She moved behind the chair of her sleeping father. He had snuffed the life out of the tiny rabbit that she had loved so well. She arranged the rope across the front of his throat. He had traded his daughter so that he could enjoy his money-losing gambling. Yazmin crossed both of her hands behind his head and took up the slack.

He had taken from his daughter the will to live.
Not poetic justice this: retribution was its name: vengeance.

She jerked the rope viciously. Holding the rope locked tight, Yazmin saw, with calm indifference, that the diameter of the scrawny neck below, was compressed to just a fraction of its norm. He died without even fully waking.

Leaving the rope in place, Yazmin went to the knife drawer. The selected knife with the pointed end was always kept sharp. It was definitely more than long enough for the job at hand.

With a final look at the Virgin and the Saint on the wall, Yazmin crossed herself, placed the point of the blade to the left of her sternum, and calmly fell forward, skewering herself when hitting the ground.

CHAPTER 40

"Good evening, flower." He closed and locked the door behind him. She looked up briefly from her book and mumbled something.
"OK then?"
"I am hungry."

"Would you like a take-away, petal?"
"Oh yes please, Brad. Can I have a Chinese?"
"Tonight you can have whatever you want – within reason."
"Great. I want it on a proper plate not in a plastic tray, and with some Soy sauce, and some chips and mushrooms and …"
"Wait, hang on. Tell you what, I will get their menu."
Bush returned with a card. When she had heard him say he would fetch the menu, Karen hoped to be able to see the name of the take-away. It would have to be a local one. She might be able to approximate where she was being kept. He ambled across to the pile of magazines and books and selected a magazine. Sitting at the table he began to browse the menu whilst keeping it shielded inside the magazine. Her captor was brighter than he looked.

"So what do you like, Karen? They have the usual; seafood, chicken, pork, beef, chop suey, chow mien, English meals……"
"I should like Chicken Chow Mien, mushrooms, chips and pretty please can I have some Foo Yung as well?
"Christ, I shall need a mortgage for that lot. No rice?"
"No. Chips, I like chips. Will they deliver?"

"I am going to fetch them. Have you ever had Wandering Dragon, Karen?"

Was he kidding? Is this some type of smutty sex thing? She glared at him shaking her head and hoping to look disgusted.

"I am not kidding, my love, it's number 53. It will have meat and prawns and a mixture of things. I am having that. Tell you what, we will share, you can have some of my number 53 and I will have some of your chips, can I? They always give you loads."

"OK, Brad but please be quick, I am starving."

"Me too; not had a Chinese for months. See you soon."

*****

Downstairs it was a normal night at *El Retiro*. Liquor was swallowed, girls ogled and stroked, music played: everybody was speaking with nobody listening. The ladies of the establishment, some of them not yet strictly old enough for that designation, moved confidently around seeking likely meal-tickets. They sat on knees, nibble ears, allowed breasts to be handled, and attempted to coax customers to more private facilities. An amenity of relaxation and entertainment for the men of the locality, it was as popular as always.

If Adam Smith had been an observer on that night, he would have been delighted to confirm that the principal of supply and demand was still in full swing, over two centuries after his death - and Economic theory might have become illustrated more convivially.

From time to time Alegria put in an appearance. She would circulate for ten minutes checking that her girls were as active as required. The girls were allowed to keep thirty-five per cent of the "service fees" from each of their punters. The house, Alegria, took the rest.

Alegria herself no longer sold her favours; and very rarely bestowed them at all.

Cameras were discretely positioned so that Alegria could watch activities on screens in her private quarters. The private Paradise Rooms were free of cameras; all that is, except for one of them.

One frequent non-paying patron, who was there that night, was Sergeant Tamayo. With him for the first time at *El Retiro* was Gelsen Jara. The young agent looked around with a smile on his face. The sergeant had promised him a lively evening, a perk of being a friend of Sergeant Tamayo. What he saw did not discourage him. He was happy to be his friend; on this night anyway. His father, Emiliano Jara, had cautioned his son to be wary of Tamayo.

"Observe him. Learn from him. Get to know the angles, the systems and the fixes. Never trust him; not with a peso, certainly not with your life. Listen well son. The man is poison."

*****

It had seemed a long time that she had sat there in the gloomy room, waiting. Very few sounds could be heard on that highest floor. Once someone had walked to a nearby room and Estella had heard the opening and closing of a door. A few minutes later they had come out and walked away heading downstairs.

She had been planning the details. The only door opened into the room and was hinged on the right as she looked at it. She decided where she would need to stand. Picking up the plastic water bottle, she dribbled the little water that remained onto the wooden floor at the spot she must stand. Estella sat again and removed her shoes. She would run faster and quieter shoeless. The she sat again to wait.

******

They had finished eating and sat for a while in silence, lost in their own -respective thoughts.

Karen knew she must have lost weight. Even if the food her captor was usually providing had been better she realised that this terrible ordeal and the worry had affected her appetite. Now, though, she felt a feeling of some satisfaction brought on by eating the first food she had enjoyed since being brought there.

Looking at Karen but not seeing her, Joel Bush was already in San Diego. In his mind's eye they were in a Diner. Music played in the background, sometimes drowned out by laughter and ribaldry coming from other customers. Bush had a gigantic steak with a fried egg on top, onion rings, fries, beans and mushrooms. Francis had double cheeseburger and fries with lashings of some kind of sauce running down his jaw. Uncle Ulanski had an omelette salad. Bush could see himself with his new family, welcomed and comfortable in California. It was not long now.

He stood. Karen watched him piling the leftover food and the crockery onto a tray. As he opened the door he turned. "Tonight I am going to watch some films with you down here Karen. It is time to widen your knowledge. School is not the only place you can learn. I have some educational videos we can watch together. See you later, petal."

The look on the face of her captor had made it clear to Karen that the content of tonight's educational videos, would be unlikely found on a degree course of any English university.

*****

"I have some business upstairs, Gelsen. Eat, drink, and choose a female. Everything is free when you come here with me."

Tamayo ascended the stairs. Estella, who had been sitting silently sobbing, tensed. Footsteps were coming along the corridor. The room had become so dark that she could no longer see the mark of the water on the floor. Was this her opportunity?

The first bolt slid. Quickly Estella stood, picked up the chair, and positioned herself, she hoped, at the spot she had decided. The second bolt rattled, the handle turned, and the door was pushed slowly open. Estella raised the chair as high as she could above her head

The light from the corridor enabled Tamayo to see into the room. She was not where he had expected her to be, sitting on the bed. He took a step into the room and reached for the light switch with his left hand. A bottle of beer was in his right.
Estella summoned as much force as she could and brought the chair down. Her target was his head, but he had turned towards the light switch and it was his left shoulder that took the blow. It staggered him. The bottle of beer fell and Tamayo's knees buckled.

Estella rushed past him. She realised he had come alone. Estella turned right, swerved out of the door, and ran silently and as fast as she was able, to the end of the corridor where she thought the steps were. Tamayo awkwardly regained his feet and began an ungainly chase. Two stones overweight, averse to exercise, and still affected by the blow, there was no way a limping middle-aged man would be fast enough to catch a fit teenage maiden fleeing for life and honour. He began to shout.

Estella had descended two flights before she saw anyone else. A woman was supporting her punter as he attempted to negotiate the steps to paradise. The pair almost filled the stairway. Estella did her best to squeeze past, but the man was not so far gone that he did not recognise a good thing when he saw it. He grabbed Estella. The woman did not appreciate the competition and she pulled him off. Estella slipped but resumed her flight. Tamayo's shouting had had no effect on that pair. He also was delayed when he encountered them.

In her lounge Alegria saw on one of her screens, a young girl in school uniform running shoeless, pushing past the couple. Alegria's quarters were on the first floor. She went to her door, and stood in the doorway. When the hurtling Estella was almost opposite her door, Alegria stuck out a leg.
Estella fell heavily. Completely expressionless, Alegria stood over the shaken girl until Tamayo arrived, gasping and sweating. Like a fish floundering out of water, Estella lay open-mouthed, soundless and stranded.

Wordlessly the pair bent together and lifted the youngster to her feet, to begin the frogmarch up the three flights of stairs, to the room for "Recruits". The two females would have completed the journey in half the time, but they were hindered by the gasping, maladroit male. Eventually they arrived and the girl was dropped unprotestingly onto the bed.
Estella's failed flight had daunted the girl. She simply lay where she had been released. As the autumn leaf descends forlornly to the ground, never to rise again to be fanned by summer breezes, Estella wilted.
She felt defeated, hopeless. She capitulated; broken.

The woman manoeuvred the school blazer off, smiling sardonically at Tamayo who was by then edging slowly towards winning the struggle to regain a normal breathing pattern. As the pair began to move to fasten the restraining

straps, Alegria who was still vexed by Tamayo's incompetence, barked, "Face up or face down?"
"Down."

The one word reply was all Tamayo wished to offer at that point. As for the capitulating girl, there would be no slipping out of the strong leather restraints. Alegria buckled three and Tamayo one. Estella simply lay there with her face into the cotton sheet of the mattress. Her four limbs were easily spread to their extremities.
Sarcastically, and without any trace of humour, Alegria remarked, "Suitable for your purpose, Sergeant? Are you sure you are in condition? Perhaps you should appoint your young colleague to stand in; or perhaps up, for you?"

In reply he hobbled angrily to the door and opened it wide indicating her departure. As she moved to leave, Tamayo hissed, "It will go hard for this youngster this night."

Alegria laughed. Once she had witnessed his battle for hardness.
"Be sure to let me know when you have finished with her. Others, younger and much fitter are in line for this little treat tonight."

The door closed and Tamayo picked up the chair which had damaged his shoulder, and sat down heavily upon it.

Aloud, Estella muttered to the Holy Mother and beseeched for divine deliverance that never came.

Somewhere along his panting way to fulfilment Tamayo made a mental note to find out if lovely little Estella had any sisters.

Eventually, Tamayo left the pillaged maiden for the next man.

CHAPTER 41

"Right, that's it for now."
Detective Chief Inspector Mallard watched the detectives
in his much reduced Schoolgirl Team making their
respective ways back to their desks. Two were pretty
cheerful: DC Cropper had a weekend break organised and
DS Tate was flying to America tomorrow.

Philippa Tate went over to him. "Is it OK if I get off now,
sir? I still have loads to do before I set off for San Diego
tomorrow."
"You are not taking Frank with you are you? He has been
like a dog with two tails all week."

Try as she may Sergeant Tate could read nothing in his
face. Was he serious? They all knew where Frank was
taking his wife for her birthday; all, that is, except his wife.
Frank had told his wife they were going to Scarborough
for the weekend to watch Yorkshire thrash Lancashire at
cricket. On hearing the news of that outing his wife had
been very lukewarm about the idea. Since it was not
unknown for Yorkshire to be on the receiving end of a
thumping by Lancashire, his wife had qualms about
Frank's subsequent mood. If she had known about the
luxury spa weekend in York that Frank had secretly
booked for them she would have been delighted.
"Do you not know where Frank is going?"
"No Philippa I don't."
She told him.
He smiled. Was it relief?

"Have a successful family holiday. Philippa. Please give my very best wishes to your brother and everybody. Then come back to us poor sods here who toil in your absence. Seriously, Philippa I value the work you do here. For the first time in quite a while I am happy with my teams. Have a safe journey."

Mallard turned abruptly and went to his own office. There, briefly he contemplated his own immediate out-of work arrangements. It did not take long. He had none.

*****

In San Diego, Catalina Cruz stood in delight at actually being in the USA. She crossed herself and gave thanks to her Maker for a completed, safe journey, and for making her visit possible. Rosa and Luis had hugged her and been delighted to see her when they met her at the bus station. She was sure she would be happy in this lovely house in America. How could she remain there? What could she do to avoid going back home and to those dreadful men? Could she find a husband in America? She must do everything possible.

When she had finished unpacking, Catalina went to her knees. At home, before she had left, in that small room she called home, she had dropped to her knees and supplicated for a full hour asking for blessing, to come to America. She had been blessed; she was there. Now she beseeched to be able to stay.

*****

By Sunday night, Francis Ulanski, Philippa Tate, and Catalina Cruz, like pieces on a chess board, were all successfully and separately located in San Diego.

Sergeant Diego Tamayo was at that moment finalising his preparations to journey there to further his private business interests.

In two more days, one Joel Bush, would arrive and be the catalyst for momentous changes to the lives of the five of them – and others!

CHAPTER 42

Joel Bush was on holiday and he was excited about it. At 35,000 feet he adjusted his headphones, fiddled with the on-screen choices and found some music to which he could relax without effort. Francis had reassured his cousin that Lucek Ulanski was coping and that it was Joel's visit that was a major factor in his reasonable condition. Bush leaned back in his Club World seat, took another generous slurp of dry red Bordeaux wine, and stared out into a blue cloudless sky. Into his mind came imagined images of his uncle. Should he have many of the characteristics of his father, they would get along just fine. Bush gradually drifted off to sleep.

He was in the wood. Karen was with him in the wood. It was cold and gloomy for the sunlight which had been so bright on the journey, could barely penetrate the canopy of branches in that copse.
When he had lifted the blindfolded, gagged, and trussed girl from the back of the van, he knew he was holding Karen for the very last time. It was so entirely regrettable. What he was about to do chilled his heart. With Sophia it had been different. He remembered lifting Sophia in the pouring rain, dropping her, and staggering to discard her into the lonely field. Then he had felt only a panicky relief to be rid of her. Karen was different. Over the past several days he had wondered if he actually loved that girl. If it was not love, it was probably the nearest he was ever likely to get to it! Her body thrilled him; but there was so much more to this girl that enchanted him. It was amazing how positive she had kept throughout her captivity. He had tried to imagine himself in a similar situation. By no means

could he have kept up his spirits like Karen. Her intelligence and sense of humour had dazzled him. Now he had to do this. Bush was glad that Karen could not see the tears in his eyes.

As he looked at the helpless girl he had placed so gently onto the ground, there was a scream. It terrified him. It had not come from Karen, but it was right in his ear. It was screeching, deafening. The voice spoke; no bellowed, and then he recognised that voice. It was Sophia! She was with them. There were three of them in the wood now. Sophia was pleading.
"Bring me back, please. It is so dark and hideous in this place. Why have you done this to me? It is just a little scar. Please let me come back."

Maureen Winter glided silently up alongside the passenger and removed the wine glass and bottle. In her eleven years of long-haul service with BA she had seen pretty much everything. It was not unusual for sleeping travellers to kick and jerk quietly in a troubled sleep. This one, so far, was enduring the experience in silence. If he threshed around, as they sometimes did, she would wake him.

Bush suffered in silence as the two lovely faces of both schoolgirls floated before him. Presently though, they morphed into macabre dripping skulls. They hovered menacingly with gaping mouths which opened and closed, intent on devouring him.

Maureen Winter heard the scream and hurried back.

*****

Limping slightly, Sergeant Tamayo selected a seat in a corner and looked around *El Retiro* which was busy as usual that Saturday night. He watched Alegria who acknowledged his arrival with just a slight nod of her head. Smiling she went over to Estella whose formerly pristine school uniform was showing the effects of the attention of many a customer's interest. Alegria spoke to the girl who looked over at Tamayo. After just a brief but stimulated argument, Estella walked dejectedly towards his table. Tamayo took hold of her arm and guided the girl to sit on his knee. She leaned back as she had been trained to do on her first day of working in the main salon. Though the girl hated Tamayo she had no choice.

Not for the first time Tamayo wished he could manoeuvre Alegria into taking him in as a part-owner. The place was a gold mine..
All was ready for his journey to San Diego. Tamayo would not take his own vehicle which was police property, to the USA. If anything went wrong it was better not to involve the force in any way. He had organised a Buick LaCrosse Premium II. With its owner locked away for further investigations there would be no need to hurry to return the car.

Tamayo relaxed his clutching hands and allowed Estella to sit upright. Told to fetch him another beer, the girl stood, felt the routine buttock patting, and made her way to get it. Tamayo watched her young haunches jiggle as she walked on the three inch heels. Perhaps he would spend some time upstairs with her later.

*****

"Terminal 2, Meeting Zone R, this is it."
Joel Bush pushed his trolley past all the other passengers with their bulging trolleys. He slowly looked around and saw it almost at once. A large white cardboard sign with his name written in blue felt tip was being waved in a huge arc,
"JOEL WELCOME"

They embraced, Francis Ulanski smiling warmly and trying to hold the big cardboard sign out of harm's way, whilst a relieved and emotional Joel Bush clutched his cousin in a fierce grip almost amounting to passion.
His relief that the journey was over was palpable. The nervousness that something would go wrong and he would not meet up with Francis has started well before he had left home. Then that nightmare on the plane, and the awful mindfulness of having lost Karen for ever. That had stayed with him throughout the flight. Francis could feel the acuteness of his grip.

"Come on Cus. Time to move on. Let's be off to meet my father."
The moment was over. Bush regained his control and followed his cousin. They left the building and made their way to Ulanski's car.

"Good flight?"
The car was eating up the miles and it simply purred along with barely a sound from the engine or road. Bush felt so much better being with Francis.
"Better now it's over. How is your dad?"

"He is hanging on. The doctor seems surprised he is doing so well. He can't wait to meet you."

"Same goes for me. He is the only one I know who has any experience of the country where my existence started. Where my parents grew up. Sad really."

Francis turned on the CD player. A jazz tune came from the four speakers as Stompin' at the Savoy resonated throughout the car.

CHAPTER 43

They insisted on buying everything. All that food piled
onto the first shopping trolley which Luis now pushed,
steering it effortlessly through the thinly populated mall. It
would have taken Catalina six months to earn that money.
The second trolley was being used for clothing as Rosa
excitedly babbled with her younger sister, choosing for
Catalina item after item of tops and skirts which she really
must have in her armoury if she was to trap an
unsuspecting husband in quick time. The two had
discussed and schemed all the previous evening. In three
weeks time Catalina would be home in Sanorias City
unless a miracle happened. They had prayed, down on
their knees for much of the evening.

Prayers were all very well, Rosa had remarked at one point
whilst rising from her knees, but it would be skillful wily
outfits, and what went inside them that would put the Holy
Mother on the road to snaring a man for her innocent
worshipper. Catalina had winced when she had heard the
word innocent. She had no intention of revealing how she
had been outraged.

Luis was happy. Next weekend there was to be no
"collection" over the border. As a consequence, Alfred
Walberg had decided that it was time he kept his hand in
himself on the collection of spares in Mexico and he would
make the run next weekend. Walberg had notified Luis
that he could take the weekend off.

Into the shoe section they went. Luis was proud to be able
to accompany the two bright-eyed attractive females and to
comfortably be able to meet the cost of the mounting
expense as the pair carefully chose another artful piece of
leather sculpture for Catalina's feet. As she giggled and

gushed, hardly able to get her words out quickly enough, Catalina stretched and angled her legs to display each particular shoe. Her movement was noticed.

Little Philip simply must have new shoes for the Christening. David and Lauren Tate made their way slowly to the seated area and began a methodical search for a suitable pair. David Tate had seen Catalina first as she studied how the shoes looked on her feet, his attention caught by her shapely legs.
Luis saw and recognised David Tate. As neighbours, they had waved to other each from across the road, but never actually met. Luis walked across. After introducing themselves and chatting for a few minutes, they shook hands and Luis went back to his females. By then there were four pairs of shoes in the trolley; one pair of white stylish sandals, and three pairs of sexy stilettos.

"Honey we have been invited to our neighbour's party on Sunday. Their son over there is being christened and we are invited to join them all when they come back from church."
Rosa and Catalina looked across at the Tates, gave a friendly wave, and then quickly renewed the quest for trainers.

*****

Whilst her brother and his wife were shopping, Philippa Tate had been busy on her computer creating a Holiday Diary. When they returned with provisions the pair proudly showed Philippa the little shoes they had bought for ten months old Philip who was asleep by then.

Obviously he was not excessively impressed with the purchase.

A short time after resuming her Diary, Philippa was stopped in her tracks. The computer screen froze. Nothing she did over the next half hour improved the situation. Whilst she was adept at inputting and using computers of various types and sizes, she was no technician. Philippa was stumped.

Her brother could not rectify it either.
"The guy next door is a wiz with computers. I will see if he is in. He will probably be able to fix it, sis."
"Can we? Will he mind?"
"I think he will be pleased actually. He lives alone; I should think he appreciates some company from time to time. I know I would. We were at school together for a time so we know each other from way back."

He picked up the phone.
"Is he coming on Sunday?
"Never thought to ask him. I suppose I should, next door neighbour and all."
Lauren Tate had put Philip in his crib and came into the room.
"David, ring him and ask him to come on Sunday. Then ask him if he is free to look at Philippa's computer sometime."
"Women! How sneaky the species can be. No wonder you run rings around us guys."
The two women just smiled and watched him dial.
After a brief conversation David announced that the guy was on his way.

David went to meet him at the door and showed him inside. Within two minutes the next door neighbour said he could almost certainly fix it, but he needed the software which was at home. He would be happy to have a crack at it at home. Philippa could see he was keen to help. The man was a little older than her but not by much, she judged. She saw him look at her. He wanted her to go round. Would Philippa like to come round whilst he fixed the computer? He needed to be off to his father's house soon but ought to be able to fix it before he went.

Philippa looked at her brother and sister-in-law who were looking relaxed. She looked again at the rather good looking neighbour. Should she go?
"That is very kind of you."
Smiling winningly, Philippa saw a happy grin spread across the man's face.
"Right, let's go, then," said Francis Ulanski as he walked towards the door carrying the computer..

*****

"Hi, it's me. Everything OK, Joel?"
"Brilliant. We get along just fine your dad and me, Francis."
The sick old man looked over to Bush and his eyes could just make out his nephew standing with the phone to his ear.
"But I think he is getting a bit tired, mate. You coming soon?"

"Setting off now, but I have some news. I have just met the sister of my next door neighbour and she is a bit of a looker. More than that though they have invited us to a party next Sunday at their place. Pretty cool eh?"

"Yep, sounds great."

"See you in ten."

The phone went dead.

CHAPTER 44

Inspector Nina Hussein specialised in sex crimes. Her colleague Detective Sergeant Beth Jones had a degree in psychology. They sat in separate chairs opposite the settee. They had moved the two chairs together so that both of them could easily be seen. It was the sergeant who spoke initially.

"Are you completely sure that you are up to talking to us right now? We do not want you to feel under any pressure. If you do not feel you can, it will be OK another time. The sooner we have the information, though, the better we will be able to act."

The girl nodded. Sitting beside her on the settee her mother squeezed the hand of the girl.

"I don't want to talk about anything, you know, I mean I can't, not personal, not yet, not now."

"That is fine, love. It is perfectly understandable. I would be the exactly the same. Talk when you are ready. Only talk now about what you feel you can talk about, love."

"I don't know where to start. It was so awful. I can't believe he let me go. I thought he was sure to kill me."

"Tell us about how he let you go, Karen, love."

"I was watching some old film on TV."

The two police officers jumped. Inspector Hussein reacted first.

"He let you watch TV, Karen?"

She must know about Sophia then.

"Not TV proper. Just the set, with no aerial but with a DVD player."

The officers sat back. They did not want to reveal yet what had happened to her friend.

"He came in and I could see he was all agitated. He kept walking up and down, sitting next to me on the bed ..."

"Aaaagh, oh God."

The wail from the mother had stopped the girl's flow. The officers had wanted to keep the mother out of the interview but she was having none of it. It took several minutes to calm things down.

"He just said I am letting you go tonight, in half an hour. Dress yourself in your skating outfit. I will come back soon. I got dressed; I mean I changed into my skating things."

The officers could tell she was saying it like that because her mother was there. Next session would simply have to be without the mother. No girl is ever going to be completely frank about an ordeal like this with the mother there. The account would be drastically expurgated.

"When he came back he tied my hands behind my back, tied my ankles, blindfolded and gagged me, and put a hood on my head. Then he carried me to his vehicle and told me not to make a noise. He wouldn't tell me where he was taking me.

It seemed he drove, like ages, and I was scared stiff but we got there and everything was quiet. He put me on the ground and took off the hood, the blindfold and the gag. Then he told me we were in a wood in Derbyshire. He was going to free my wrists but leave my ankles tied. I had to untie the knots around my ankles myself. This would give him time to get away. When I had done that I was to walk out of the wood. He pointed to me where to go; there was a path. I would come to a road. I was to stand there and wait for the police. In half an hour, he said he would dial 999 and tell them where to find me.

It was funny in a way. I don't mean funny, I mean strange. He was really concerned because he said if any car or vehicle came I was to hide. He said it was not safe for a girl dressed like me, short skirt and everything, to be alone out there. Don't get in any vehicle unless it is a marked police car. He was just like my mom or some teachers at school. He was worried for me. Can you imagine? What he had been …"

Karen stopped and looked anxiously at her mother. Karen did not need to say any more. The two officers could imagine what he would have been doing.

CHAPTER 45

Rosa and Catalina had experimented and pondered all
Sunday morning but finally the decisions were made. Their
outfits for the afternoon party were elegantly laid out on
their respective beds and they sat talking in the garden.
Luis Vasquez wondered what on earth women find to talk
about ceaselessly. If he could have heard them he would
have known of the partial revealing of her tribulations at
the hands of the police. Rosa learned some of Catalina's
experience but the account was sanitised. They both agreed
she could not return.

As always on Sundays, Luis washed and leathered his
vehicle. As he leathered, a beautiful new saloon purred
sedately and almost regally along the road. He recognised
the type. Since he was a boy, he had always taken an
interest in cars. He was given his first car ride by his
brother who had just "acquired" it. That acquisition was
soon to lead to his brother, minus four teeth, enjoying the
hospitality of the Federal Centre for Social Rehabilitation
for two years. Luis watched the Buick LaCrosse Premium
II pull into the small SD Dream Hotel seventy five yards
away from where he stood. He was interested to see which
lucky man had that desirable motor.

Sergeant Tamayo slowly climbed out, stood, stretched
himself in the sunshine, and ambled into the nondescript
hideaway.

Luis Vasquez was too far away to recognise him.

Tamayo was completely unaware that at that very moment,
a small gathering of locals was formed back in Sanorias
City. As the central living character, the priest spoke
solemnly and with extra sincerity, for the widowed mother

had managed to convey to him, even through her uncontrolled tearful outbursts, the circumstances which had led up to that outcome. The funeral service of Yazmin Gonzales and her father was brief but poignant. As the priest watched the mourners depart he wondered, not for the first time, if his god would ever intervene and bring just a little degree of humanity to the authorities in his country.

*****

When a church service of an infinitely more joyful kind had ended, baby Philip and his proud parents emerged into the morning sunshine followed by Philippa Tate, the mother of Philippa and David, and other invited relatives.

They made their way back to complete the preparations for the afternoon celebration. David Tate went to ignite the Bar-B-Q. An Englishman, a butcher, had volunteered to oversee the charcoal–smoking, slow cooking of the meat and fish. This meant an early lighting. David Tate also needed to check that the cleaning of the swimming pool had been completed. The bar staff were due to arrive in one hour and the entertainers in two.

Bush's father had loved Bar-B-Qs and had prided himself on his knowledge and inventiveness in both cooking and presentation of all types of foodstuffs. Meat would have been selected and brought from his own shop. Joel had been a keen observer of everything his father did and had himself become proficient. Joel Bush was in his element explaining to David Tate what he proposed to do with the available food. David Tate watched. This cousin of his neighbour Francis Ulanski seemed to know what he was doing.

Francis Ulanski had arrived with Joel and was sitting alone by the pool, hoping that Philippa would arrive soon so that he could spend some time with her before the other guests arrived. She had made an impression on him. He wondered what she did for a living; probably something like teaching. A lot of teachers were on vacation and the chances were she taught – maybe at a private girls boarding school. Hopefully she liked men. What he had seen so far had given him hope.

Philippa Tate checked her image in the full length mirror in her bedroom. She wore a white sunhat with a large brim, a thin yellow, décolleté cotton blouse which she had aligned well down her arms leaving the smooth white skin of her shoulders entirely bare. Her short cotton, slightly flared skirt of white, was exactly the shade of the sunhat, and a pair of smart heeled sandals completed her outfit. She could smell the charcoal smoke and guessed that the Englishman she had not yet met would be attending it. Francis would have arrived with him. Satisfied with her image, she picked up her shades, twirled them between her fingers, and set off to find the interesting Francis Ulanski.

She saw Francis as soon as she left the house. He was reading something. Philippa did not approach him, but took the long way, strolling around the pool, as if idly ambling with time to kill. With peripheral vision Philippa watched him as she sauntered. He spotted her and stood. She smiled, flushing inwardly as she pretended not to notice his eager attempts to attract her attention. When she *accidentally* looked his way, she waved back and walked towards him. From his position behind his glowing fire, Joel Bush figured that the girl would be the Philippa that Francis was keen on. He could see why.

*****

Except for the accumulation of money, Sergeant Tamayo had one other obsession, and one hobby. The obsession was regularly satisfied by willing and, more often unwilling, females in Sanorias City: although in America his lust usually went unfulfilled. Horseracing was his hobby. It was his intention to visit the Del Mar racetrack, twenty miles north of downtown San Diego. First though, must come completing the final arrangements for his new business. That would be done tomorrow.

Moonlight Beach was one of the reasons Tamayo chose Encinitas to stay when visiting San Diego and at two o'clock he threw the towel, with his swimming trunks wrapped inside, into the back of the car and drove from the parking area of the SD Dream Hotel, heading for an afternoon of lazing and a little swimming.

Even though the house in which Catalina was staying was less than a hundred yards from the SD Dream Hotel, it was altogether a matter of great coincidence that he should be driving down that road at the instant that she began to cross it, heading for the party. Excitedly gushing out her words, to which her sister was paying scant attention, Catalina was barely aware of a car which passed safely behind her and continued down the street. She was completely oblivious of Tamayo who stared at the girl in disbelief.

Throughout the Drive to Moonlight Beach, Tamayo's mind schemed and sought a way to ensnare the desirable girl to pacify for a while, his non-monetary obsession.

CHAPTER 46

Small talk had turned to innuendo with a good measure of lingering eye contact. Each of them was verbally fishing and exploring the other. Neither was disappointed or discouraged: they were bonding well. Both realised that quite soon, the touchy-feely, tentative first stages would increase, leading to more physical closeness. People were filtering in but the pair did not notice. It had been quite some time since Philippa had been romantically attached. She was pleased she had chosen the off-the-shoulder blouse. Philippa could see the eyes of the man opposite admiring the view of the vivacious young woman before him. If, as was likely at some point, this man told her how lovely were her shoulders, he would not be the first.

"That meat smells delicious." Philippa had consumed only a little orange juice and the waft from the Bar-B-Q was tantalizing.
"You are not a vegetarian, then?"
"Certainly not. You?"
"No way."
"The chef is your cousin is he?"
"He is. Have you met him yet?"
"No. Maybe we should go and use your influence to jump to the head of the queue. I am ravenous."
"Are all your appetites as keen as your hunger?"
Philippa regarded him coyly.
"My temper can be if some forward libertine irritates me."
It was said with laugh and accompanied by Philippa slipping her arm through that of Francis as they began to slowly wander the length of the swimming pool towards Joel Bush and his white-hot charcoals.

Bush noticed them approaching and felt a pang of envy. Francis had only met her last night. It brought back the memory of his Karen. The sun beat down on the pair but there was a welcome breeze. The girl was dressed for the summer heat. The big white hat heightened her femininity. Not that she needed help. Whoever this girl was, she was a cracker.

The couple stopped, or at least the girl did, and Francis was jerked to a halt.

"Francis, where does your cousin live?"

"Bloody hell. You stopped a bit quick. England."

"Where in England?"

"A place in the North called Sheffield. Why?"

"When did he come to San Diego, Francis?"

"What's that got to do with anything, Philippa? Come and meet him."

"When did he leave England?"

"Last Tuesday."

"What is his name, Francis?"

"Joel Bush."

Francis Ulanski was perplexed. The happy smiling relaxed Philippa had gone. In her place was a frowning troubled female who had released his arm and stood three feet away from him. What in the world had he done wrong?

"Will you excuse me Francis? I need the Ladies Room."

Francis looked at his cousin. By his gestures Joel was enquiring why the girl he had not recognised had suddenly dashed away. Ulanski shook his head and shrugged.

*****

Luis and Rosa Vasquez were with Catalina seated at a table which was some thirty feet away from the Bar-B-Q. Luis had shovelled down a decent quantity of food and had begun to wash it down with the iced bottles of beer he kept fetching from about thirty feet away. As he fetched another, the girls were whispering. That big fellow with the unfortunate looks kept looking across at them whenever he took a rest from serving the food. It was highly likely that it was Catalina he was really looking at. Luis had no inkling. To test out the supposition, Catalina had walked absent-mindedly around the pool. Rosa watched Bush. Sure enough the chef's eyes had travelled with Catalina – or, more accurately, on her. The girls now knew. Was he alone, or with his wife? Information was required. Rosa went to the Bar-B-Q and whilst she chose food she engaged the chef in conversation.
She returned.
The bad news outweighed the good. He was not American and he was on holiday. Holy Virgin, but he was not a pretty sight either. Also he must be the wrong side of thirty years old. The only good thing was that his wife had not come with him to America because he had no wife. Catalina must look elsewhere for a man.

*****

He had swum a little, lazed a lot, watched the volleyball and dined well in one of the restaurants at Moonlight Beach.

Back in his hotel room Tamayo sat on the bed and rang Gelsen Jara.

"How are things, Gelsen?
"Same as ever sergeant. A little crime, a little punishment, and a little commission."
"How much commission?"
"Exactly as last week, senor. They all paid me. I told them you would be here next week and would be most unhappy….."
"Yes, yes. Listen Gelson. I have seen a girl here you will like. Her visa expires after one month and she will be with us again. You remember I told you about Catalina Cruz? She is living just down my street here in San Diego."
"No shit"
"Right. When she gets back home she must come and see us, eh amigo?"

Some time later on his hotel roof he could see and hear a party in the distance. He finished his cigar and returned to his room. It was almost dark and he was bored. Tamayo decided to take a walk down in the direction of the party to see what was happening. Perhaps he could gatecrash. It would be better than spending the rest of the evening alone.

CHAPTER 47

Tamayo could clearly hear the gaiety from the street. Chancing his luck he climbed the four steps and slowly, confidently sauntered into the pool area. He chose a seat at an unoccupied table, sat down, and fished in his shirt pocket for a cigar. He was in.

Out, was Catalina. Joel Bush was the only one at that moment who had been paying any attention to Catalina. He had seen the look of pure terror and unmistakable consternation, transform her features. He turned to where she had been looking and saw Tamayo, still engrossed with his cigar. Bush shot out of his seat and chased after Catalina. He found the girl hiding behind the house.

After half an hour together inside the house, Bush obtained some of the story. It was nothing like a full account of what had happened to Catalina, but it was a general graphic tale of the experiences commonly suffered at the hands of the authorities in her town. Bush was incensed. This lovely girl was here at a family party in America, and was terrified because of this man. He, Joel Bush would protect her! And he meant it. He would.
Catalina looked at the man. She saw the features which she and Rosa had already disparaged: but now she saw something else too. She saw concern; in his manner, his voice, and especially his eyes. His brown eyes looked into hers with genuine feeling. She had seen feeling in men's eyes before, of a quite different persuasion. Never before had she known a man who had consideration *for* her. This man had. It was a revelation. He was a big man; strong looking. Catalina felt safe with him.

This man earlier had been looking at her a lot. Could she overlook his features?

"Stay here. I will get rid of him."

Bush went outside and spoke briefly to David Tate, checked that the man was not an invited guest, and walked over to Tamayo who by then had a beer, his cigar and his feet up on another chair. His eyes were half closed as he listened to a gentle song of unrequited love, into which the female singer was putting her heart and soul. Holding Tamayo by the neck from behind, Bush lifted and propelled the much smaller man to the top step leading down to the garden and the road beyond. Down they went at a pace. Tamayo was ignominiously shoved off the premises falling in a heap in the road.
The words he heard from Bush, fell short of a civil good-night.
"Fuck off, and stay away."

Catalina had crept apprehensively out of the house to watch what Bush would do. As he walked nonchalantly back up the steps he saw Catalina waiting for him. She had decided.
The tender kiss on the cheek of Joel Bush, as she stood high on tiptoe to reach him, was the precursor of others delivered later elsewhere, and with more fervour later that night.
His cousin received just a polite chaste peck on the cheek from Philippa when he departed, uncomprehending and disillusioned.

*****

When Francis had left, Philippa went straight to her computer to check online for developments in the Schoolgirls case. The information obtained from Karen was listed. Philippa noted down the items she wanted.

Big man aged up to 40. Brown eyes
Big hands. Rough hands. BO. at times
Yorkshire accent probably Sheffield
Ten minutes drive from Arena.
Kept in basement. Basement 14 steps down.
Few street sounds. Good crockery.
Given female clothes which fitted (Sister? Wife?)
Chinese take-away nearby. Not in remote area, then.

Joel Bush?

Was it really possible? Bush was here, no doubt, but was it fate that had brought her close to him again?
She considered the facts about him that she knew.
Fits the CCTV at the skating rink.
Big man, up to 40, brown eyes, big rough   hands
Yorkshire accent
In England when Karen held captive.

Every item she had just written obtained from Karen fitted.

They had suspected him before. Nothing known about him would rule him out. He must surely be considered a suspect.

She remembered her Harvard days. Think clearly they had emphasised. Cut out the deadwood. Look at the wood not the trees. Remember Ockham's razor.

She was clear. Sergeant Philippa Tate was not going to let this go. She resolved to investigate Bush more.

Reluctantly she decided she must definitely not date Francis.

CHAPTER 48

Mallard had been furious but was unable to prevent it. Her parents had taken Karen to Crete. All three of them, they had insisted, needed to get away from everything and have a complete break. It was a two week long holiday, and another nine days before they came home. There was so much more Mallard and his team hoped to learn from Karen.

His team stopped what they were doing when Mallard walked into the Incident Room. His face told them that whatever it was, it would be bad news. He uncharacteristically seated himself on the corner of a desk. It was clear that he could hardly speak.

"She is dead. Karen died this morning in Crete."
Mallard stood and slowly, with a heavy tread, retreated to his office.

The officers quickly discovered that she had been swimming in the Carpathian Sea when two youths on a jet ski ran into her. At the hospital she was pronounced DOA. There would be no ID parade or further information obtainable from Karen.

CHAPTER 49

Joel Bush lay in the shade and reflected on the past two weeks of his life since he had first met Catalina. She lay asleep beside him on her sunbed. It had been a whirlwind two weeks during which he had learned more of Catalina and the dilemma that she faced; fallen in love with her; bought the engagement ring, had heard with delight her acceptance of his marriage proposal; and proudly taken her to meet uncle Lucek.

Five days later there had been a sadder appointment; the funeral of the seventy-one year old Lucek.

After the engagement, firm plans were made and decisions taken. After the wedding Bush would have to fly home to attend to his business. Catalina was not returning to Sanorias. They would marry in Mexico City and had already engaged a wedding planning agency to arrange both the paperwork and the wedding. The wedding needed to be legally accepted in the UK and would take place at a civil registry the following week. A church wedding would be arranged later. The couple would live together in Sheffield when immigration for the wife was accepted. They both wanted children.

*****

Philippa Tate did not want Bush to recognise her and had to keep her distance. She reasoned that she must also keep only an arm's length connection with Francis. Her best source of information had to be Catalina, and Philippa was doing her best to foster a close relationship. It was not a simple matter because Bush was almost always there. On the evening that the two cousins had arranged to catch a baseball match, it enabled Catalina to go over.

They had been sitting by the pool, drinking a little wine and chattering a lot. Philippa kept steering the conversation round to Joel but had learned nothing of value. Catalina was engaged; she would move to Sheffield, have babies and live a wonderful life. It was all so staggering. Philippa knew probing further that night would be a waste of time and relaxed. She went off-duty, and they spoke of men in general.

"I get so mad when men look at me and strip me with their eyes. It happens all the time, at work, in the street, on a bus, everywhere." Catalina was feeling the effect of the white wine and venting a long-standing annoyance. Philippa was rather more used to wine and was more philosophical, although she too attracted plenty of attention from the opposite sex.

"Calm down, Catalina. May I tell you something quite true? One day when I was on the New York subway, I happened to be sitting next to a well dressed lady of about middle age. I noticed her shoes were expensive and her clothes were good quality. She had an attractive hairdo and tinted, brown hair. Her make-up was discrete and effective. She had looked after herself and watched her weight because I could see she still had a good figure. Probably on her way to some event or other, her total appearance was excellent. I was going home from college and was dressed in the baggy comfortable clothes I had worn all day. My hair was untidy and I was hot and tired and ready for the shower. I was about your age.

Further up the train three men had their backs to us and they sat and talked quietly about a football game. When their station approached, they walked down and had to pass by us to reach the doors. They were all of a similar age to the woman next to me. As they approached all three men fixed their eyes on me, looked me up and down, and virtually undressed me. Their eyes never went to the other lady. As they got off the train I hissed quietly through my teeth,

"Bloody men!"

Although I had intended to say it to myself it had come out loud enough for the lady to hear. She turned to me and smiled.

"Young lady, it does not last. There comes a time, quicker than you expect, that you find you have become older. When you have reached a certain point, men stop looking. You may well discover, as I do, that you look back on the attractive times with nostalgia. Enjoy it while you can. When it is gone, it is permanently gone. Beauty is a fleeting thing - like a ripple on a rolling river."

Then she stood and she too was gone.

Now when men look, I remember her words – and I relax."

"I will try to remember, but I bet will still get angry."

"I hope we can be friends, Catalina when you get to Sheffield."

"Oh I want that too. I will not know anybody over there, and my English is not so good. I speak some but cannot read."

"Your English is fine. Your accent is attractive. Don't try to change it. Enjoy your culture."

CHAPTER 50

It felt weird being in the house alone. A feeling of complete and unreal fancy would come over him at times. Like that time he had been in the air going to America. It felt as though he had just awoken from another fitful, seven-mile high, dream and that it had all been just pure reverie. Until he looked down. There it was in plain sight: it was real. He could touch it, feel it, turn it round, and twist it on his finger. It was no dream. That wedding ring was proof. The lovely Catalina had placed it lovingly upon the marriage finger of his left hand. She now wore his. His wife, HIS WIFE, wore his ring!

He regretted that their wedding in Mexico City had been over so quickly. Still, it was all properly legal.

Yet now he was alone. One of them at least should be with him. He had barely given a thought to the youngster Karen, such had been the breathtaking tumultuous speed of recent events. It had been the hardest thing he had ever had to do, parting with Karen. Where was she now? On that late September evening, where would the youngster with the winning smile and smart intelligence be? Of course she would have told the police about their time together: that was inevitable. Their time together had meant a lot to him, but for the girl? There was not much chance of that. Could she have revealed anything that would lead the police to him? Maybe, but he could never countenance ending that sweet life. But could she? If they were on his trail they would know he was back. They had not come. It was only the first day, but they were not there. Strange he had never even thought about it when away. Too late now anyway.

Still there was an important job to do; not until tomorrow though. It would have to wait. Getting rid of everything from that basement would not take too long, but it needed cleaning and decorating before his wife arrived. He could still hardly believe it.

*****

"It was started deliberately according to the Fire Officer. We are looking at murder. I want another Briefing here at 2000 hours."

Chief Inspector Mallard needed another murder enquiry like he needed a hole in the head. This was the third serious crime in a week. He had managed to duck the second but not this. With seven people dead it had landed fairly and squarely with him.
He was nearly back to his office when DS Tate intercepted him.
"Can I have a word?"
"Come in, Philippa. What is it?"
"Thursday is the funeral of Karen Clayton at last. I think I should attend."
"The family managed to get her body back from the Greek authorities, then? About bloody time too. Yes you should go. Look sit down for a minute. The family will ask where we are with finding the swine who took her. We have nothing to tell them."

"I have been through everything since I returned from California and it seems we are left with just one possibility, unless he snatches another girl."

"Go on."

"Bush."

"Bush? Ah yes Mr. Bush. The man we are warned by the ACC to leave alone. That Bush?"

"Yes, sir. Joel Bush. A man we identified as a possible, way back. A man whose size fits the CCTV at the skating rink. A man with a van of the type Frank saw in Hagg Hill. The description Karen gave fits him; big man, heavy, big hands, rough hands, Sheffield accent."

"It will not have bypassed your undoubted intelligence that the description you just gave, except for Hagg Hill, fits hundreds of men in Sheffield. Also we are free to investigate the entire population of Sheffield except one: Joel Bush."

"I know, sir."

"You have a bee in your bonnet, sergeant. Do you also have a plan? I think I know you well enough to think that you would not be pulling my strings like this unless you also have something up your sleeve."

"We are certain that the same man, who abducted Karen, had snatched Sophia the previous week. Remember we have the DNA of a man from Sophia's bed? Well if we can prove it is Bush by getting his DNA then we have him."

"And Bush of course is going to turn up here one bright morning and give us a sample do you think?"

"No sir, we have to arrest him first."

"I think you need another holiday, sergeant. I am being patient with you but it is wearing very thin"

"You know from the report I sent you whilst I was there that Bush was staying in the same street. Whilst he was there, after my report, he met a girl and married her. Well, I went out of my way to make friends with Bush's wife in San Diego. They are trying for her to come and live here in Sheffield. When she comes to Sheffield we have agreed that we will meet up, not with Joel Bush there of course. Catalina does not know I am a detective.

If I can get into their house when Bush is out, I can get a sample of his hair, analyse it in the lab, and we can arrest him on suspicion if it is positive, and Bingo. You will have to dream up a reason to arrest him. Don't leave all the clever stuff to me, sir."

Mallard looked at the beaming Philippa. He walked over to her, reached out, and gently squeezed her shoulder. He did not need any words. Philippa uncharacteristically blushed.

Out in the general office, the office filled with diligent crime-fighters, the office in which no-one misses a trick; in that office eyebrows were raised, and another rumour was born.

*****

Sergeant Diego Tamayo knew Catalina should have returned home from the USA. Her visa which had been valid for one month had already expired. The two men he had sent round to her address had reported that there had been no sign of her. They had entered her room and seen her belongings. The neighbours expected her at any time. She would be back. But was she dead? He checked a list of known deceased females. That she was not on the list was far from conclusive; he knew that better than most. He could wait; he would invite her for another interview when she returned. He smiled; his new partner Gelsen Jara was learning to be an enthusiastic interviewer in that special, quiet office.

CHAPTER 51

Catalina's sister Rosa went and collected all of Catalina's belongings three days later. There was not much. She and her husband loaded them into their car and took them to San Diego.

Catalina knew improving her English would be much easier once she was living in England. Each morning she attended a small class in Mexico city where she was taught English along with five other pupils. All of the other students had to go to work, but not she.

In the afternoon she had computer lessons in a different place. There, in an attic room, she was being taught by a woman with only one leg how to use her brand new laptop. Catalina was the only pupil and it was apparent that the woman was glad of the company. She was an American who had married a Mexican singer. She had been widowed for over twenty years and had been obliged to work after the death of her husband. One day making her way to work on a small motorbike, she had been struck by a lorry that had come straight out of a side road. That was how she lost her leg. She had been depressed after the accident and had taken to the bottle. The woman still had a sense of humour, though.

"I was legless in more ways than one for a time" she had told Catalina.

Already Catalina could use a Search Engine. Soon she would learn how to use Skype. When she could do that she could talk to Joel and see him on the monitor. Joel had shown her and they had spoken to Francis on Skype for ages – and it was free, absolutely free. It was amazing. She was learning everything as fast as she could.

Catalina Bush was loving her new life in Mexico City. Her husband had found her a room and paid rent for a full six months in advance. They had opened a bank account for her which she had never had before, Catalina had a debit card but he would not let his wife have a credit card. Every week lovely Joel transferred money into her account and all Catalina had to do was to skip to the bank and fetch some money. She must always use the ATM inside the bank and not the ones on the pavement outside. Others were nearer to where she lived but her husband had insisted she must use that particular one, inside that particular bank. She must put the money safely in her purse before leaving the bank. No problem, her husband provided money and she did not have to do any work. This was heaven.
Joel had bought her a Samsung Smartphone and she spoke to him every day.

She could phone her sister anytime. Rosa had been to Sanorias with Luis to fetch Catalina's belongings. Catalina would never have to go there again.

She must keep her husband happy of course; but that should be easy. He took care of her so well when he was with her, and Catalina was determined she would take care of him.
She had been so surprised how emotional Joel had been that first night on honeymoon after the wedding in Mexico City. She had happily surrendered her virginity and he had been delighted to be the first.

Now she was pleased that those two brutes, animals that they were, had left her intact. That was not the reason that Joel had been emotional, though. Over the hours and days they had lain together, Joel had told her of his life. She understood and was pleased she could end his loneliness for ever. All because she went to America: lovely, lovely America.

*****

The basement was almost bare. Even the TV and DVD player that he had fetched downstairs for Karen to watch, had been dumped in the council tip. He knew he would never have been able to look at them again without being reminded of her. All the walls and the ceiling needed emulsion. Should he paint it himself? No; ring a decorator. The basement was priority number one; he must be sure there were no traces of either girl. The carpet upon which he stood was barely worn at all and could stay. Ok, he had vacuumed well; now a painter was needed .
Their bedroom must be sorted out too, but the basement was first.
He went upstairs and found the number of his usual decorator. The painting was fixed for two weeks hence. Should he buy a new bed? He would.

Then he rang his wife. Catalina had been waiting. She answered immediately.

*****

At breakfast Bush mechanically shovelled spoonfuls of cereal into his mouth whilst he scanned the morning paper. He usually began at the sports pages at the back. It was habit and a masochistic one. A Sheffield man from birth, he would have loved one day to be able to pick up the paper and read something cheerful about football. Sheffield has two allegedly professional football teams. It was always a waste of time expecting good news from either.

On his second cup of coffee, the cup stopped abruptly, midway to his lips. He did not believe it. There at the foot of page two, in a single column, was a three-inch piece referring to the funeral later that day of a schoolgirl killed on holiday on a Greek island.

*****

Many of the people present had to listen to the service outside the church. There was a huge number of pupils and staff from her school, together with her relatives, her friends, and other people who had simply read of her and wept. Once the church was full, the others stayed outside. Two such mourners who stood for tactical reasons outside were DS Philippa Tate and PC Trevor Higgs-Whitethorn. In an unmarked police car, parked so as to be ready in case of emergency were four officers. The police hoped that the abductor would attend. Two more officers with powerful film cameras were filming everyone through the open window of a house opposite the main entrance to the church. A police helicopter was on standby. Philippa looked for Bush. She would recognise him with or without the disguise. Karen Clayton was laid to rest within the church grounds. Many a tear fell. None belonged to Joel Bush. Conquering his instincts he had wisely decided to stay home.

CHAPTER 52

At exactly 10.00 p.m. Bush went to his computer, accessed Skype and waited for Catalina to answer. It was 4.00 p.m. in Mexico City and she should be home. Since they had tearfully parted, the routine of his wife for five days every week had not varied; morning English, afternoon Computing. She was learning very well and they used Skype every day now.

"Hello darling."

Her face smiling on the computer looked as lovely as ever. Time was passing so slowly for Joel. He was an Englishman, born and bred in Sheffield. All his life he had worked hard and paid his taxes. Yet the government, his government – he had voted for this lot – would not let him live in England with his wife. She was in Mexico, he in England. Two people who loved each other, they were married not just living in sin, two who were married were being kept apart by the government, not her government – his!
Bastards!

"Hello Catalina darling. It is so good to see you. I have been thinking of you all day."
It was true: he had.

Catalina needed to be able to declare on the Home Office application form VAF4A that she had passed an English Language test in Mexico.
"Do you know yet when they will let you take the test?"

"No. I am not ready yet. The teacher says wait and she will tell me."

"What about the others. Anybody ready?

"Oh yes. Three will take test next Tuesday."

"How many are with you and still learning?"

"Fifteen I think, maybe sixteen. Everybody wants to come darling, to UK. We work very hard but is difficult."

"I don't understand this. You and me we speak together and we understand each other. What else do they want? Some people who were born here, not immigrants either, they come into my shop and are as thick as pig-shit and can hardly ask for what they want."

"Darling, what is pig sheets?"

"It means they are stupid, Catalina."

"How you spell pig sheets? I must learn. I write down, darling."

"No, no darling. It is not very nice. It is swearing. You remember I told you about swearing?"

"Ah yes. Like fuck-pig sergeant Tamayo, you say that is swearing."

"Oh hell, I had better be careful what I say. Sorry darling I will try to be careful and not swear. I will try to use only good English with you. Listen; tomorrow I want you to ask the teacher how long before you will be ready. I am going mad here. I want you here with me. I love you so much."

"Ok darling I ask tomorrow. I love you too. I cannot wait to come and live with you. We will have a good life and babies, yes?"

"Definitely darling."

The conversation went on for another hour or so. When he closed the connection and the screen was empty of her face, he sat in morose silence. The empty house did not bother him before. It did now. He was alone now because of paperwork and rules. If Catalina had been Romanian or Greek or American, she would be with him in England. But she was not. She was an undesirable. Catalina was a Mexican. He had married someone who was inferior according to the rules.

Bush had not been interested in literature at school. Yet something had struck a chord with him. There was a passage from the Merchant of Venice that they had made them learn. Always something of an oddity because of his looks, that passage fitted himself, he had realised. It had stuck with him. Now it seemed appropriate for the "inferior" Catalina.

"If you prick us, do we not bleed? If you tickle us, do we not laugh? If you poison us, do we not die? And if you wrong us, shall we not revenge?"

Bush knew what Shylock was talking about. He was alone still; and he did not like it.

He clicked on the Skype address of Francis who had returned to San Diego.

They spoke of this and that for a while and Bush gave Francis a résumé of progress, or lack of it, it Mexico.

"Joel, would you like me to go down to Mexico City to see if I can find a way to hurry things along for you?"

"What about your business? Can you leave it?"

"Not much on just now. To tell you the truth I need a change of direction; new pastures and all that. I am winding up my business. I want to travel the world."

"Will you really go Francis? I am going out of my bloody mind here being kept apart from my wife. I love her to bits you know."

"Leave it with me Joel. I will arrange it this week. I can book into a hotel nearby Catalina. Is there anything you want me to take her?"

"If you are going by car will you take her things which Rosa is keeping for Catalina? Your help with that will be really appreciated."

"So be it. Say no more. Signing off now. Cheerio, as you English bods say."

CHAPTER 53

Before he was in his teens, Trevor Higgs-Whitethorn had made the decision to follow his father into the police force. It simply appealed to him. He had decided it would be better to chose a force in which his father had not served. Detective Chief Superintendent Lawrence Higgs-Whitethorn had spent the latter part of his career in the West Yorkshire force. He had in fact, for a time, been the superior officer of Assistant Chief Constable James Fisher. He selected South Yorkshire Police. It admitted him without fuss. Trevor had not needed to pull any strings. He interviewed well and his academic credentials were definitely acceptable. He now lived alone in a smart comfortable flat in Broomhill, Sheffield.

He had expected the possibility of some resentment and backbiting from some quarters. It was not much of a problem. He intended to do well on merit, as his father had, and if some small-minded sods resented him – no worries. That was their problem.

Although it was quite late when he had left work, he had met some friends in their regular coffee bar in Broomhill. For the first time, one of the regulars, Jessica, had brought her sister Monika. The girl was recently discharged from a prolonged stay in hospital. A keen cyclist, a year earlier Monika had been struck a glancing blow by a car as she had raced along a country road. It was a regular training route for the team. The driver had not stopped but the collision had left her with a broken back. She had made a full recovery and was back in training. Trevor liked Monika immediately. The girl had not paid him any particular attention, but Trevor decided it would be agreeable to rekindle his boyhood liking for cycling. That he no longer owned a bike was a bit of a disadvantage. Or was it? Not at all.

At the coffee shop he had steered the conversation round to one of his specialities. Now, as a result of that discussion on internet privacy, Trevor sat at one of his computers at home. To each of those coffee-bar friends he sent an email.

As I said in the coffee bar, major search engines have quietly created the largest database of personal information on individuals ever collected. This data can all too easily fall into the wrong hands. Every time you use one of the popular search engines, your search data is recorded. Major search engines capture your IP address and use tracking cookies to make a record of your search terms, the time of your visit, and the links you choose. Then they store that information in their giant databases. Those searches hold a tremendous amount of your personal information. Your interests, financial queries, family and friends, searches of all types, political leanings, medical conditions, etc. can all be accessed. This information is available to be interrogated by hackers, advertisers, criminals and government officials. Imagine how at risk you could be, if someone got their hands on **all** of your search data. They can. This is a reality. Do please use the alternative search engine I wrote down for you tonight.

This topic was of a particular interest to him. At university he had learned much. It was his intention to have more than one string to his bow. If the police career proved a disappointment, he knew he would specialise in computer security. Much of his leisure time was devoted to it. It was his hobby.

Hobbies can be useful in many ways. Trevor Higgs-Whitethorn was patting himself metaphorically on the back. His strategy had been to discover the email address of the attractive, and very fit looking Monika. He looked down at the piece of paper on which the girl, with a look in her eyes that showed him she suspected what he was up to, had written her email address in a very neat, feminine hand.

Trevor needed a new bike. Perhaps Monika would help him choose one. This second email to Monika alone, took him until the wee hours before he had a version he thought might do the trick. Even then he saved it in his draft folder. Unsent, it parked there. After breakfast the next morning, following two amendments, he clicked the Send key.

*****

It had taken some time but she had slowly begun to admit it to herself. Philippa Tate found herself looking over at Trevor with increasing interest. He was not handsome in a heart-throb way at all. You barely noticed him among a crowd. It was his vitality and mental agility which Philippa found attractive. It was madness. It was utterly against the very first rule she had made before joining the force. There were bound to be many more men than women at work. Never get involved at work. Philippa was looking at him as his fingers flew across the keyboard. He was lost somewhere inside the electronics of that beast. She could picture herself sitting on a rug in front of a log fire in a remote country cottage with a thatched roof. Just the two of them would sit there sipping cocoa or wine, it did not matter. Oh, the conversations they could have. The many wonders of the universe as yet undiscovered that they could speculate about. They could sit cosily in the warm comfort of each other. Philippa's eyes had gone misty. "Oy! Come on you lot. It is POETS day. Anybody for the Huntsman?"

Philippa snapped out of her musing. Brownose was halfway to the door.

"Poets day, what are you talking about, sergeant?" Higgs-Whitethorn's question was aimed at the retreating back of Sergeant Brownlow.

"Tell him, Frank."

"Oh ignorant child." Frank grinned.

Philippa was pleased it was Trevor who had asked. She was clueless as well.

"Today is Friday - POETS day. Stands for Piss Off Early Tomorrow's Saturday."

Frank left them with that thought as he hurried to the Huntsman.

"You going to the pub, Trevor?"

"No. I have to do some things on the way home before the shops close. You going, Philippa?"

"Not now," is what Philippa would have said if she could have spoken openly. Instead she just shook her head, collected her belongings and walked as brightly as she could out of the door.

Trevor Higgs-Whitethorn, completely oblivious to her mood, as men usually are to the deeper mysteries of the opposite sex, continued inputting.

Philippa walked to her car and put the matter out of her mind.

She wished to maintain contact with Catalina and tried to speak to her at least once every week. She resolved to ring her later that night.

CHAPTER 54

Joel Bush was in the process of sending another email to his wife. One obstacle to Catalina being able to obtain the essential visa was that they had known each other for such a short time. Some of the staff of the UK Border Agency might allow that there could be love at first sight; relying on that would not be wise. They were indoctrinated to err on the side of caution. They saw many sham marriages, and they needed to assume a short relationship before marriage and a speedy visa application was likely to fall into that category. There were quotas and political pressure to limit immigration. Anyone with a passport issued by "acceptable" developed countries will never experience the difficulties which face those holding passports issued by countries outside that category. For Bush, a holder of a British passport, it had been a total shock when he first learned that his wife would not be automatically allowed to come with him to his home.

Effort needed to be made to be able to convince the Border Agency that the relationship was genuine. Speaking on Skype every day was all very well, but there was no evidence that Catalina would be able to provide that those contacts took place. Phone records of their contacts between her and Bush, together with emails, when printed out and produced to the Agency would be evidence. Letters would be some help but the post took an age to arrive. Emails were best now that Catalina was competent enough to use the laptop.

Bush sent the email.

Now the part he had looked forward to all day. He connected onto Skype for his nightly chat. Already two months had passed since they had been together. Time seemed to have stood still for Bush.

The connection was successful and The face of his lovely Catalina appeared.

She told him immediately. She had the date for the interview.

*****

More paperwork; Tamayo hated it. Information required for the British Embassy pigs. The Western big shots thought they ruled the world. They came into Mexico always complaining about something or other. The day would come when they got their comeuppance. He only hoped he lived long enough to see it. The South American countries were not powerful enough yet to oppose them with force. It would need to be force. They would not change otherwise. His neighbours the Argentinean fools had tried when they tried to get back the Malvinas. "The Falklands are ours" said the British Prime Minister – a woman, a bloody woman. The Argentineans got their arses kicked double quick. The day will come, though.
Glumly Tamayo checked the names on the paper. He worked his way through the official circulatory language.

Stupid language; what they mean is have these got a criminal record? Yes or no. Simple enough if you know what to say. The document showed two were women, each applying for a marriage visa to live in the United Kingdom with their husbands:

Ana Magana and Catalina Bush, both residents of Mexico City, but one of them had been formally a resident of Sanorias City.

With his pen poised to countersign what an agent had already checked, Tamayo halted. He knew a Catalina who had not returned to Sanorias City. One of these applicants was called Catalina.
He rifled the papers until he found her full details. Well, well, well, little Catalina Cruz had got herself married. Her name now was Catalina Bush. She had naturally been afraid, as they all were, and had kept quiet about her interview downstairs. Tamayo had no complaints on that front.
It would be interesting to see the girl again for another talk, this time with Gelsen.
Mexico City was quite a way south, though.

Tamayo was reluctant even after all those years to go to Mexico City. He stared at the ceiling as if he could see those events pictured up there, passing again for him to review. It was years since he had thought of Felice. Where would she be now? She had been his first. As a new police officer of six months he had cut a dashing figure. The family was proud of him. The youngest of five children he was the only one with a genuine job. His mother had brought them up as well as anyone in their circumstances could. Father dead just after Diego Tamayo was born, she had worked hard for her five children. The eldest was Sebastian and he had assumed the father's role when he became fourteen. Sebastian had married at eighteen and had four children. They lived next door after he got married.

The trouble came when Sebastian's eldest child was fifteen years old. Felice was a lively innocent child but maturing physically. Tamayo had noticed her. In turn, Felice was fond of her uncle Diego and when she saw him in his smart new police uniform she always stayed near to him. The fateful day was a school day. But for a sprained ankle Felice would have been at school with the others. When Tamayo went next door that day, still in his uniform, and innocently wanting to speak with Sebastian who was usually there in the daytime, Felice was alone. It was just three days later when Felice had an argument with her mother that she shouted out to her mother that uncle Diego loved her even if nobody else did. Her mother saw a look in the eyes of her daughter and pursued the matter. Tamayo had to leave Mexico City and had never been back. He missed his family but he was an outcast.

Maybe Catalina could be persuaded to make the journey north. It was worth a try. He smiled and signed the paper anyway, knowing he could keep track of her.

*****

Francis Ulanski was enjoying his time in Mexico City. It was he who had inputted most of the emails which Catalina sent to Bush. He gave her extra tuition in using her computer, and helped Catalina with her learning to read and write English. She had not had many years at school and her education was very rudimentary, but she was eager to learn and at nineteen years of age, receptive. There was nothing deficient with her memory, and Francis found it most gratifying to see how his instructions on both computer and English produced such quick results. Francis had always been something of a loner. His business was entirely a one-man affair. To be working with, and seeing the results blossoming in, another person was rewarding in a way which delighted him. It crossed his mind that he might take up teaching, perhaps in an undeveloped country.

Joel Bush was pleased to hear how well Catalina was progressing. He kept to himself his nervousness about the length of time the two were spending alone together, and he was constantly on alert for any sign from either of them that there was hanky-panky taking place.

Bush need not have worried. Francis was attracted to Catalina but had no intention of betraying his cousin. Catalina, for her part, had her mind set on going to England. The pair got on well together; that was all. In any case, Joel was coming soon. It would be good to see him again.

******

Janet Cropper watched her man stride purposefully and brightly to his car, waved back to him as he pulled away from the kerb, and brushed a tiny proud tear away from one eye as she watched the car drive out of sight. She would never know how hard Chief Inspector John Mallard had pushed for it. What she did know was that her man deserved it.

The day passed routinely, as countless others had, and in the evening the "gang" assembled and downed a few refreshing welcome draughts of their chosen liquid. Newly promoted Sergeant Frank Cropper was paying for the first three rounds so they were downed in a most pleasant fashion. That he had been promoted back to his previous level before his indiscretion with that Norfolk inspector, now a Superintendent at the NCA, gave him a feeling of relief, pride, and justice. Sergeant Frank Cropper was happy to buy the ale that evening.

It was on that occasion when Sergeant Philippa Tate informed Mallard that Catalina Bush could well be arriving in England soon. She updated him on her frequent phone contact with the girl. Mallard bought the next round.

Quite a few of them had arranged taxis for later in the evening so they could drink without having to drive. It was a lively atmosphere. Sergeant "Brownose" Brownlow had a very pleasant voice and it was he who was first performer on the Karaoke stage. As the alcohol flowed and was downed there became an increasing number of crooners. The absolute star on the stage was a lass by the name of Monika. The now regular girlfriend of Detective Constable Higgs-Whitethorn was applauded loudly. Detective Sergeant Frank Cropper looked around at his colleagues and was a happy and contented man. He knew that when he arrived home the love his life, Mrs Janet Cropper, would be waiting for him. It was not unknown for him to need a little bit of assistance with his balance after a drinking session.

CHAPTER 55

He had chosen to fly with Lufthansa as this gave him the most convenient times as well as the shortest journey time, even though it meant changing planes in Frankfurt on the outward journey, and Munich coming home. He managed to sleep on the flight and this time his dreams were pleasant enough. There was the worry of Catalina being refused the visa at the interview, but his mind was on simply being with her again. It had been a period that had seemed an eternity.

Arriving at Terminal 1 in Mexico City was seamless and soon he was pushing his trolley towards the meeting point. The touts were out in force recommending hotels, offering cheap transport into town, and journeys to shops with special bargains for visitors to Mexico. Almost everybody just ignored them; and so did he.

Francis was to accompany Catalina and Bush's eyes scanned the hoards of people waiting to greet passengers. As when Bush arrived in San Diego, Francis was holding a distinctive home-made cardboard sign. He saw it. His heart leapt once more when he spotted the sign, and even more when he saw the wide smile of his lovely wife.

The couple hugged and Joel Bush kissed Catalina. When they separated Bush embraced his cousin.
What Bush did not see was the ordinary looking man watching him from a distance of some twenty yards. Neither did he see the camera in his hand that took several photographs of him from various angles. When the three of them made their way to the short term car park where

Francis had left his hire car, the man had his phone to his ear. As he followed them, the phone was used to guide a car to a point which the three would need to pass. The car followed them when they exited the car park. Francis drove straight to Catalina's rented flat whilst the unobserved tail kept a discreet distance behind. The driver saw the three enter a building which contained just four flats. They already knew that this was the woman's address..

Sergeant Tamayo received the phone call and the photographs that same afternoon. When he saw the picture of Bush he went icy cold. He well remembered his humiliation at the hands of that swine. For quite some time Tamayo sat pondering. Unmistakably this was his chance of revenge. Bush was not in America now. He was in Mexico – his country. He would have to go to Mexico City.

*****

Three days later, the morning dawned and they both rose from sleep which had been fitful. The interview was set for 9.30 a.m. at the British Embassy. After breakfast the couple picked up the file of paperwork needed to show to the officials. Their taxi arrived and off they went. Catalina was smartly dressed in a modest dress of good quality and looked as fresh and pretty as ever. Bush was uncomfortable. He was determined to make an impression

He had only one suit but it was a good one. The problem was that the suit was made in England and designed for the weather there. As he wriggled about in the taxi he was hot. The driver had the air conditioning on, but it was set at a comfortable heat for Mexicans. Bush sweated.

The security at the British Embassy was manned by Mexicans whose English competence left much to be desired. Despite that and Bush's disdainful manner with them, they managed to gain entrance. Hotter than ever, Bush found seats for them in a waiting area which seemed to be carefully designed to display how unimportant were the people who came into that room. Bush felt as though he should have brought a begging bowl. He was determined to stand no nonsense in the interview.

Eventually the name of Mrs. Catalina Bush was called out and they both stood and hastily made their way to room number three. Bush followed Catalina into the tiny room where there sat at a desk, a man who looked British, dressed in an expensive suit, and a woman who was obviously Mexican also in a suit.
"Mr. Bush?"
"Yes."
"Please wait outside."
"I am with my wife."
"Please wait outside."
Bush had to leave Catalina alone with them.

He sat with the others outside in that Spartan room whilst the bastard in the suit decided his future. Bush was not allowed to accompany his wife and help her. The destiny of Joel Bush was in the hands of a man he had never met, and whom he was not allowed the opportunity to convince of his utter sincerity. It reminded Bush of his time when he had been at the hands of that teacher in the gym. He was hot, miserable and extremely nervous. Bush watched the faces of the ones who came out of their interview rooms. A few were smiling; others were in tears. His guts churned.

After twenty minutes Catalina came out. Bush jumped up trying to read her face.

It was OK. Catalina had a two year visa.

CHAPTER 56

It should be simple enough. He would catch him alone and shoot him. The bastard Englishman deserved to die. It had meant travelling down to Mexico City but it would be worth it. As he stood that afternoon watching the entrance to the flats, Tamayo weighed up the possibilities. The British Embassy could turn very awkward when annoyed so it was best to be careful. If the man had been Mexican, eliminating him would be no problem. A foreigner though needed care. He could not enlist the help of anyone else in the elimination. The two contacts who had followed Catalina Cruz, now Bush, to the airport would say nothing about that. It would be most unlikely that they would ever connect the man at the airport with a death some days later. If they did they would keep quiet, but if they were involved with the killing they could not be trusted. He would act alone.

There was a big problem. How to get the man alone. Newly married to a Mexican girl in a country which was comparatively strange to him she would be at his side the whole time. Catalina knew Tamayo; she must not see him. Wait. There had been another man at the airport. How did he fit in? Who was he? Tamayo must watch and wait.

Tamayo followed them when the couple went out, but they mostly spent a lot of time alone together in the flat. When they did go out, it was to eat. Then they returned. It was frustrating. Tamayo considered simply walking up to the flat, knocking on the door, shooting whoever answered and then going inside and shooting the other. The problem with that was the stairs. He could meet somebody going up or coming down. Also there were CCTV cameras high on the stairs. There was no way of knowing if they worked; they might be working, it was too risky. If they had lived on the ground floor he could have done it through the window. The first floor was inaccessible except with a ladder or those stairs.

There was one chance that he had recognised. The rubbish bins were in a corner of the front space that was mostly used as a car park. From time to time people came to the bins to empty rubbish. It was rare but it happened. They never came in pairs. It was fifty-fifty that it could be the man. In Mexico it was always the women who did that kind of task: but Englishmen were supposed to treat women better. It just might be him. Tamayo decided that he could wait to see if an opportunity came along within the next two days. If not he would run up the stairs and shoot the pair of them in their room. Decision made Tamayo settled down again to wait.

*****

The following day it had rained for most of the time and Tamayo had sheltered in a passageway. Wet, cold, and miserable Tamayo was losing patience. Then his luck changed. It was early evening and Bush came out of the building alone. Nonchalantly he swung a black plastic bag containing the household waste, and he stopped to take in a deep lungful of fresh evening air. They had been inside every bit of the day and he welcomed some air. He was looking forward to an evening with his cousin. Catalina wanted to wash her hair so she would be happy enough alone for the evening. Francis and he would find a few bars and relax. He would be arriving soon.

It was obvious Bush was about to head for the bins. Tamayo took out his gun. He crouched lower behind one of the parked cars. This gave him a clear view of the bin area and the flats behind. Everywhere was deserted, People were indoors. There was only that idiotic big Englishman around.

"Come on you fool." Tamayo was screaming inside with tension.

Bush stretched again. Looking up at the stars he headed for the bins. Tamayo brought his other hand to join the first. Holding the weapon with both arms outstretched in the classic hold, Tamayo began to slowly rise.

"Remember your breathing. Slow and even, no jerking the weapon, bring it smoothly to bear on the target, take a final aim."

Tamayo remembered every word like it was yesterday. He had the big bastard clear in his sights. He would get it right between the eyes. He always had been first grade with weapons and this was a simple target. Gently squeeze the trigger. As he had been taught, all his concentration was focussed, on his enemy. He had not heard it.

Bush had. As the taxi turned into the parking area Bush turned toward it. Tamayo's bullet passed by his ear.

Francis leapt out of the taxi and shouted.

"Down Joel down."

Tamayo whirled around, saw the taxi screeching off like a bat out of hell, saw a man shouting, and brought the gun to bear on the newcomer. Bush did not take the advice of his cousin. He did not get down. His mind flashed back to a passage in a book he had read by one of those ex SAS guys. When you are outgunned – attack. Do the thing that the enemy least expects.

Bush attacked. Head down and crouching low he bolted straight at the man with the gun. Tamayo was in a frenzy. He was aiming at the new man. Indecision gripped him for just a second and then he turned back towards Bush. Too late: Bush hit him with his head aimed directly at Tamayo's chest. Ribs cracked and as Tamayo hit the ground his head met the asphalt. He was stunned though not out cold.

It was only then that Bush took a good look at the gunman. He recognised him. He had never expected to see the man again but there he was; and he had tried to kill him. Francis walked across and, using his handkerchief, picked up the gun. Bush still stared at the man remembering that night by the pool.

Although Francis had seen Joel throw the man out at the party, he had not looked closely at him and did not recognise him.

"Why is this man trying to kill you?"

"Fuck knows. I threw him out of David Tate's party but that is hardly a reason to murder somebody."

"What do you want to do, Joel?"

Bush kicked the man with the toe of his right shoe as hard as he could.

"I think we had just better let him crawl away, Joel. Come on pal. This is Mexico not England and he is in police uniform. Being innocent might not help us here. He is not getting this gun back, though."

Bush bent, took hold of the man's shirt and lifted him off the ground.

"If I ever see you again I will kill you. Piss off out of here."

He flung him away from him. In pain, Tamayo slowly hobbled away.

CHAPTER 57

An hour later they were nearly ready. When his blood had cooled Bush had listened to the words of his cousin. They were in Mexico and Bush had just beaten a policeman. The couple should get out of Mexico as fast as possible. If the authorities apprehended Bush he would be taken away and in all probability never heard of again. Get out of the country. It was unlikely that the police knew who Ulanski was. Nevertheless he would head for Cancun and fly out back to the United States from there. It would be safer if the three of them were not together.

The packing was completed. Bush double-checked that he had their passports and all of the paperwork relating to Catalina's visa, and the couple sat down in silence to await Francis who had gone to find a taxi. When it arrived, the three said their goodbyes. The couple set off for the airport where Bush hoped to find two seats on any aircraft flying to anywhere in Great Britain. He would take any aircraft in any class, whichever was first available.

It was a United Airlines flight to Heathrow via Houston that had ample seats available in cattle class. The aircraft had taken off slightly less than three hours after they arrived nervously at the airport. They would never know, but three hours after they had taken their taxi, the police had arrived at the flat, smashed through the door and found it unoccupied. Seeing the criminals had fled and taken all of their belongings, they correctly assumed they would be flying to safety. Contact was made with security at the airport to search for them. By the time the Mexican police had discovered the pair were already in the air their plane was touching down at Houston. Tamayo had to be kept in hospital.

His condition did not improve when they broke the news.

*****

By the time Bush had escorted Catalina to Passport Control in Terminal Three at Heathrow, breezed through, thankfully confirming her visa was in order, had the Tuberculosis X-ray for immigrants which proved clear, and stood weary, relieved, and relishing his accomplishment, it was early evening on that bright, clear Spring day.

They had won; free of Mexico, clear of Home Office hurdles for the time being, and on the threshold of beginning a new life together, Bush was overjoyed and Catalina was still having trouble believing how her fortunes had completely changed. They stood in the hectic Arrivals area and hugged each other.

Bush decided they should spend a few days in London before travelling to Sheffield. He chose a good hotel, and in a very satisfactory room they ordered room service and ate a snack. Soon afterwards they went to bed. Both of them slept, each in his own way, free of fear and uncertainty for the first time for what seemed like a very long time.

CHAPTER 58

Mallard was writing when Philippa walked into his office. Another day, and items of paperwork were stacked in his pending tray awaiting his "urgent" attention after he had finished the current tome. Detection he enjoyed, meeting people and gathering evidence was an enjoyable essential. Paperwork was a bind and it increased constantly as each new broom that entered the chain of command wanted to make his own indelible, individual mark.
He wished some of them would heed the words of the White Rabbit. "Don't just do something; stand there." It would make a welcome change.

"The man Bush is back. Catalina phoned me yesterday. They have been in Sheffield now for seven weeks."

Mallard looked up. It took a few seconds for him to make sense of her words. Inside he was still striving to resist the urge to respond frankly to the request for his opinion on a suggestion that, in order to produce an enhanced degree of cooperation, detectives should dress in casual clothing when dealing with members of the public. Suits and ties could raise barriers of resistance in some quarters.

Without realising it, the fingers of his left hand were touching his tie as the significance of his sergeant's words sank in.
"Sit yourself down, Philippa."
Mallard placed his pen carefully on top of the half-written reply as he collected his thoughts.
"It has been too many months since those two girls were treated so abominably, and we have just one hope of

catching the criminal; this man Bush. Without him we have nothing; you agree, Philippa?"

"I do, Sir. Unless the man, if it turns out not to be Bush, unless he snatches another we are not likely to catch him."

"How did Mrs Bush sound?"

"Extremely happy. She gets a bit bored sometimes but she can't believe her luck. Back home she was working and sleeping with no time for anything else. In Sheffield it is the complete opposite. Bush does not want her to work because he has enough money without his wife needing to work. She does not wish to argue with that. Sir I should like your advice on something that is troubling me."

"Fire away, Philippa."

"When I recognised Bush at my brother's house I told everybody outside my family that I was a teacher in Leeds and I kept out of the way of Bush. Catalina thinks I am a teacher. Should I tell her the truth?"

"Oh boy, that is a tricky one. You should of course tell her, but can you ask her not to tell her husband?"

Philippa nodded.

"Has she invited you to the house?"

"No, I have spoken to her just once, yesterday."

"I don't think we can get his DNA without you going there. Can you think of any other way?"

"I thought of asking her to contribute some items to charity. If I take a collection bag from Oxfam or somewhere and give it to her to fill we might get some of his things in it."

"We will keep that in reserve. I suspect she will simply say that they get bags from Oxfam and everybody else all the time. I know I do. Why should they fill yours? No you need to be in there. A quick visit to the bathroom, find one of his hairs in a brush or somewhere, and bingo our lab will do the rest."

"That will be the sure way. I will try to wangle an invite. But should I tell her I am a detective?"

"What will you say when she asks you why you said you were a teacher. Not only that, why did you hide the fact that you were from Sheffield? I know why, but what can you tell your friend? Is she really a friend by the way, or is she someone you are cultivating?"

"These are the hard questions, Sir. It has been going round in my head ever since last night. I need to think some more about it. I must admit I have really just been friendly for our own ends here."

"I can't tell you what to do for the best, Philippa because there is no easy answer. On balance I think it best to continue to be a teacher. If it turns out that Bush is our man there is no way she will be your friend after you trap him and make her, to all intents and purposes, a widow."

"With no husband to support the girl the Home Office will probably withdraw her permission to stay in the UK as well. The poor girl will be sent back to Mexico. Her fabulous new life here will be destroyed, and she will be back home again to fend for herself. I feel terrible."

"Remember the Pearson and the Clayton families, Philippa. Do you feel worse than them? That was a cruel rhetorical question, but I mean it to be helpful and to give you some perspective. You have my sympathy, Sergeant. I am sorry though I really need to finish this lot."

He tapped the papers.

Sergeant Tate left his office.

*****

"Darling I am fourteen years older than you, and it is a fact that women live longer than men. When I die, hopefully not for a long time yet, everything I have will be yours. It will be yours then. For now I want it where it is."

Catalina thought it was beautiful. She had seen pictures of famous people and girls modelling clothes. Often it was the first thing that Catalina noticed. It was a great shame that it hung up there on that wall when it was made to hang around someone's neck; especially the neck of a devout Catholic girl such as she. Catalina pulled a face and wanted her husband to see it.
The crucifix would be much better placed around her neck. This was the third time he had said no. She would wait and one day if she found him in an especially good mood, perhaps he would change his mind.
Bush grimaced when he saw Catalina's expression. He wanted her to be happy. She was not having that crucifix though, not until he was gone.

"Joel I am meeting my friend Philippa tomorrow. Can I have some money please? We are going in to town for some lunch. Can I look around the shops with her and maybe buy a few things, please?

"Who is Philippa?"

"She is that girl we met in America."

"I don't remember, oh wait a minute. Do you mean the sister of the people who had the party?"

"Yes."

"I never got anywhere near her. She seemed to keep out of my way. No I don't want you to meet her.

Make some new friends over here."

*****

"Philippa I have a problem."

"What is it Catalina?"

It was the morning that Philippa Tate had arranged to meet Catalina for lunch. She had decided to keep up the pretence of being a teacher. They were to meet, have a look around a few shops, and then have lunch somewhere. Philippa was looking to see where in town there was a restaurant serving Mexican food.

"What is wrong?"

"Joel says he does not want me to meet you."

"Did he say why?" She was apprehensive. This could be a showstopper.

"Not really, he said to make other friends here."

"Are you going to come anyway, Catalina? This is England. You do not have to do what a man tells you in England. You are free to please yourself."

"That would be nice. To please myself. I would like that. I want to come but it is a very long way to walk to town. I have no money at all. I cannot come on the bus. It is impossible."

"Oh no it is not. I will send a taxi for you. If you want to come, come. I can afford a taxi. I want to meet you too."

"I don't know, Philippa. I love my husband. I don't think I can come."

"If you want to come you should just come. You are an adult. You can make up your own mind."

"I must think about this, Philippa. But today I will not come. Not today. I must think. I am so sorry."

"Are you sure?"

"Yes. I am sorry, Philippa. I will ring you sometime. Bye bye."

Sergeant Philippa Tate swore an uncharacteristic oath.

*****

"We need an alternative strategy."

"That is stating the obvious. I am surprised at you sunshine."

DS Frank Cropper looked at Trevor expectantly. Had he thought of something?

"A party, a knees-up, drinkies or something. Can we devise something where we can invite both of them? Get Bush's glass when he puts it down and whisk it away."

"Go on then, son. Devise something."

"That, oh beloved sergeant is the hard part."

"Just ring him up, tell him it is Chief Inspector Mallard's birthday, we are throwing a surprise party and can he come and bring his lovely young wife with him. Where is the party? Oh, yes, it is down here at police headquarters. We can send a car for you if you like Joel."

"Bollocks, sergeant."

*****

The days passed quite slowly for Catalina, but not the evenings. They would sit side-by-side on the settee and either just talk about their past lives or simply lean back and watch TV. Catalina particularly loved some of the films. She had hardly seen any in Mexico. Time and money had been in such short supply. Those evenings were the best time. Catalina was happy. The films were all in English and so helped her to learn the language. She was also thrilled that she might become pregnant soon. Her husband wanted children too and now it was just up to the Holy Trinity to whom she prayed so earnestly several times a day. The crucifix was her focal point when she was on her knees to the Holy Virgin.

The films on TV during the day time were old ones and a lot were in black and white. Joel had showed her this small collection of DVDs and he had chosen some for her that she would like. She had played one each day all that week. He had thrown some others into the bin when she had found them in that drawer in the bedroom.

Catalina selected one of the DVDs for the morning's viewing. She picked South Pacific; that might be OK. Before she could open its case the phone rang. It had been weeks since Catalina had spoken to Philippa.

It was Philippa. She was on holiday that day and would be passing close by Catalina's road. Could they meet for a coffee? After some wavering Catalina agreed but it would have to be in the afternoon. Joel came home sometimes for lunch so that Catalina had some company a few days of the week. It depended how busy the shop was. She never knew until he got home because he liked to surprise her. They agreed that Catalina would be at the bottom of Beech Street at 2.30 p.m.

Catalina put down the phone and opened the South Pacific DVD case. She took out the disc. A piece of paper dropped out of the case. It appeared to be a piece torn from a magazine and on it there was some handwriting in red ink. Joel must have left it there for something and forgotten it. She tried to read the writing but it was not printed clearly and she could not understand it. She would show it to Joel when he came home. So she would remember, she placed it in the pocket of her blouse.

The South Pacific film started and Catalina loved it. It was by far the best film of them all. She cried in parts. When it had finished it was nearly midday. She had plenty of time before she was to walk and meet Philippa. She wondered if Philippa had seen South Pacific. It really was marvellous. Dare she lend the DVD to Philippa? Joel would not notice, surely.

*****

Philippa Tate left the police station and set off for her meeting with Catalina in her own car. If she could get inside the house for just five minutes that would be enough.

When she arrived Catalina waved happily. She looked a picture of health and happiness. What a difference those intervening months had made. Her black hair shone in the watery sunlight and reached half way down the pale green blouse. She wore a knee-length cream skirt. The cool weather that day did not seem to inconvenience Catalina.

Inside the nearby coffee bar their animated chatter livened up the otherwise hushed room. Older customers watched the decades younger pair talking excitedly. It was some twenty minutes before Catalina reached into her handbag and brought out the DVD.

"This film is South Pacific. It is a very old film have you seen it, Philippa? It is lovely."

Philippa had heard about it but never seen it.

"No."

"You can borrow it if you like."

"Thanks, Catalina that is very kind."

"Joel does not know but I can sneak it back when you have watched it."

"Are you sure? What if he sees it is missing?"

"He does not watch them. It will be OK."

"Right OK, thanks." Philippa placed the DVD case into her bag.

"Oh, I forgot about the paper. You'd better give it back to me. I am stupid. Sorry Philippa."

Philippa reached into her bag for the DVD.

"Wait. Maybe you can tell me if it is important."

Catalina took the piece of paper from her blouse pocket and gave it to Philippa.

"I cannot read it can you?"

Philippa straightened out the paper. It was a small piece torn from a magazine.
"What does that writing in red say, Philippa?"

An expression came across her face as Philippa Tate realised what was written. She looked at the innocent face of the girl waiting for an answer. Then she smiled and said, "It is just somebody making marks. Perhaps they were testing a pen or something. It is nothing. Come on Catalina, I had better be on my way."

She folded up the small piece of paper and put it back inside the DVD case which she placed back into her bag. Philippa took Catalina back to the bottom of Beech Street.

Although they said they would meet again, they never would. It proved impossible.

CHAPTER 59

Alegria watched her video screens and picked disinterestedly at her food on the plate before her. She saw the girl Estella sitting alone in a corner of the lounge. It was quiet tonight and that was a pity. Perhaps it would liven up later; she hoped so. If not she would wait for another night when it was packed. That way the bidding would be lively. Estella was beckoned and Alegria saw the girl put on a fixed smile and saunter with hips swaying across to the men. There were four of them. The youngster was doing very well. What would her reaction be when she found out her sister was in the room for Recruits? Malevolently Alegria jokingly considered passing by her table and whispering the news in her ear. Alegria liked to dream up ways to liven the solitary hours she spent alone in her room. On her own, staring at the screen sometimes drove her nearly mad. When it got really bad she would force herself to think back to the time when she had been in a position similar to that of Estella's sister now. Her mood lifted. If she could survive the experiences that these girls underwent, then they could too. She had not only survived but had overcome and flourished. It was not easy; but it was not impossible either.

The four men had been joined by three more girls. None of the girls had a drink. Alegria rose and went down into the lounge. There she wandered over and began to chat with the men. Before long not only had each girl been bought a drink but Alegria had one too. Mission accomplished Alegria made an excuse, circulated for a while, and later made her way towards the door. As she passed by the table she bent and whispered into the ear of Estella, "When you are free I want to see you upstairs."

Some time later when her "escort" had finished with her, Estella went along and knocked on the door of Alegria.
"I have some news for you my girl. Listen carefully. There is someone upstairs who you know. In a few days after her initiation I want you to take her under your wing and show her the ropes. Show the girl how to become very popular with my customers. That is all."
"Can I ask who it is?"
"I don't see why not. It is your sister Tyona."
"No! Little Tyona, no!"
"She is not so little your sister. She will do very well here."
Estella was mortified. Tyona was two years younger than her.
"I hear your special friend agent Tamayo is out of hospital now. Perhaps he will appreciate her as much as he enjoys you, girl. Off you go and earn your keep. Ah, ah, who is this hobbling into the lounge?"
On a screen, Alegria had seen Tamayo enter. He was making his painful way to the nearest free table.
"Off you go. It looks as though he needs someone to look after him.

Estella did not just go, she fled. How bad could this life get? Her sister was up in the Recruits room and Tamayo was downstairs. This was just too much. He just could not do to Tyona what the beast had done to her. It was just not fair. At the foot of the stairs she paused, took a deep breath, and then walked into the room.

Immediately Tamayo summoned her. She sat with him. He was obviously in a good deal of discomfort. His broken ribs were still very painful and he was taking strong painkillers. Strong was simply the word used by doctors. They were no use to him. He was in pain and his mood showed it. Estella just had to sit there sipping a drink and smiling as ever. She hated the man. She hated him for what he had done that first night and for all the other things he kept doing to her. He choose Estella more than any of the others. What about Tyona? Would he want her? She knew the answer.

El Retiro gradually became busy. Two minibuses had arrived and business was good. At the next table was a group of rough looking men. There could be trouble later. Three of them had hunting knives sheathed at their belts.

Alegria judged there were enough customers there to fetch a decent price. When she made the announcement that a new girl had arrived and was upstairs awaiting her first customer, Estella nearly died. It was going to happen. The bidding for the virgin started, became extremely lively and the price rose. Estella was relieved that Tamayo had kept silent.

"Now gentleman, I know you can do better than that. Such a lowly price for a fresh one. I know how much you all like fresh. What about you Sir? You have not bid."
She was pointing to Tamayo who sat immobile. Whenever he moved the pain racked his body. The alcohol would deaden it better than those useless tablets. He kept sending Estella for more drinks.

"Are you not interested, Sir? Perhaps you may be if I tell you who I have upstairs."

Tamayo sat unmoving whilst Estella held her breath.

"I have upstairs the little sister of the girl at your side that you are so fond of."

Tamayo stiffened. He stared at Estella.

"Is this true?"

She did not reply but Tamayo could see from the expression on her face that it was.

He smiled and nodded. He had bid. The bidding continued until there were just two bidders left. Alegria was delighted. Tamayo had spent weeks in hospital but he received full pay throughout and had plenty of legitimate money in his pocket. Gelsen had managed the private business well enough in his absence. He was pleased he had recruited Gelsen after Rufino's departure. In the end it was inevitably Tamayo who was the winner. It would be difficult to climb three flights of stairs but he was motivated; and he had an idea.

"Come little Estella. You and me have an appointment with your sister. You will help me climb the stairs. Whilst I get to know your sister I shall want you to stay. You can fetch my beer as the night progresses. If I am pleased with your sister I may buy drinks for both of you. Come girl, help me."

There is a breaking point.

When it is reached the unexpected can happen very quickly. Interrogators see this often, even with the most difficult of prisoners. Eventually a point arrives when the body, the soul, the will, and all reason, buckle. The prisoner begins to talk. He talks and he talks and all the interrogator need do is to listen. He will unburden himself. With soldiers who are tough but rebellious to authority, when their spirit is overcome they change and behave like the others, subordinate and biddable. They can turn into the very best of soldiers.

Estella had reached her breaking point. The thought of having to assist Tamayo whilst he availed himself and abused her younger sister was simply unbearable. It would not stand. It must not happen.
Tamayo was leaning on her with his arm over her left shoulder. She was really supporting him as, groaning, they drew alongside the table where the newly arrived rough men were sitting with girls on their knees. The customers were fully preoccupied. Estella simply had to bend just a little, take the knife at the man's belt from its sheath, and she had the weapon. It happened totally unexpectedly and nobody really saw her do it. Knife in hand, Estella turned towards Tamayo and thrust it into his abdomen.
It was an exceedingly sharp knife. There was no resistance. It really was too easy. The knife slipped in and became embedded up to its hilt, right in the centre of his abdomen, some four inches below his sternum. The aorta of Sergeant Diego Tamayo was sliced completely in two. One does not live long in that condition. He was practically gone by the time he had crumpled slowly onto the floor, in a comically ungainly fashion.

Tamayo would not abuse her sister.

The second highest bidder would climb the stairs later that night. Estella would never know. She had already been strangled.

CHAPTER 60

"Sir, we have got him. I think you should get the team together and stand-by uniform and ART."

"Hold on a minute Philippa. Slow down. Are you talking about Bush?"

"Yes. Sir. I have proof; definite proof."

"It will need Forensics to make it definite.

"No sir. I am on my way. This is urgent; top priority. Please sir!"

"How long before you whirl in here Sergeant?"

"Twenty minutes, no wait. There is a lot of traffic ahead, make it thirty, Boss."

Philippa Tate was excited. She was certain she had with her the vital piece of evidence that would convict Bush. The sense of triumph had completely over-ridden her consideration for Catalina Bush. That young woman was forgotten, for the time being at least. Thoughts of the girl, how she had looked when Philippa collected her from the bottom of Beech Street, the excited friendly gesture of lending a DVD to her one friend in England who she was meeting behind the back of her husband, would resurface later, and would continue for the remainder of Philippa's life. But not then.

As she drove ignoring the words of her Chief Inspector, threading her way through the very busy Sheffield city centre at speed, all thoughts were on the next steps they would need to take. She hoped Mallard was moving as she had suggested. It had sounded as if he hardly believed her. Should she call him again? Should she call Frank to ask him to check if Mallard was acting? There was some

370

danger. If Catalina rang Bush and told him what she had done even though Catalina did not realise its significance, Bush would act. There was no time to waste.

*****

There was no phone call from Catalina to her husband. Yet Bush left his shop just as Philippa Tate was arriving at the police station. It was exactly nine months to the day since the Christening and Bush had first seen the girl who had become his wife. The day needed marking. Catalina should have flowers. She should have a lovely necklace as well. It was not a busy day and his two assistants could easily manage without him for an hour.

*****

Mallard was alone in his office awaiting the arrival his female Sergeant. Would this be the day the case turned? He had alerted a team of fifteen men but decided against armed response. The fifteen had been given no hint for which case they were standing by. Security was usually excellent at the station, but he erred on the side of caution. When he saw the pride on the face of Sergeant Philippa Tate as she raced into his office he knew.

"Look at this John."

She took out the piece of paper from the DVD case and smoothed it out on Mallard's desk. It measured no more than six square inches but it was momentous. Written in red, were just four words.

HELP ME

KAREN CLAYTON

The Sergeant and the Chief Inspector looked from the piece of paper into each other's face. For a moment there was a stunned silence.

Thereafter there was frantic activity.

*****

With a bunch of flowers in his vehicle, Bush drove contentedly to the jewellery shop to which as a schoolboy he had been with his mother. Magdalina Bush would often go there just to look at the window display. Standing at the window outside, she would pick out some items and describe to young Joel their usefulness, and she would invent stories for him about the earrings, or the necklaces, that she would herself have loved to be able to buy.

Today Mrs Catalina Bush would wear one of those items. Money was not a problem. Listening to the radio tuned into Radio Sheffield, Bush spied a parking place and manoeuvred into it.

When he left the shop with a necklace he drove home to give it to his wife. It would perhaps appease her for being refused the crucifix.

*****

Three police vans with lights flashing headed for Beech Street. Mallard was not with them. Two cars headed for the butchers shop where they expected to find Joel Bush. One car contained Mallard, Tate and the driver. The other, in addition to the driver contained three big, fit, uniformed coppers, one of whom was a sergeant. If there was bother these men would handle it. When the cars parked near to the shop, two officers were sent round to the rear to prevent an escape that way. Mallard and another officer entered the shop leaving Philippa Tate and the sergeant outside. Darryl was in the shop alone. There were no customers at the time. Mallard went into the back followed by a protesting Darryl.
Bush was not there.

The senior officer in the vans which raced up Beech Street was Sergeant Frank Cropper. The officers surrounded the house quietly and one of them was lifted up by two others so that he could peer into the front lounge. From that vantage point he observed Bush with his wife. At his confirming signal, he was lowered to the ground and

Sergeant Cropper walked to the front door and rang the bell.

Inside, Bush muttered. He expected it would be some kind of nuisance call. It was unlikely to be those kids but he peered through the window in case. He saw a big man on his doorstep. Bush stared. Although it had been many months since he had been visited in his home by the fellow with the stranglers hands, it was a visit he would never forget. Recognition was instant.

"Tell them I am not in, Catalina. I don't want to see them. Hurry darling. I am not in."

Catalina went to the door. The officers pushed past and walked quickly inside. Bush had retreated to the far corner of the lounge. Once the officers were inside Bush was arrested, cautioned and handcuffed.

Catalina looked on uncomprehending. She saw her husband in handcuffs flanked by two burly police officers. Without them saying a word to her. They began to usher Bush towards the door. Two female uniformed officers stayed as the bewildered Catalina watched her husband taken away.

There was jubilation at the station. Bush was processed and then led into an Interview Room. They left him alone for ninety minutes before Mallard and Cropper interviewed him.

The Forensic investigation of the house subsequently retrieved two tiny pieces of toenail clippings embedded in the basement carpet. His vacuum cleaning had been thorough, but Bush should have replaced the carpet. The clippings had belonged to Karen Clayton. Without that evidence Bush may have been able to concoct a story that could possibly have raised an element of doubt regarding the note in some of the jury.

Testing of his DNA confirmed that the trace of sweat found on the bed of Sophia Pearson matched that of Joel Bush. With a conclusive link to the second girl and the DNA evidence from the bed of the first, the verdict would without doubt be a formality.

CHAPTER 61

For the police investigation of the house to be concluded, Catalina Bush was made to vacate her home during the first week after the arrest of her husband. Her first cry for help was to her only friend in England, Philippa. Her friend did not answer. For three weeks she kept ringing her friend Philippa at different times of the day and night. She was never to receive an answer.

Catalina tried to visit Joel every day during that first week, and did succeed twice. He denied to Catalina that he had any knowledge of those schoolgirls. How could the police set him up like that? With her experience of the police in Mexico Catalina could believe anything of police.

Bush continued to deny any connection with the girls and he remained uncooperative with the police. He was stricken with the knowledge that his wife was utterly alone, for he had discouraged Catalina from being out of the house without him. Consequently she knew nobody except that Philippa who refused to answer her calls. His earlier concern for her wellbeing in the strange land to which he had brought his wife, meant that she only knew that one other person in England.

When Bush was able, he told Catalina to contact his cousin Francis in San Diego. Catalina telephoned her sister Rosa, and during a tearful, heart wrenching conversation, poured out her misery. Rosa agreed to walk across the road and talk to Francis Ulanski. It was several days before he returned from Tallahassee where he had been researching his notion of becoming a teacher of English, overseas. He was dumbfounded at the turn of events which had overtaken Joel, and over the following few days he had several conversations with Catalina. Ulanski arrived in Sheffield a few days later.

After holding out for three weeks, on the advice of his solicitor and faced with undefeatable evidence Bush agreed to plead guilty. The families of both girls would be spared the ordeal of a lengthy trial.

When Catalina, and Francis, heard from the police that Bush had admitted to the murders they were stunned. Ulanski was staying in the Bush house, using one of the other bedrooms. They had to both come to terms with the intention of a guilty plea. At first, even Ulanski had been more inclined to think it was a mistake by the police than acceptance of the likelihood of the guilt of his cousin. A conversation with his cousin eventually settled the matter. Ulanski was staggered.

Except for one person, who would sometimes awake in the wee small hours and lie sleepless in the darkness, no-one else gave much thought to the plight of Catalina Bush. The wife of a murderer receives scant sympathy.
A more than occasional tear was shed for the girl, by Sergeant Philippa Tate in the quiet darkness of her own solitary bedroom.

CHAPTER 62

The trial had finished on a Friday afternoon. A life sentence was imposed on Joel Bush with a recommendation that he serve at least twenty-five years. Those who had been most involved with the Schoolgirls Case throughout, assembled the day after for a final end-of-case drink.

It was a double celebration. There was also a presentation made to the Pathologist, Anthony Pemberton. Unlike on several previous occasions, they had reason to be cheerful. Frank Cropper had been thrilled that it had been Philippa Tate who had made the breakthrough. Coaxed by Trevor into reminiscing about his army career, Cropper had the floor.

"This new Captain was assigned to our army outfit in a remote post in the North African Desert. During his first inspection, he noticed we kept a camel hitched up behind the Mess Tent and he asked the sergeant why the camel was kept there.

Our sergeant said: "Well, sir, as you know, there are 250 men here on the post and no women. And sir, sometimes the men have "urges". That's why we have Molly The Camel."

The Captain says, "I can't say that I condone this - but I understand about "urges", so the camel better stay, I suppose."

About a month later, the Captain starts having his own "urges". Freaked out for sex, he asks the sergeant to bring the camel to his tent. Putting a ladder behind the camel, the Captain stands on the ladder, pulls his pants down and

has sex with Molly The Camel. When he's done, he asks the Sergeant:
"Is that how the men do it?"

"No, not really, sir. They usually just ride the camel into town - where the girls are."

*****

Just the two of them remained. Nearly everybody else had things to do early that Saturday afternoon. With no partners to return to, or commitments to fulfil, the two bachelors could relax.

"So, why Nepal, Anthony?"
Doctor Anthony Pemberton was pleased to be alone with Mallard. They found it easy to talk. The brief retirement presentation at the station was behind him, the flock of colleagues had drifted away from the Huntsman pub, and he would take a taxi home when he was ready. His half of bitter was before him on the table and he stared into it for a while before answering.

"My youngest sister first went there some ten years ago straight after qualifying, and she goes there as a volunteer every few years, to spend a month carrying out surgery at a medical camp in Bumburi. I have been cutting up corpses for fifteen years and am ready for a change of direction, something different, something constructive. In Nepal I will heal and improve people. The medical camps over there attract local people from miles around, many of whom walk for hours, and sometimes days, to get help at the camps. I know that after just a few days there I will feel valued. I will value myself in a different way."

"Medics are fortunate in that they can take their skill with them anywhere in the world. Don't know what I will do when I retire."

Each sat with his own thoughts.

Eventually, "That man Bush, got life didn't he? You got him in the end."

"Yes we got him. I suppose we had some luck, but we need some now and again: deserve some. That writing in red on that magazine cutting turned out to be blood. I suppose she had no pen so she wrote in blood using a fingernail or toothpick or something. Clever that girl was. And again, Anthony, if I had not let Philippa go to the Christening in the States we probably would never have caught him."

"That other schoolgirl who's neck he broke, remember I did the autopsy?"

"I remember."

"What was her name?"

"Sophia Pearson. Sixteen years old."

"That's it Sophia. A really lovely girl. Do you know, John, it was that autopsy that finally decided me I had had enough. Such a fearful waste: to see a young person like that discarded, in the prime of life, dreadful."

Minutes of sombre rumination passed until the two friends shook hands and went their separate ways.

In the ensuing years Mallard was to serve with the South Yorkshire Police until he retired.

Pemberton never left Nepal. He derived much personal satisfaction from the constructive healing medicine he practised in the same locality in which his sister showed up regularly. He also met and married a local nurse.

When the lamp is shattered
The light in the dust lies dead -

Shelley

EPILOGUE

6 Years later.

The little boy teetered across the room intent on reaching his favourite little leather stool. Sometimes the journey was successful. More often, as now, he fell with a bump. The polished wooden floor may well have damaged an adult, but not this supple, fifteen-months old pioneer. The boy looked around to see if his mum was watching and he waited for her familiar approach to pick him up. When she did not come he pushed himself off the floor, stood, and resumed his quest. Sitting on his stool he saw his mother enter the room, wave to him, and walk outside into the garden. Jarek stood and toddled to join her. The beauty of the cherry blossom on the trees was what had drawn the woman into their garden. It would be April in two days and already the trees were resplendent in full riotous bloom. On Sunday next, April 1st, there would be a festival in the Fujikawaguchiko local park, with food, drink, and music. Beyond her garden trees the woman's gaze focused on Mount Fuji in the distance. This was a truly magical place to be. A tear of joy slowly crept down one cheek.

*****

"Who can name three, don't put your hand up unless you know three, three airports in England?
The class consisted of ten thirteen year-old boys. It was a mixed ability, fee-paying, class and the pupils were well-

382

behaved and attentive. Five arms were raised to answer. Four of them could have been expected as they belonged to the leading students, but Yuito was a surprise.

"Yuito, what are your three?"
"London, Manchester, Arsenal, sir."

"Hassan, what are your three?"
"London Heathrow, Gatwick, Manchester, sir."
"Correct. Who can tell me what is wrong with the answer of Yuito?"

Hands raised and answered.

"Yuito, this time, name me three English football clubs." The boy listed eight correctly and was in full flow before the teacher stopped him. It was approaching the end of the school day. As he often did, Francis Ulanski dismissed the class a little early this Friday.

The boys filed out of the classroom in the customary orderly Japanese fashion. What a difference there was to the discipline, behaviour, and attitude to be found in American classrooms.
Next year when the boys were fourteen, they would be offered the chance to visit America and spend one month being educated in America. Ulanski was delighted to be one of the teachers participating. Much as he enjoyed teaching in Japan, there were aspects of America that he really missed. He appreciated the huge difference in life in Japanese education, to that in America. He watched the last smartly uniformed pupil carefully and quietly close the

classroom door behind him. It would be important that the boys did not catch bad habits over there.

*****

The drive home would take twenty-five minutes. He was looking forward to his three-day weekend. He did not work on Mondays. Whilst Ulanski waited for the traffic lights to change, a man crossed the road. As he watched the man, he noted the similarity in stature to his cousin Joel Bush. With a start Ulanski realised it had been a long time since he had even thought of him. How long had it been since the police had arrested him? The seven years had flown by.

When he had been with his cousin, he had seemed a normal guy. That he had done what he had done to those two young girls had been as contemptible as it had been stupefying. Ulanski was ashamed to think he was a blood relation of his. When he had learned that his father had stolen the crucifix of Magdalina Bush, Francis Ulanski had felt shamefaced. After the admission by Bush of his guilt, he felt anguished to be a relation.

To his credit though, Bush had done the right thing towards his distraught, isolated wife. He would be in prison with no chance of release for many, many years, perhaps forever. His young wife would be bound to be forced out of England when her visa expired. She must surely hope to find another husband one day and have the babies she so desired. Bush agreed to an uncontested divorce, and indeed helped her all he could from prison. Ulanski kept away from visiting Bush. He and Catalina lived in Beech Road, at first in separate rooms. Soon, though, they became close.

By the time the divorce nisi was issued, a new bed had been installed and the pair shared it. Marriage followed. Immediately afterwards, matters were commenced towards permission for Catalina to go with Francis to live in the USA.

The traffic lights changed and Ulanski drove, still reminiscing. He thought of his cousin locked away in his new humdrum existence, and the astounding contrast that had occurred between that marriage in Mexico to the wonderful girl he had found, and then having found his dream, it had led within months to his deserved capture. "Follow your dream" can have many outcomes. For himself, life was brilliant. He was satisfied and content teaching, and especially in watching the knowledge he had imparted, blossom within his pupils. He was fulfilled.

*****

Francis Ulanski parked the car in his drive, retrieved his briefcase from the back seat, and looked expectantly at his front door. An enormous pride and jubilation mounted in his breast. There, as she did every single day, stood his own angel beaming her delightful smile.

Catalina Ulanski held young Jarek clutched lovingly to her breast. She was taking care to keep the boy's bouncy feet, off her stomach. As Catalina watched her husband walk his lively walk towards them, she was looking forward to breaking the wonderful news to her man when they were alone.

She kissed Jarek.

THE END

Nothing ever becomes real 'til it is experienced.

John Keats

15989011R00218

Printed in Poland
by Amazon Fulfillment
Poland Sp. z o.o., Wrocław